Praise for the Crochet Mysteries

"A gentle and charming novel that will warm the reader like a favorite afghan. Its quirky and likable characters are appealing and real."

—Earlene Fowler, national bestselling author of
The Road to Cardinal Valley

"[A] charming mystery. Who can resist a sleuth named Pink, a slew of interesting minor characters and a fun fringe-of-Hollywood setting?"

—Monica Ferris, *USA Today* bestselling author of
Knit Your Own Murder

"Crochet fans will love the patterns in the back, and others will enjoy unraveling the knots leading to the killer."

—*Publishers Weekly*

"[These] characters are so unique that they are not easily forgotten! They are witty and charming, a perfect group of crafters to have an armchair adventure with . . . Absolutely stunning."   —Open Book Society

"Betty Hechtman does it all so well: writing, plotting and character development."   —Cozy Library

"[An] enjoyable series with likable characters."

—The Mystery Reader

"Crocheters couldn't ask for a more rollicking read."

—Crochet Today!

"Betty Hechtman has written an enjoyable amateur sleuth featuring a likable lead protagonist who has reinvented herself one stitch at a time."   —Genre Go Round Reviews

"Combining a little suspense, a little romance and a little hooking, Betty Hechtman's charming crochet mystery series is clever and lively."   —Fresh Fiction

Seams Like Murder

BETTY HECHTMAN

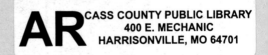

BERKLEY PRIME CRIME, NEW YORK

**BERKLEY
PRIME
CRIME**

An imprint of Penguin Random House LLC
375 Hudson Street, New York, New York 10014

SEAMS LIKE MURDER

A Berkley Prime Crime Book / published by arrangement with the author

ISBN: 978-0-425-27944-1

PUBLISHING HISTORY
Berkley Prime Crime mass-market edition / May 2016

PRINTED IN THE UNITED STATES OF AMERICA

10 9 8 7 6 5 4 3 2 1

Cover art by Cathy Gendron.
Cover design by Rita Frangie.
Interior text design by Kristin del Rosario.

Penguin
Random
House

Acknowledgments

It can't be easy starting out with the tenth book in a series, but my editor Julie Mianecki did an amazing job. My agent Jessica Faust as always is there with advice and help.

Molly has been almost arrested a number of times, and I've had to imagine how she was handcuffed to a bench. No more. Lee Lofland once again put on a fabulous event called Writers Police Academy at the Fox Valley Technical College Public Safety Training Center in Appleton, Wisconsin. They actually had a whole mock-up of a booking area, and I got to see firsthand what that bench looks like. I also went into the cell she might have ended up in.

Thank you to crocheter extraordinaire Amy Shelton of Crochetville.com for including me in the NaCroMo blog tour. What a way to celebrate National Crochet Month. Her talents inspire me. Delma Myers, another crocheter extraordinaire, has been my guide to the yarn world and keeps me posted on what's going on.

Linda Hopkins is my crochet angel. She helps with the patterns and so much else.

Thanks to my knit and crochet group Rene Biederman, Alice Chiredijan, Terry Cohen, Trish Culkin, Clara Feeney, Sonia Flaum, Lilly Gillis, Winnie Hineson, Linda Hopkins, Reva Mallon, Elayne Moschin and Paula Tesler for all the yarn fun. Roberta and Dominic Martia remain my cheerleaders. And hugs to my family—Burl, Max and Samantha.

CHAPTER 1

"No!" I YELLED AS THE SMALL GRAY TERRIER MIX took off across my living room with a ball of blue yarn in his mouth. Cosmo, a black mutt who resembled a mop, was on Felix's tail, and I was running after both of them. The lid was off the plastic bin I had so carefully packed, and balls of yarn in blues, greens and lavenders were all over the wood floor in various stages of unravel.

A growling Cosmo caught up with the offender, and the terrier dropped his trophy at my feet. Not long ago I'd been concerned that my life was too quiet, and now it had gone in the opposite direction. This chaos was just an example.

"Felix, you're adorable but completely naughty," I said, shaking my head at the gray dog. "It wouldn't be so bad if this yarn was mine," I added as I began to retrieve the colorful balls of fiber and rewind them, checking for damage. Yes, I could certainly afford to lose a few skeins from my overabundant stash. Actually, overabundance was an understatement.

"But this belongs to the bookstore," I continued, picking up the ball of royal blue mohair. Was it my imagination, or did the dog give me a quizzical look? Did he wonder what a bookstore was doing with yarn?

It all started when my husband, Charlie, died and I'd had to start a new chapter in my life. I'd gotten a job at Shedd & Royal Books and More as the event coordinator. Soon after, I discovered that a group of crocheters, the Tarzana Hookers, met at the bookstore. They offered just what I'd needed— friendship and something else to do with my hands besides ferrying homemade caramel corn to my mouth.

In those days, the "More" in the shop's name referred to things like journals, writing supplies and a small array of chocolates. But my boss, Mrs. Shedd, was always looking for new revenue streams, and she realized that the crocheters bought yarn and attracted yarn buyers to the bookstore. The next thing I knew, we had a yarn department and I was in charge. Then we started putting on crochet parties, in addition to all the author events and writers' groups I was already running. I suppose it was only natural to come up with our newest offering: the Yarn University. Yarn stores often offered series of classes that included making a project. I'd observed how they handled things, and the idea for Yarn University had been born.

The Tarzana Hookers were loaded with talent and all ready and willing to be teachers. Strike that—all but one were ready, willing and able. I had talked Sheila, the youngest Hooker, into teaching a class on her special technique, which incidentally had the most people signed up. Since she had no experience teaching, my best friend and fellow Hooker Dinah Lyons had worked with Sheila to come up with a plan. Everything seemed to have been okay, but now that it was getting close to the actual beginning of the class, Sheila was getting cold feet. Actually, more like frozen feet. She was shy and had anxiety issues, and thinking about being in front of a group of strangers was freaking her out.

"This yarn is for Sheila's rehearsal," I told the dogs, examining the ball of yarn in my hand for damage. I'd come up with a plan to have her do a practice class, hoping it would calm her down. Secretly, I hoped it would calm me down as well. Since I'd talked her into it, I felt personally responsible. And there was something else, too—Mrs. Shedd had no idea there was any problem. I picked up another ball of yarn out of the bin.

"Can't use this one, either." Somebody had pulled the ball apart, and the fine yarn was a tangled mess. I looked at my two cats, who were perched on the back of the reddish brown leather couch. They blinked and closed their eyes, as if to proclaim their innocence. Cosmo danced around my feet, trying to show off that he'd rounded up the offender.

My other dog, Blondie, had just come into the room. Her strawberry blond, wiry hair might say terrier mix, but her personality didn't at all. She didn't mingle with the others much and spent most of her time in a chair in my room. She glanced at the rest of the animals, sensed something was going on, and retreated to her spot.

After I'd placed all the usable yarn back in the bin, I closed the top, this time making sure it was completely secure. I picked up the bin and started across the living room, followed by a parade of pets who knew what was going on. *Here we go again*, I thought.

"I'm sorry, but I have to leave." I said it without looking back. I couldn't bear to see the looks on their faces. Sometimes I wondered how I'd ended up the mistress of this menagerie.

It had just been me and Blondie at first. After Charlie died and I was feeling very alone, Blondie and I sort of found each other at a dog rescue. I was pretty sure she had been adopted and returned—when I first saw her, she looked totally woebegone, and she seemed to feel as abandoned as I did.

I quickly found out that she was the Greta Garbo of dogs—she preferred to be alone. She'd already returned to her spot in my room and wasn't part of the parade that was trailing behind me.

The rest of my pets pretty much chronicled the changes in my life. Cosmo really belonged to Barry Greenberg, my ex. I refuse to say ex-boyfriend, because it just seems weird to call a homicide detective in his fifties a boyfriend. It figured that a cop's dog would be the one to catch up with the yarn offender.

Barry's son, Jeffrey, still came by once a week or so and acted like Cosmo's owner. The dog seemed to play along, but as soon as Jeffrey left, Cosmo made it clear he was all mine.

The two cats' names were Cat Woman and Holstein, which at some point had morphed into Cat and Mr. Kitty (don't ask). They'd come courtesy of my son Samuel, who had moved in and out a few times, eventually just leaving the cats here.

And finally there was Felix, the gray terrier who, unlike Blondie, definitely knew he was a terrier. He'd arrived with Samuel the last time he moved back in with me, when he and his girlfriend Nell broke up. Thank heavens Samuel had stayed this time. Managing all these animals on top of everything else was a little much. Though at the moment, my son was on the road. His day job was head barista at a coffee place, but at heart he was a musician.

My mother was part of the She La Las, a girl group from back in the day who had one hit—"My Guy Bill." The group had turned the public's nostalgia for the song into a gig as part of an oldies show touring performing arts centers across the country. Samuel had been hired as their musical director and roadie.

I got to my kitchen and set the bin down. The air smelled of the freshly baked biscuits that were cooling on the counter. Thankfully Felix hadn't learned yet how to get up on the counter, or they would have been history.

"Presentation is everything," I told my animal audience as I put a checkered cloth napkin in a basket and loaded it with biscuits before covering them with another napkin. I also had several small brown paper bags on the counter—I used a couple of paper napkins to line them, making sure the white corners showed at the top before adding biscuits to each. Finally, I loaded everything into a recycled plastic shopping bag.

This was the hardest part. "Sorry, guys, but I have to go." I picked up the yarn bin, balancing the bag of biscuits on top, and took it all outside. When I came back in to get my jacket and purse, my pets were gathered near the door with sad faces. Guiltily, I reached for the treat jar and gave a biscuit to each of the two dogs and a tiny cat treat to each of the cats. My plan was to hustle out the door while they were eating. It had also been my plan to have them associate me going out with them getting a treat. Unfortunately, neither plan worked very well—they'd finished chewing before I'd slipped on my jacket, and when I looked behind me through the glass door, Felix had his paws up, as though pleading to go along. I steeled myself—I had places to go and people to see.

It was March in Southern California, and the winter rains had left everything green. The orange trees were in full blossom, and their wonderful fragrance perfumed the air as I hurried across the yard.

It took just a few minutes to drive to the heart of Tarzana. Once upon a time the whole area had been part of a ranch owned by Edgar Rice Burroughs. Creating the Tarzan character was his main claim to fame, so it made sense he would name the area after him.

These days, the ranch feel of the area was long gone, and the grasslands where sheep had grazed were all filled with houses. A few holdout areas still had a rural feel, though, complete with horses and chickens. Tarzana was quirkier than the surrounding San Fernando Valley communities, which suited me just fine.

Shedd & Royal Books and More was located on Ventura Boulevard, the main drag, which zigzagged along the south end of the Valley. I pulled into the parking lot behind it and fished through my stuff for my ever-present canvas tote and one of the small brown shopping bags. The smell of the biscuits made my mouth water—it had been all I could do not to sample them when I'd taken them out of the oven. I was saving them to share with Dinah, who was already waiting outside the store. She eyed the small bag in my hand, and I opened it for her inspection.

"Those smell heavenly. I'm glad one of us still cooks," she said, licking her lips. Dinah was somewhere in her fifties, though she wouldn't say exactly where, even to me, since she was convinced that people judged you once they knew your exact age. I always thought she was brimming with so much energy and such a sense of adventure that no one could possibly think of her as over-the-hill. Besides, didn't Liam Neeson just say that sixty was the new forty?

Now that Dinah had joined the crochet group, she made all of her long trademark scarves herself. They were all skinny, and sometimes, like today, she braided two together. Today's combination was burnt orange and turquoise.

"Before we go in, let me drop off these." I pulled out a stack of flyers about Yarn University that listed the classes and our upcoming event to promote them. I'd added photos to illustrate some of the class projects. The crochet hook with a strip of single crochet stitches done in pale blue cotton yarn was for the beginning crochet class. A small red bag with a navy blue flower showed off what felting was all about. The basket of coasters and pot holders in bright colors was from our quick and easy class. Finally there was a hazy green, blue and lavender piece that we were calling "a Hug" from our specialty class. I'd already left some flyers at most of the stores on the street, but I hadn't been able to connect with the new nail salon on the corner.

We walked past the bookstore and continued to the corner. A "Grand Opening" banner hung above the entrance of the Nail Spa, but the sign on the glass door declared it closed. I checked to see if there was a list of their hours but didn't find one.

"I'll have to come back," I said as we turned to retrace our steps. "It just seems like the perfect place to leave some flyers. People are thinking about their hands when they go in there, and we're offering something else for them to do with them."

"Good thinking," Dinah said with an approving nod.

We headed back to the bookstore, and as I crossed the store on my way to the café, I stopped to adjust the poster near the cashier stand promoting Yarn University. It was similar to my flyers and was positioned in front of a display of knit and crochet books. I made a mental note to add another poster in the yarn department and straightened a copy of *Hooray for Crochet!* as I let out a worried sigh.

"Don't fret. There will be lots more sign-ups, and the classes will all work out." Dinah grabbed my hand and pulled me toward the café. "The world will look rosier after you have a red eye."

"I swear, nobody makes coffee at home anymore," I said when I saw the long line to the counter. Bob, the barista, looked up with an apologetic smile.

"That's because we're all hooked on lattes and espresso drinks," Dinah said. "A cup of plain coffee seems so yesterday." I had to admit the smell of brewing espresso was intoxicating, and a shot of it definitely offered more of a jolt than a plain cup of coffee.

"Thanks for all you've done with Sheila already," I said, thinking of our newest teacher. "At least she has a class plan, but I wish you were going to be there this morning. Just in case she has trouble." Dinah was an English instructor at the local community college. She was known for taking freshmen who were still immature—big babies, as she put it—and turning them into real college students.

"I doubt anybody in a crochet class is going to give her problems like my students. They insist on wearing their baseball hats in class and throw fits when I tell them to put away their phones. Sheila just needs to be in front of a group and have it go well, then she'll be fine for the actual class."

"I'm sure you're right. Or I hope so. Sheila's class has the largest number of sign-ups." It was easy to see why. Even in the small photo on the flyers, the beauty of her project was evident. It wasn't that the shawls and scarves she made had intricate stitch patterns—it was all about the colors. She mixed shades of blues, greens and lavenders, and the results were pieces that had a soft, hazy coloration similar to an Impressionist painting.

"Anyways, I'd rather be spending the time hanging out with the Hookers than giving a pop quiz to my class. Can you believe that they keep asking for do-overs? All I can say is I hope none of them become surgeons." As soon as Dinah stopped speaking, her expression faded and she seemed upset.

"What's wrong? Can't think of what to order?" I teased as the line moved up a bit. "It looks like we'll have plenty of time to decide." I glanced past the people ahead of us as a man in white shorts and white cable-knit sweater draped over his shoulders stepped up to the counter.

True, it was March and the weather had gotten milder, but the mornings were still chilly, and I shivered seeing his bare legs and arms. The man leaned on the counter and scratched at his arms. Even from this distance, I could see he had a rash. Bob saw it, too, and instinctively backed away. The man picked up on Bob's reaction and seemed annoyed.

"Relax, man. It's just an allergy. You're not going to catch anything," the guy in shorts said.

"I don't think Bob bought it," I said to Dinah, motioning to where Bob had taken another step back from the counter as he took the guy's order.

"Huh?" Dinah sounded mystified. Her reaction surprised me, as it wasn't like her to be oblivious.

"Okay, I'm guessing there's more on your mind than whether to have a medium or large café au lait," I said.

She let out a heavy sigh, and I felt something big coming.

"I'll tell you when we sit down." The three people ahead of us placed their orders quickly, and suddenly we were at the counter. Bob saw the small shopping bag on my arm and eyed it suspiciously.

"What's in the bag? Are you bringing in your own treats again?" he said in mock annoyance, gesturing toward his array of freshly baked breakfast bars. "Mrs. Shedd frowns on such things." I opened the bag and took out one of the biscuits.

"I won't tell if you don't. Here's your payoff," I said, offering him a biscuit with a conspiratorial grin.

He took a tiny taste, and his eyes opened wider. "You'll have to give me the recipe. We're definitely adding these to the menu." He asked Dinah and me for our orders. I opted for my usual tall red eye—the coffee with a shot of espresso would definitely open the blinds of my mind. Dinah almost ordered something different, but in the end she got her usual café au lait. It seemed almost counterproductive to dilute the caffeine with steamed milk. Wasn't hot milk something you drank to fall asleep?

As soon as we got our drinks, we gathered up some packets of honey and a lot of napkins and found a table. I was waiting for Dinah to say something more about whatever was on her mind, but so far she hadn't started to talk. Dead air always made me nervous, so I tended to fill it with chatter.

"I brought some biscuits for the group," I said. "And another bag of them for Mason. I'm going to stop by on the way to Sheila's practice class."

Mason Fields was the man in my life. I had thought that once I made the choice that he was the one, it would be all clear sailing. But life never seemed to sail clear for me. Just when we were about to go off on a wonderful trip, he'd had a car accident. His car had been totaled, and Mason had almost been totaled, too. I still got a sick feeling when I thought about seeing him in intensive care, hooked up to a bunch of machines. And yet I also got a warm feeling when I remembered the look in his eyes when he saw me there. It was amazing how much emotion he managed to pack into his gaze.

He'd had a whole laundry list of injuries, from a punctured lung to a broken leg and foot. Luckily they were all things that would heal. By the time he'd been released from rehab, he was already back to his usual upbeat self. He was doing the last of his recovery at home—his home. We'd used his dog Spike not getting along with my assorted animals as an excuse, but I don't think either one of us was ready for him to move in to my place or for me to stay at his. I shook my head just thinking about the complications of middle-aged relationships. Anyways, Mason was getting stir-crazy from being housebound for so long, so I knew the baked goods would be a nice treat.

"Okay, I can't take it. Whatever's on your mind, please spill it now before I ramble on anymore," I said. "What is it? Another student trying to pass off text talk in an essay?" I meant it as a joke to lighten things up, but it was something that definitely bugged Dinah. Her students were so accustomed to using shortened versions of words on their phones, they didn't seem to understand that it didn't work in a paper. Dinah said she felt like a code buster sometimes, and that was without considering the slang they threw in. "Sick" was supposed to be a compliment now?

I was relieved when she smiled. "No, it's not a student. It's Commander." Commander Blaine was the man in her life. None of us knew if his first name was really Commander, or if it was a nickname or a title, but we did know that his wife had died a few years ago and he owned the local Mail It Center. Dinah had been divorced when I met her—her husband had been a jerk, and so had most of the men she'd met after they had separated. So even though Commander was a total non-jerk, she had trouble believing it.

"You're not breaking up," I said, looking at her with concern.

She laughed at my furrowed brows. "Quite the opposite. He says he wants us to make a commitment."

This time I laughed. "You mean like going steady, or is

he going to give you his class ring to wear on a chain around your neck?"

"Actually, he's talking about putting a ring on my finger." She held up her left hand and wiggled her fingers to make sure there was no doubt about what he meant.

"He wants to get marr—" I couldn't get out the whole word before she shushed me.

"I can't even say it out loud," she said, and her expression got serious. "I don't see why we can't leave things the way they are. I like his company, but I'm used to my life, my house, having my ex's kids over."

"Tell me about it," I said. That had been part of the problem with my ex Barry. He'd wanted to get married, and I was still figuring out my life after Charlie died. "What I have with Mason is perfect. Or it will be, when a few things get straightened out."

"Commander is really serious about it. He said he needed time to get over his wife's death, and now he's ready to move on. And we all know he's a proper sort of guy, down to the way he dresses."

I nodded in agreement, thinking of how Dinah had been put off at first by the razor-sharp creases in his khaki pants and the way his oxford cloth dress shirts were tucked in so perfectly that there wasn't even a stray wrinkle.

"I wish he wanted what you and Mason have," Dinah said. I knew what she meant. Mason and I had started out as friends. He was a fun person and never seemed to take anything too seriously, including relationships. He'd said he was just interested in something casual. No titles, no strings. But when it came down to it, we'd both realized that just being ships that passed in the night—or I guess the more contemporary term was friends with benefits—wasn't really what either of us wanted, and so we'd agreed to belong to each other.

"What did you say to him?" I asked. She took a sip of her coffee and grinned.

"I used to see old movies where women responded to proposals this way, and I thought it was silly and something I would never do." She shrugged with a sheepish look. "I told him I'd think about it."

CHAPTER 2

A HALF AN HOUR LATER I WAS DRIVING ON THE back roads of Tarzana with my last bag of biscuits on the passenger seat. The winding road that ran along the base of the hills leading up to the Santa Monica mountains was my route of choice. The houses were all different along this road, rustic with large grounds and trees that made a green canopy. I thought of how much nicer it was than taking Ventura Boulevard even though the busy commercial street was more direct. Finally I turned onto Mason's street.

His ranch-style house was done in dark wood that almost seemed to blend in with the trees and elegant landscaping of the front yard.

I parked in front of the house and went up the walkway. Mason had insisted on giving me a key, but I still felt funny about using it, though it turned out not to matter. The front door was slightly ajar. I pushed it open and heard frantic barking coming from Mason's dog, Spike, a toy fox terrier who thought he was a Doberman. Worried that something was wrong, I started down the hall, following the noise.

I heard voices above the barking as I approached the living room, though they stopped abruptly when I became visible. Spike even stopped barking long enough to run up to me and give my ankles a once-over. Mason was standing with two women. I recognized both of them. It was no surprise to see his daughter Brooklyn. As soon as she'd heard about his accident, she'd dropped what she was doing in San Diego and moved in to take care of him. That was all I really knew. Mason had never said anything about what she'd abandoned in San Diego or even how he felt about it, and I didn't ask.

When I'd first gotten to know Mason, he had a thing about keeping his family separate from his social life. I suppose it was because his relationships had been so casual, with no strings, so there was no reason to involve his daughters. But that didn't work for me, and eventually he'd introduced me to his daughters. And even his ex.

The one thing I did know was that Brooklyn didn't like me. Every time I came over, she treated me like an intruder. If it had been his other daughter, Thursday, there wouldn't have been a problem. She had actually been pushing for me and Mason to get together. We got along fine and even crocheted together sometimes.

So, it wasn't the cold stare from Brooklyn that was the surprise. It was who was with her and why.

What was Jaimee Fields, Mason's ex-wife, doing there? And why was there a suitcase next to her? If Brooklyn's stare was cold, Jaimee Fields's stare could have made an ice skating rink in hell.

"Sunshine, you're here." Mason was all smiles as he moved away from the group to give me a welcoming hug. His ankle and foot were still healing, and he couldn't put weight on one leg, so instead of hobbling around on crutches, he'd opted for a scooter. Basically, the scooter had a cushion where he could rest his knee, three wheels, and a basket. Typical for Mason, he'd jazzed it up a bit and added an old-fashioned bicycle bell. He saw the small shopping bag I was holding and looked inside with a grin.

"Biscuits, my favorite!" he said. He put the bag in the scooter's basket and gave the bell a pull and it made a happy sound. He was chomping at the bit to be recovered, but in the meantime, he was doing his best to make it fun to use the scooter.

I wanted so badly to demand to know what was going on, but there was no way I could ask. When Mason had finally opened up to me about his family, he told me the divorce had been peaceful, as far as breakups went. The marriage had ended once their two daughters were on their own and Mason and Jaimee had realized they didn't have much in common anymore. They were leading separate lives already, so they decided to make them completely separate. It was conscious uncoupling before anybody knew what that meant.

Jaimee was doing her best to not look at me or at Mason's arm around my shoulder. Their breakup might have been amicable, but it didn't erase all the years they'd been together, and she didn't seem particularly happy that Mason had found somebody else.

"I'm here to help Brooklyn take care of you. You know I would have been here sooner, but I just had so much going on," Jaimee said.

What! I froze at her words. She might have been avoiding looking at me, but I had no problem looking at her. I know it was supposed to be true that people keep picking out the same kind of person, but that couldn't possibly have been the case with Mason. Jaimee was all boutique clothes, perfectly highlighted hair and expert makeup. And I was in my usual classic khaki pants and cotton shirt, topped with a black V-neck sweater. The orange crocheted cowl had a subtle touch of sparkle and added some zip to my plain outfit. I was happy with my non-highlighted brown hair, and as for makeup, I'd say the best description of my look was subtle.

"I appreciate your offer," Mason said. "But as you can see I'm almost one hundred percent." He did a little cha-cha with the foot that was on the ground to show off how well he was.

Jaimee's face clouded over and she looked perturbed. "I can't believe you're turning down my offer. You've probably run poor Brooklyn ragged. She needs some help."

Brooklyn stepped a little closer to her mother and nodded in agreement. I tried to keep a benign expression so I wouldn't give away how ridiculous I thought the comment was. I knew for a fact she hadn't been run ragged. The biggest thing she did for him was to act as his driver. I actually had the feeling Mason was letting Brooklyn stay more because she seemed to need it than for any help he required.

Mason cut right to the chase. "Jaimee, why are you really here?"

Jaimee seemed offended by his comment. "I thought it would be a win-win sort of thing. I could help look after you and have a place to stay while my house is being redone."

Mason still seemed skeptical. "What about Todd? Can't you stay at his place?" Even though their divorce had been amicable, there was a certain level of hostility in Mason's voice when he said her boyfriend's name. I didn't think it was jealousy, but more irritation at what kind of person she'd chosen to take Mason's place. I'd seen him once from a distance. All I remembered was that he was younger than she was and some kind of tennis pro. Personally, I thought her money had a lot to do with her allure. Maybe Mason was thinking the same thing. Either way, I don't think he wanted to consider that he and Todd were alike any more than I wanted to believe Jaimee was like me.

Mason and Jaimee had been married a long time, and it seemed that there was bound to be emotional residue. I just didn't want to be in the middle of it. I tried to pull away, but Mason held on tightly to me.

Jaimee threw Mason an exasperated glance before she continued. "If you must know, we broke up. Well, actually, I broke up with him."

This was starting to get more and more uncomfortable. "I just came to drop off the biscuits, really," I said, managing to pull free this time.

"Please stay," Mason said with a smile. "I'll make cappuccinos." Jaimee seemed impatient with our little moment and started talking again.

"I'm pretty sure Todd was cheating on me," Jaimee said. The comment had the desired effect, as all three of us turned our attention to her.

"You tend to overreact sometimes," Mason said. "I'm sure you can work things out."

Jaimee made a face. "I should have figured you would say that. I don't overreact. I don't know why you keep saying that. He went somewhere Thursday night. He said it was business, but he wasn't dressed for a lesson. Besides, he's been cancelling students, saying he doesn't have the time. I know because I answered his cell phone a few times and these people started yapping at me—he's such a great teacher, their game is going to suffer if they don't have their weekly session, blah, blah, blah. When I brought it up to him, he got mad at me for answering his phone. Then he said he had invested in some kind of business and had a partner and that was why he wasn't doing so many lessons anymore. He wouldn't give me any more details than that. The final blow was when I suggested staying at his place while the work was being done at my place. He said no, so I said go."

"What about a hotel?" Mason said. "I'll even make the reservation." He was already pulling out his cell phone.

"No," she said vehemently. "I can't be in some public place. I need to hide out."

Brooklyn held on to her mother's arm sympathetically.

Jaimee seemed to sag. "I was dropped from *The Housewives of Mulholland Drive*. The producer said there wasn't enough drama in my life to keep the audience interested. Once they heard I broke up with Todd, I was just an overdressed woman remodeling her house."

I couldn't see Mason's face, but I had a feeling he was rolling his eyes. I was sure he was about to talk Jaimee into going to some spa in the desert to hide out, but Brooklyn stepped in.

"Dad, you should let her stay here. This house is huge. She can stay in the room next to mine, and you'll never have to see each other."

"She's right," Jaimee said brightly. "It'll be like we're girlfriends. You won't even know I'm here." Mason might have stood his ground with his ex-wife, but once his daughter got involved, he gave up. I wasn't happy with his decision, but I understood, though I had to press my lips together to keep from asking, if Jaimee was going to be so invisible, how was she going to help take care of him? As if that was ever really an option, anyway.

When we were just friends, before we got together, Mason and I had a fun sort of relationship. Casual, with no baggage. But all of that had changed, and if we were going to belong to each other, as we'd put it, it meant accepting everything that came along with the other person, including an ex-wife and a hostile daughter.

"All right, then," Mason said, putting his hands up in capitulation. Jaimee had a triumphant smile as she made a move to pick up her suitcase, but Brooklyn grabbed it first, and the two of them walked away down the hall.

"That was not supposed to happen," Mason said, shaking his head at the receding figure of his ex-wife. "I thought I had disconnected all the buttons she knew how to push."

He made another offer of a cappuccino, but I was already overdue for my next stop and still buzzed by the red eye. "You're not sorry about us, are you?" he asked, looking intently into my eyes. "I promised you a wonderful trip and then got in a car accident. I promised you lots of fun and good times and now we're stuck with Jaimee."

"She won't be here forever," I said, and Mason brightened.

"And then it will be time to let the good times roll," he said, and he gave me another warm hug.

CHAPTER 3

I WAS RUSHING WHEN I LEFT MASON'S. I BACK-tracked through Encino to Tarzana and onto a road that ran into a secluded street. The houses here were more like estates, and the lots were irregular sizes due to the ravine that ran off Corbin Canyon. It was also darker here because of all the trees. Only a few lost their leaves over the winter, so there was a lot of foliage even now.

I pulled in front of the stone pillars that marked the entrance to CeeCee Collins's place. A wrought-iron gate closed off the driveway, and a wall of tall, neatly trimmed bushes marked the boundary of her yard.

The expansive property definitely suited our celebrity Hooker. CeeCee Collins was a veteran actress, known for her sitcom *The CeeCee Collins Show* as well as multiple movie and TV roles and cameos. Then her life had changed. First she'd become the host of a reality show, then she got the part of Ophelia in a movie called *Caught by a Kiss*. The movie meant a lot to all of us because its hero, a vampire named Anthony, crocheted to control his blood lust. The book series it was based on was a bestseller at the bookstore, too.

And then, after way too long a time of hearing about "Oscar buzz," CeeCee had actually been nominated for best supporting actress.

I wouldn't say all this had gone to her head, exactly. She had always been a little self-absorbed, and yet she was the leader of the Hookers and the one in our group who was always most interested in making crocheted items for charities.

I hit the intercom, and her unmistakable voice answered. She always sounded happy and merry, and she had a laugh I could best describe as tinkling. As soon as she heard it was me, she buzzed the gate and it swung open.

I always thought of fairy tales when I came over to CeeCee's place. Once you were inside the gate, it was like the outside world didn't exist. I had to pass a small forest of trees to get to the house, which resembled a stone cottage, though a rather large one. A stepping-stone path led the way to the door, and with all those trees and the basket of biscuits I was carrying, I almost felt like Little Red Riding Hood, except I wasn't wearing anything red and I certainly hoped there weren't any wolves hiding behind the trees.

CeeCee was standing in the doorway, and I saw her eye was on the basket I was carrying. "Thank you for letting me hold Sheila's practice class here," I said when I got to the open door.

"Of course, dear. You know I love helping Sheila. And I understand your predicament. There's no reason for Mrs. Shedd to know there's any problem." While she was talking, she lifted the checkered napkin on the basket. "Oh good, you baked something."

CeeCee was always concerned about being photographed by the paparazzi, and so she was always dressed for the possibility, but at the same time, she had a famous sweet tooth and was constantly battling her weight. "Oh, they're not sweet," she said, sounding disappointed, just for a moment. "But we can add butter and honey," she decided cheerily.

As we spoke, CeeCee's two Yorkshire terriers ran out the door and began carefully sniffing every inch of my shoes and ankles. By now I had a whole cornucopia of animal scents on me, thanks to my own menagerie along with Mason's dog Spike.

"There's just one thing, dear," CeeCee said as I handed the basket of biscuits to her. "It shouldn't be a problem, really, but there are a few extra people. And I have something exciting to present to the group."

I assured her that everything would be fine and said I would get the supplies from my car. The dogs had tired of sniffing my shoes and took off for parts unknown while CeeCee took the basket inside. When I returned with the bin of yarn, the dogs were heading back to the house, one of them carrying a fuzzy-looking ball in her mouth. They started yipping as they followed me inside.

I went straight to the dining room and set the bin down. There were already three women sitting at the table, and I realized they must be the extra people CeeCee had mentioned. I recognized two of them. "Kelsey Willis and Pia Sawyer," I said in surprise. "I haven't seen you in ages." Ages might have been a little extreme, but it probably *had* been close to twenty years. We'd all volunteered together in the old days, when our kids had gone to Wilbur Elementary.

It amazed me to think about it, but there was an "in" crowd even in the PTA. They were part of it. I wasn't. All of them had even looked about the same. They had blond hair—not natural—wore similar fashionable clothes, and drove whatever style of vehicle was in at the moment. In those days it had been minivans. These two had always considered themselves on a level above me. Kelsey's husband was an executive at one of the studios, and Pia's husband produced all of Flynn Huntington's movies, while my husband had just had a public relations firm. Executives and movie producers trumped lowly PR guys on the status scale.

Amazingly, Kelsey looked just the same as she had when we'd volunteered at the school together. She was still tiny with sharp features, and her blond hair was in the same shoulder-length style. She still had the kind of figure that could pull off wearing clothes designed for a twenty-year-old and not look like she was trying too hard.

The two women looked at me blankly. I started to explain that we'd worked together when our kids were young, hoping to jog their memories. It was kind of odd that I remembered them so clearly, and they seemed to have no recollection of me. Finally, Pia's eyes lit in recognition. "Polly, isn't it? You worked in the school library with us."

She nudged her friend. "You remember her. We worked with the kids, and she put the books back on the shelves."

Kelsey looked at me closely but still didn't seem to recognize me. "Maybe this will help," I said jokingly, turning and pretending to be pushing a library cart.

"Oh," she said finally. "Now I do remember you."

The third woman was a complete mystery to me, but she actually recognized me. "I know who you are," she said in an excited tone. "You work at the bookstore on Ventura Boulevard. Shedd & Royal, isn't it?" she asked. She didn't wait for an answer before going on about bringing some children to story time and the wonderful woman who made it all so dramatic. She abruptly stopped herself and looked at me.

"How silly of me. Of course you don't know who I am." She held out her hand. "Babs Swanson." Barely taking a breath, she continued as she glanced in the direction of Kelsey and Pia. "I talked them into coming with me. It seemed like the neighborly thing to do when CeeCee told me about the problem you have."

CeeCee was rolling her eyes out of sight of her guests. "Molly, dear, come into the kitchen so that we can make some coffee to go with these biscuits." I wanted to laugh. The only thing CeeCee knew about her kitchen was where it was. It was rumored she could burn water. And make coffee? No way. We passed through the swinging door into the other room just as Rosa, her proper-looking housekeeper, came in the back door. She stopped in her tracks, startled to see us in her domain.

"We're just making coffee," CeeCee said to Rosa, who wore a gray uniform and sensible shoes. I watched as CeeCee surveyed the kitchen and finally found the coffeemaker on the counter. She pulled out the glass pot and then seemed at a loss as to what to do. Rosa gave just the slightest amused shake of her head before offering to take over.

CeeCee seemed relieved to relinquish the pot. "I'm sure you'll do a better job than I would," she said. "We have these biscuits, too. They need something. . . ."

Rosa took the basket from CeeCee's arm. "Don't worry, Miss CeeCee. I know what you like. I'll bring in some honey, butter and the strawberry jam Mr. Tony had me get." I'm sure the housekeeper was hoping we'd leave now that she'd taken over, but CeeCee looked around in a dither.

"What did I come in here for?" She turned to me with a question in her heart-shaped face.

"It was something about the women in the dining room," I said.

"Yes, that's right," CeeCee said. Her expression faded slightly. "I'm sorry, but I couldn't stop her."

"You mean Babs?" I asked. CeeCee was momentarily distracted as Rosa opened a jar of fancy-looking strawberry jam. Rosa offered her a taste before adding it to the tray she was setting up. CeeCee smiled, which I guess meant it got her approval. Rosa seemed unconcerned with CeeCee's interference, but then she was probably used to it.

"Yes, Babs. She's visiting—well, no, actually she's living with her son and daughter-in-law." CeeCee made a broad gesture that I imagined was in the direction of their house, though I couldn't tell where she meant. "She's from Iowa City, where everybody is friendly and stops in for coffee unannounced. When she first got here, she made the rounds to all the houses—with brownies. Very good brownies," CeeCee added, sounding a little guilty. "Since then she's always stopping by with something to be neighborly. I don't know how to tell her that she isn't in Iowa City anymore and people don't do that around here. She certainly doesn't like that the houses around here have high fences. Apparently, where she comes from fences are in bad taste. Well, dear, as soon as she heard I was helping you with Sheila's lesson, she volunteered to be a pretend student. I don't know how she got the other women to come along. Babs said something about one of them living nearby. One of them said she'd invited Tony and me to a party." CeeCee shrugged in a helpless manner. "Of course," she said, her face lighting in recognition. "That must have been the party the other night. Tony told me it was being thrown by someone he was hoping to get involved with his new project. He went, but I stayed home." She went back to talking about Babs. "I know she means well, but she just keeps popping over and telling me all about her situation. Her son and daughter-in-law both have big jobs, so she came to look after their kids. But, they have two nannies—one for each of the kids, so Babs has a lot of time on her hands."

By now the coffee was dripping into the pot and Rosa was putting the finishing touches on the accompaniments to the biscuits.

Babs picked up where she'd left off when we returned to the dining room. "It is so exciting to have a real actress as a neighbor," she trilled. She sighed as she looked at the mural on the wall. It had CeeCee as the character she'd played in *Caught by a Kiss*. Anthony, the vampire who crocheted, was featured next to her, complete with a crochet hook dripping blood. It was a pretty good likeness to Hugh Jackman, who'd played the part in the movie. The hook was more for effect than accuracy—the fictional Anthony had never harmed anything or anyone with his crochet hook. CeeCee had left an empty section at the bottom for an Oscar statue in case she'd won, but now that she hadn't, it had been filled with the words *Academy Award Nominated*, which from now on would be part of her title.

The Yorkies went crazy as the intercom buzzed. I went to answer and a few moments later opened the door to some of the Hookers. Rhoda Klein came in first. She was solidly built and had a no-nonsense air about her. She was dependable, though a little blunt. She went directly into the dining room and looked around. "Is Sheila here yet?" she asked, looking at the three strangers. Rhoda had lived in Southern California for twenty years or more but still had a thick New York accent.

"Not yet," I answered, trailing behind her.

"Are you new Hookers?" Rhoda asked the three women. She began to unload some items from her tote bag and set them on the table.

Kelsey and Pia blanched at the title, but Babs stepped in

and explained to them that Tarzana Hookers was the name of our group.

"I brought along some samples of felted items," Rhoda said. She looked at Kelsey and Pia. "So, are you joining us?"

Kelsey took on the role of spokesperson. "No. We're not joining anything. I'm not even really sure why I'm here." She glanced in Babs's direction. "Pia and I were out at the street getting my mail, and Babs came along and said CeeCee Collins needed some help."

There was an awkward moment before I explained what the gathering was about. I might have gone into a little too much detail about the bookstore and the events we had before getting to Yarn University and Sheila's class. Kelsey was twitching in her seat and was clearly impatient. "When is this supposed to start?" she asked. "Babs talked us into coming." She glanced toward the door, making it pretty obvious that she wanted to leave.

Babs blanched at the comment. "I didn't have to do much convincing. You both said you'd always wanted to see the inside of CeeCee's house."

Kelsey shot Babs an annoyed look, but CeeCee stepped in and turned on the charm. "Let me give you a tour. Where did you say you lived?" Kelsey smiled and explained that her house was on the street behind CeeCee's, and Pia's was farther down the same street.

"If you lived in Iowa City, you'd be old friends since you live so close," Babs said. "You'd be doing block parties together, planning your decorations for Halloween together. Not like here where you people all keep to yourselves. I plan to change all that," Babs said gaily.

I'm not sure if Kelsey and Pia heard the end of Babs's comment, as they were already following CeeCee, who had offered to show them the living room and the den. I went back to setting out the supplies, and a few minutes later the three came back into the dining room.

"I'll show you the guest apartment with the rest of the group," CeeCee said, but the two women didn't sit down again. "We can't stay," Kelsey said, fumbling over an excuse. You didn't have to be a detective to realize she just wanted to get out of there. They started for the door, but then Pia stopped and nudged Kelsey. I heard some mumbling about being tired of the same old thing.

Pia stopped in front of me. "You said something about doing handicraft parties at Shedd & Royal." She gestured toward Kelsey. "That would be perfect for Erin's baby shower. It would be something different. You could start a trend, Kelsey." Kelsey suddenly seemed interested and asked for my card, handing me one of her own in exchange.

"I'll talk to my daughter. She will want to stop by and see what you offer, Polly."

"It's Molly! Molly Pink!" I called after her.

The door had only been shut for a minute or so when it opened again and Adele Abrams came into the house. "Those blond women let me in the gate," she said. We all loved crochet, but Adele was by far the greatest champion for the hobby. To her it was the only yarn craft worth anything. As usual, she was decked out in some of her handiwork. She saw Babs at the table, and her face lit up.

"Hello, let me introduce myself." She shot out a hand toward Babs. "I'm going to be teaching the beginning crochet class at Crochet College," she said.

"We're really calling it Yarn University," I corrected, and Adele glowered. Babs seemed thrilled to be meeting yet another new person.

"My name is Babs. I'm just here to be a pretend student. I used to knit, but I haven't done it for years."

Adele shuddered at the word *knit*. Babs leaned a little closer. "You're going to do fine. I don't know why your friends think you're too shy."

Adele seemed mystified, and I tried to stifle a laugh. The idea of someone thinking Adele was shy was too funny. "This is Adele Abrams," I said. "We're still waiting for Sheila.

"And that must be her," I said as we heard the intercom buzz. We all looked toward the entrance hall expectantly, but when the door opened, Elise Belmont came in. She was a small woman who had a birdlike voice and who looked like a good gust of wind could blow her over. Elise often came off as a little vague, but in truth she had a steel core. She had turned her obsession with Anthony, the vampire who crocheted, into a business. She kept the bookstore stocked with a constant supply of kits to make "all things vampire style," as she called it. She was teaching a class in Literary Crochet. But of course, the only books involved were the Anthony series. She looked around at the group. "Where's Sheila?"

Exactly what I was thinking.

CHAPTER 4

"MAYBE SHEILA ISN'T COMING," ADELE SAID. "I can take over the class if she's chickened out." To illustrate the point, Adele pulled out a crocheted scarf done in shades of blue, but it was all made of one type of yarn, and the texture was nothing like Sheila's pieces.

"Nonsense, dear. Sheila will show up," CeeCee said, giving her mouth a dainty wipe. We had decided not to wait for Sheila to eat. Rosa had taken the presentation up a notch, putting the jam and honey in china bowls and the coffee in a silver pot alongside my basket of biscuits.

"We might as well work on our own projects until Sheila gets here," Rhoda said. She had already taken out hers. Babs examined the royal blue piece and asked what she was making.

"Just a vest," Rhoda said. When Elise inquired who she was making it for, Rhoda seemed almost perturbed and dodged the question by looking to the beige strip of crocheted yarn that Adele was taking out of her tote. "What's that?" Rhoda asked.

"It's a bow tie for Cutchykins." Adele turned toward Babs to explain who she was talking about, but before she could say anything, Rhoda spoke for her.

"We all know your pet name for your fiancé," she said.

"When's the big day?" Babs asked, eyeing Adele's engagement ring.

Adele's face clouded. "Eric and I are still working on the date and venue," she said, and she quickly changed the subject to the bath mitt she was making for her soon-to-be mother-in-law.

Rhoda leaned toward Babs. "Eric's mother is trying to put the kibosh on the wedding, so Adele's attempting to win her over with crocheted gifts."

Adele overheard and was starting to argue that she didn't have to win her over when we were interrupted by a white-haired man sailing into the room with Sheila in tow.

"Look who I have," Tony Bonnard said, unlinking his arm with Sheila's and giving her a soft push closer to the group. I was never sure how to describe Tony's relationship with CeeCee. It seemed absurd to call him her boyfriend, but I couldn't come up with anything better. "She was outside the gate when I pulled in. I knew you were expecting her." He didn't say it, but I was pretty sure he'd had to coax her to come in. She looked tenser than usual, which was really something for her.

If there was one word to describe Sheila Altman, it was *anxious*. She was the youngest in our group, so we were all like a bunch of mother hens looking after her and trying to help her deal with her nerves. Sheila had been brought up by her grandmother, who'd died not long ago, leaving her feeling abandoned. She was still trying to find her place in the world, though now that she'd started working at the lifestyle store, Luxe, down the street from the bookstore, she seemed more on track. The best part of the job was that the beautiful crocheted pieces she made fit right into the store, which featured lots of one-of-a-kind items. Customers always fell in love with the lush coloring of the blankets, shawls and scarves she brought in.

With her new job, Sheila seemed to have given up on her previous desire to be a studio costume designer, despite all the classes she'd taken. The classes weren't really a loss, though—it was probably through them that she'd come up with her distinctive Impressionist style. Most of her items were crocheted, and none of us liked to bring it up in front of Adele, but Sheila did knit some of the pieces.

And now for the first time she was going to show others how to crochet one of her signature pieces using her method.

"I'm sorry I'm so late," she said, and she began reciting a list of excuses. It seemed she'd been so nervous thinking about doing the practice class, she hadn't been able to sleep, but then she had fallen asleep and overslept, which gave her a whole new reason to be anxious. "I had to sit and crochet with string for a while just so I could calm down enough to get dressed." She stopped long enough to take a deep breath. "Thank you for doing this," Sheila said, pushing her chin-length hair behind her ears to get it off her face. She put on a brave smile, but her brow was still furrowed.

Babs came up next to her and introduced herself. "I'm your volunteer student. I'm anxious to learn, and I know you are going to be great." Babs put her arm around Sheila's shoulder. If this was what they did in Iowa City, I was all for it. Sheila let out a deep breath and seemed to relax a little.

Rosa had come in with two more plates and some biscuits she had smartly set aside, but Tony held up his hand.

"None for me. I'm just here for a moment. No more cushy life of an actor for me. I'm a producer now. I just stopped by to pick something up. Then it's errands to run and people to see."

"I can't believe they canceled the soap you were on. I thought you were fabulous," Babs said.

Tony smiled at her comment. "Thank you, but such is life. You have to make the best of change." He sounded like he meant it, but who knew for sure. Acting was his trade. He certainly looked the part of a leading man with his square jaw and sparkling blue eyes, the collar of his tan polo shirt stylishly turned up. None of the other Hookers said anything, but we all traded glances. We knew that Tony and CeeCee had been a couple for a long time, but they'd always had their own homes. CeeCee hadn't said anything, but lately it had seemed like Tony was living at her place. We thought it was rude to ask, but we did wonder what was going on.

"I'll leave you to your crocheting, ladies," he said, stopping to kiss CeeCee on the cheek. He gave Sheila a pat on the back. "I know you'll knock 'em dead." He was halfway out of the dining room when he turned back. "CeeCee, don't forget to tell them about your plan."

All eyes turned to CeeCee. "Well?" Rhoda said.

"You heard Tony say he's a producer now. He's putting together a web-only series. We were talking about ways to keep the expenses down, and these days you can do so much with so little equipment. And now that my niece has moved out of the guest apartment over the garage, we thought we'd turn it into a studio. I thought we could use it to make crochet videos. Of course, I'd be the director."

"And I could be the host!" Adele said excitedly.

"We can figure that all out later," CeeCee said. "I just wondered what you all thought of the idea." We were all enthused, and Elise wanted to see the space she was talking about right away. "I don't want to take away from Sheila's time. We can look at it another time," CeeCee said.

"Why not do it now?" Sheila said, obviously stalling. I really wanted to get her practice class done, but she was already leading the way to CeeCee's front door.

"I think filming something and putting it on the bookstore website would be a great idea, though I'll have to talk Mrs. Shedd into it," I said, getting up. "She's resisting having too much of an online presence. She wants the bookstore to be a destination."

We all followed Sheila out the front door. "A video of me crocheting might bring people into the bookstore," Adele said. "We could film me doing story time, too. That would bring in customers."

I didn't say anything, but I was thinking, *Leave it to Adele to figure out how to make it The Adele Show*. Though I had to admit that she always made story time very dramatic and was known to wear costumes to match the characters she was reading about and to practically act out the books.

"You'll have to use your imagination, because we haven't done anything to it yet," CeeCee said as we walked across the front of her property. "We'll add some lighting, and Tony wants to have a green screen so he can make it look like all different places." As CeeCee talked, I looked around the yard. I loved the outdoor patio area, with its arrangement of chairs and string of lights overhead, though it seemed dark now because of the shadows from all the trees. It was almost hard to believe it was midday. We approached the garage, which was freestanding and had room for multiple cars, though CeeCee always parked in the driveway near the gate. The apartment was probably originally built to house live-in staff, but when CeeCee's career had stalled, she'd gone to having a housekeeper who just worked days. Then CeeCee's niece had moved into the space when she came out from Ohio. Nell was a bit of a sore spot with me. She had abruptly broken up with my son. I didn't know the exact details, but I gathered that she didn't want to be tied down and had simply moved on, leaving him heartbroken. My gray terrier mix, Felix, had originally been their dog. CeeCee went on about how her niece had been making a bunch of life changes—not mentioning that that included breaking up with Samuel, even though everyone knew—and had gotten a place in the Silver Lake neighborhood of L.A.

There was a stairway along the side of the garage that led to the second-story entrance, and CeeCee took the lead in climbing it. "Before we do anything, we'll have to clear out the old furniture," she said. "We haven't even bothered locking the door."

CeeCee rambled on about getting a director's chair with her name on it and wearing a baseball cap like Ron Howard did, and I listened halfheartedly as the breeze blew a whiff of a terrible smell my way. I hoped it would go away, but with each step it seemed to get stronger.

When we got to the top, CeeCee pushed the door open. It was as dark as a cave inside, and a blast of heat came out, intensifying the bad smell. CeeCee made a face. "Oh my God, what did Nell leave in here? And why did she leave the heat on?"

Babs had come around the others and was just one step below CeeCee and me. "A mouse or something must have gotten in," Babs said. CeeCee cringed at the thought and took a step back, somehow maneuvering me in front of her. The rest of the group had stopped where they were.

CeeCee dropped her voice. "Babs must be right. It's happened before." Then she turned back to the others and gestured toward me. "Molly will take care of it. She has a lot of experience with dead bodies."

CeeCee followed behind me, hanging on to my shirt until I entered the apartment. "Is there a light switch?" I asked, touching the wall. CeeCee had backed away from the doorway and either didn't hear me or didn't know the answer. There were closed shutters over the windows, but enough light came through for me to be able to gingerly pick my way across the room. I tried to deal with the smell by holding my nose, but it was no help. The awful smell still got through. I pulled back the shutters and pushed the first window open. An old-fashioned heater was on the wall near the door. I made a beeline to it and turned the dial to Off. I looked for the source of the smell next, and I gasped when I realized it was something bigger than a mouse. Way bigger.

A figure of an adult person was sprawled on the ground. I couldn't tell if it was a man or woman, but I was very sure that he or she was dead and had been that way for a while.

"Carbon monoxide!" Rhoda yelled from the doorway, pointing at a sensor on the wall. The battery must have worn down too much to sound an alarm, but there was still a flashing red light. "You better get out."

"Oh no," CeeCee yelped, staring at the body on the ground. Her knees were beginning to buckle as she stood in the doorway, and she looked pale as skim milk. I grabbed her hand and pulled her out onto the stairway with me. Babs grabbed her other arm and helped me get her back down to the bottom of the stairs, where we had her put her head

between her knees. In that moment, she was hardly the picture of an Academy Award nominee.

Sheila's eyes were as big as saucers, and she had taken
out her hook and string and started to blindly crochet in an
effort to calm herself.

"Is it your niece?" Rhoda asked the slumped-over
CeeCee. CeeCee shook her head.

"She called me last night. There's no way it's her."

"Well, then, who is it?" Elise asked. "And how did they
get there?"

CHAPTER 5

"MOLLY, YOU HAVE TO DO SOMETHING. I CAN'T have a line of police cars roaring up here with their sirens wailing like a bunch of banshees. What if the paparazzi latch on to them?" CeeCee said. "A body on my property!" And then something else occurred to her. "They'll think I'm responsible. I'll be arrested!" CeeCee had recovered enough to stand up, but now she was almost in hysterics as she thought through her predicament.

We had taken a moment to evaluate the situation. We all agreed that the smell made it clear the person was beyond resuscitating and there was no point in calling the paramedics. Adele had stepped in and taken most of the group back to the dining room, where they were trying to recover from what they'd just seen. Poor Sheila was a total wreck now. In a surprise move, Adele had put a supportive arm around our nervous Hooker and reassured her that everything would be okay. When I said we were all mother hens to Sheila, I hadn't meant

Adele. Adele always seemed most concerned with herself, but maybe being engaged was changing her. Babs, trying to be the good neighbor, had stayed behind with CeeCee and me.

"But you have to call the police," Babs said. "You can't just leave a body up there and hope it will disappear." She took out her cell phone. "I'd be happy to do it." She had her finger poised to hit the numbers.

"Don't," CeeCee commanded in a shrill voice. "Molly has connections. Let her take care of it."

I hung my head. By connections, she meant my ex, homicide detective Barry Greenberg. We'd been kaput for a while, and since the friendship idea didn't appeal to him— did that ever work, anyway?—I hadn't talked to him for a month or so. Even so, his number was still listed under Favorites in my contact list.

I hit the icon, and the phone dialed his number. It rang a few times while I reminded myself that this was all business.

"Greenberg," he said, clearly in professional homicide cop mode. I didn't mean to, but I got butterflies in my stomach at the sound of his voice.

"Is anybody there?" he said after a moment.

"It's me, Molly," I said finally. I thought I heard a little sound of surprise, but when he spoke his voice was guarded.

"Personal or professional?" he asked.

"Maybe a little of both." I paused for a moment while I collected my thoughts. "We found a body at CeeCee's. She's worried about—" Before I could say the rest of it, he had interrupted.

"A body. How is there a body at CeeCee's?" He blew out his breath. "Who is it?"

"We don't know," I said. "I'm not even sure if it's a man or woman."

"I'll be right there. Don't touch anything, and don't let

anybody leave." Just before he hung up, I heard him mutter, "You can't seem to stay out of trouble, can you?"

I sent Babs and CeeCee to join the others and hung around by the front gate until I saw Barry's black Crown Victoria pull up. He was straightening his tie as he got out of the car.

"What happened?" he demanded as I let him in the gate. There was a slight lift to his eyebrows as his gaze moved over my face, but other than that, his expression was all business. I hated to admit it under the circumstances, but I felt a kind of rush at his presence. I guess that never goes away. He looked tired, but that was how he usually looked, since he constantly worked long hours. He was clean shaven, but there were shadows under his dark eyes. He glanced at me again, and for just a moment there was a hint of emotion. Did he feel something, too?

"Why didn't you call 911? Where's the victim?" He looked around the expansive property.

I explained CeeCee's desire to keep things quiet. "A rescue ambulance and fire truck with sirens wailing would have destroyed that plan," I said. Immediately, I realized how ridiculous that sounded, and I added that once he saw the body, he'd realize there was no need to rush.

"Let me have a look, then," he said. He told me to lead the way. "You found the body?" he asked as we started to walk. When I nodded, he gave me a discouraging shake of his head. "You better tell me how that happened."

I'm afraid I gave him much more information than he needed. I don't think he cared about Sheila's lesson or CeeCee's desire to be a video director. I couldn't see his dark eyes now, but I'm pretty sure they were glazed over, though he snapped to attention at my next comment.

"I think the cause of death is carbon monoxide poisoning," I said.

"Now you're doing the work of the medical examiner, too?" Barry made a disgruntled noise, and I guessed he was rolling his eyes at my assessment. He wasn't fond of me playing detective and tried to discourage me whenever possible, so I didn't wait for him to ask me how I was so sure, but rather went right into describing the heater being on and the sensor flashing.

He stopped and turned to look at me. "And you went in there anyway?"

"I didn't see the sensor right away," I said with a shrug. "Obviously I didn't know there was a dead person in there, either. It was pitch-black."

"Are you ever going to learn to stay out of things?" he asked.

"Probably not," I said with a smile, and he groaned. I led him across the yard to the garage and pointed up at the open door. He went on ahead, and I followed him up the stairs.

We stopped at the top while he looked in, and I pointed out the carbon monoxide sensor and the open window, reminding him that I'd turned off the heater. He gave me a hopeless shake of his head and then put his arm out to hold me back as he went in. This wasn't his first go-round with the smell of death, and he pulled out a handkerchief to cover his nose and mouth.

He made a dash across the large space to the sensor on the wall, removed it, and returned to the stairway. He conveniently had a 9-volt battery in his pocket, which he placed in the sensor before plugging it back in. It didn't go off. Still, he opened all the windows to let more air in and checked the heater again to make sure it was really off.

Barry walked over to the victim, examining the area. Now that all the shutters were open and he'd turned on the recessed lights in the ceiling, I got a better look at the whole place. I didn't want to look at the body, but my eye kept going back there anyway. I glanced over the whole figure, starting with the shoes. The victim wore tan shoes that didn't give a hint to the sex of the wearer. The soles reminded me of pink erasers, except for something dark at the front of the shoes. He or she also wore khaki pants and a multicolored vest. My eye stayed on the vest as I racked my brain, trying to figure out why it seemed familiar. The head was turned to the side, and all I could see was some rust-colored hair. The shaggy cut didn't make the gender of the person any clearer, either. Barry was already on his phone as he headed back to the door, but he returned it to his pocket as he walked out. "I forgot to ask you the most obvious question," he said, herding me down the stairs. "Who is it?"

"I think it's more accurate to say who *was* it. But I haven't got a clue."

"CeeCee must know, then," he said.

We'd reached the bottom of the stairs, and he was leading the way back to the gate. "I wouldn't bet on it," I said.

"You're kidding. CeeCee doesn't know who that is?"

"That's what she said to me. She is sure it isn't her niece, though. You got a pretty good look. Was it a man or woman?"

He looked at me. "No, we're not doing this again. I ask the questions, and you answer." He went toward the driveway, and I followed. A green Jaguar was stopped just outside the gate, and I recognized Tony Bonnard's brilliant white hair as he stuck his head out and punched in a code. The gate began to slide open, and Barry nudged me.

"Who's that?"

"I guess you're not a soap opera fan," I said with a smile. Barry gave me his cop face in return. "He's CeeCee's boyfriend." Barry's eyes widened, and the cop face broke.

"You're calling him her boyfriend, but you wouldn't call

me your boyfriend? He's older than I am, so the term is even more ridiculous!"

"It's her term, not mine. And maybe she has another term for him now. We think he might be living here." Once the gate was fully open, the Jaguar pulled in and Tony stuck his head out, lifting his sunglasses and showing off his crystal blue eyes.

"Leave the gate open," Barry commanded. Tony did a double take and looked to me.

"What's going on, and who is he?"

CHAPTER 6

I<small>N NO TIME THE DRIVEWAY AND THE STREET IN</small> front of CeeCee's were flooded with police cruisers, a paramedic fire truck and a fire department ambulance. Although Barry did get them to arrive without sirens. I was a little surprised at the arrival of the paramedics. Could there possibly be any doubt that the victim was dead?

I was expecting to tag along with Barry as he took Tony to the house, but when Barry introduced himself, he gave me a squinty-eyed stare, making it clear I wasn't to blurt out anything else. Not that I had much of a chance, anyway—Barry waved over a very serious-looking young male officer and told him to take my statement. Then, before I could protest, he and Tony were already on the way to the house.

My officer was all business as he took out a metal clipboard with sheets attached to the top. "Molly Pink," I said before he asked for my name. He seemed confused about my volunteered information. "It's my name," I added. He still appeared flummoxed, and not altogether happy. I'm sure he'd been taught in the police academy that he was supposed to be in charge, and here I was taking over and offering information before it was asked for.

"This isn't my first crime scene," I said. "In fact, I'm surprised you don't have my information on file." It was my attempt at a joke, but the officer didn't crack a smile. Instead, he threw me an annoyed scowl. "Actually, *crime scene* probably isn't the right term. I mean, if the cause of death is carbon monoxide, it could be an accident."

The cop ignored what I said and asked what I was doing at CeeCee's and how we came across the victim. "Well, the Tarzana Hookers had come to help one of our own," I began. His cop face gave way to a moment of surprise at the name of the group.

"So, you're saying CeeCee Collins was operating some kind of prostitution ring out of her house?" he said.

"That's Hookers as in crochet." I reached in my pocket for a crochet hook to show him, but he put his hand out to stop me.

"Keep your hands where I can see them," he ordered.

"What?" I said, surprised. "You don't think I'm a sus—"

"Ma'am, we're just taking statements," he interrupted. "As far as we're concerned, everybody could be a suspect." He asked for the identity of the victim and made a slight tsk sound when I said I had no idea, as if he didn't believe me. Finally, he finished up, pointed toward the gate, and told me I could go.

"But I'd really like to go see my friends. I'm sure they're very upset." I took a step toward the house, but he stopped me.

"Orders are to get your statement and see you out. You'll have to check on your friends by phone." He took my arm and escorted me to the gate.

I hung around the front for a few moments, looking toward

CeeCee's. I was about to accept that there was nothing more I could do when I saw a cop walking Babs toward the gate. When she reached me, she was muttering to herself and seemed in a state.

"This would never happen back home. Being questioned by the police at a movie star's home!" She shook her head a few times, as if trying to make sense of the situation, and then looked up and noticed me.

"Are you okay?" I asked.

"Fine. I'm fine," she said. But her cadence was too fast, and her tone didn't go with the words. I wasn't feeling that great myself. True, it wasn't the first time I'd come across a body, but there are some things you never get used to. Still, I was in better shape than she was.

"Why don't I walk you home," I offered. Babs's face relaxed, and it seemed like she let out her breath. Barry had managed to keep the police cars' and the fire truck's arrival quiet, but he couldn't control the media. I heard one news helicopter then another take up positions above us. I could tell they were news helicopters, not police, because of the way they hovered in the air—for some reason hovering helicopters were far noisier than circling ones. A body found at a celebrity's house was kind of a dream story for the media.

"We don't want to see ourselves on television," I said, taking Babs's arm and starting to walk away from the gate.

Babs looked up at the helicopters. "They can't really see us, can they?"

"Are you kidding? With the cameras they have, they can practically see the polka dots on your bikini while you swim in your own pool."

"How terrible." She looked down at what she was wearing as if evaluating how it would look on a news report. "I'll take you up on your offer. It would be very nice if you'd walk with me. All this has been a little much." She gave me a spontaneous hug, which I returned before looking out at the street.

"Which way?" I asked.

"My son's place is on Stargazer Lane," she said, as if I knew where that was.

"That's a lovely name for a street, but you'll have to direct me. I don't know the street names around here."

"Sure, follow me," she said. Babs started to walk across CeeCee's driveway, and I followed as she stepped onto the grassy strip between the street and a giant hedge that surrounded CeeCee's property. I looked up at the wall of green—it had to be ten feet tall.

"Funny how I never noticed this before. I guess it blended into the scenery." I shrugged it off then explained to Babs that I usually just parked in front of the house on Greenleaf Drive and went in without much regard to the surrounding area. I'd never even noticed that Greenleaf Drive wrapped around the side of CeeCee's property before. As we walked, I tried to imagine what was on the other side of the hedge, inside the yard. The wall of bushes made it so that from out here, I couldn't see CeeCee's house or anything else to orient myself and figure out what we were passing. I don't think Babs paid any attention to what I was saying. Her mind was still on what had happened.

"It has to have been some kind of accident," Babs said. "But don't you think it's strange that CeeCee didn't know who the person was? How could somebody be up there without her knowing?"

"I don't know how it happened," I said. "The front gate has locks now. CeeCee got them a few years ago—she didn't bother with much security before she got the reality show and then the movie."

"See?" Babs said, pointing ahead to where Greenleaf Drive ended at a cross street. "That's Stargazer Lane."

When we got to the intersection, I stopped, looked to the left, and saw that the hedge continued on across what I now realized was the back of CeeCee's property. Babs saw me surveying the area.

"When I first got here, I thought it was some kind of private park," she said. I could understand why—from the street all you could see was some trees. The garage and house were totally blocked from sight.

"CeeCee's place is really an island," I said.

"No, it's more of a peninsula," Babs corrected, pointing out that there was a neighbor on the other side of CeeCee's property. "It's hard to give names to the shapes of yards around here. In Iowa City, the houses are all on rectangular plots.

"You can't see my son's house from here, but it's the third one down from where Greenleaf ends at Stargazer," Babs continued, pointing at the other side of the street. The houses were all behind ornate walls and had lots of old trees in the yards. I could also see some tall light fixtures and a wire fence with something green inside it. A tennis court, perhaps. Babs started to say something about being okay to go the rest of the way on her own, but a rumbling sound interrupted.

I looked across the street and saw that the gate on the property farther down had begun to slide open. A white BMW SUV drove out and went past us, then screeched to a stop and backed up until it was next to us. The darkened window opened, and a blond woman wearing sunglasses stuck her head out. I noticed she had a tattoo on her finger and realized it was Pia Sawyer—I'd seen it when she pointed at me that morning at CeeCee's.

I didn't understand tattoos, especially on middle-aged

women. Young people might not realize that someday their tattoos were going to fade and their skin was going to sag, making that eagle look like it had a potbelly, but anyone my age should have figured that out already. I couldn't quite tell what Pia's was supposed to be—maybe a rose twined around her finger. Or was it a snake?

"What's going on?" Pia asked. "Those helicopters are making all the dogs howl."

"You won't believe what happened after you left." Babs had recovered from her shock and once again turned into the town crier as she gave Pia all the gory details. I suppose Pia's eyes must have widened with surprise, but I couldn't tell, since she was wearing sunglasses. Before Babs had even gotten out all the details, Pia had her cell phone out and was calling somebody. I considered admonishing her about dialing and driving, but despite being in the middle of the street, the SUV wasn't going anywhere. I heard her telling somebody to come outside right away, then she threw the phone down on the seat and pulled the BMW to the curb.

The gate to the property in front of us opened with a loud groan, and Pia's almost-twin Kelsey ran out. She was a little taller than Pia, but they were so similarly styled and dressed that they really looked the same. Babs tried to interrupt, but Pia was already telling her version of the story. And, like in a game of telephone, it had already changed. Pia claimed the body had rolled down the stairs as we were on our way up. "Like it was some kind of zombie," she said with a shiver.

Before I could correct her, I was distracted by a sports car that turned onto the street and pulled up to the curb next to us. The door opened, and Kelsey made a move toward the man who got out. I had only seen Evan Willis a few times at school events and some business things with Charlie, and that had been years ago, but I recognized him right away. As he got closer, I could see that although his wife had been able to hide the passage of time with a trendy hairstyle and probably facial injections, he hadn't been so successful.

It wasn't that he had a lot of lines on his face or that his hair was thinning—to the contrary, it was mostly dark, and the combed-back style seemed almost luxuriant. I think it was the expression of his dark eyes. They seemed strained, but I suppose years of being an executive at a studio would do that to you.

"Evan, there's a dead body at CeeCee Collins's house." Kelsey waved her arm in my direction. "Polly here almost got hit by the body as it rolled down the stairs."

"What?" The tired look left his eyes, and he gave his head a short shake, as if trying to clear it. "A body rolling down the stairs? Are the cops there?"

I stepped forward. "It's Molly," I corrected. "Molly Pink. You worked on some projects with my husband, Charlie."

It took a moment for what I said to sink in, and his face grew serious. "Sure, I remember Charlie Pink. We did work on a number of things together. I was sorry to hear about his death. He was a good man."

I always felt awkward at moments like this. It had been a few years, and while I would never stop missing Charlie, I had learned to accept the situation. I wasn't sure what I was supposed to say beyond agreeing, so I just nodded.

Kelsey and Pia were fidgeting, impatient with the attention Evan was giving me and being left out of the conversation.

"Should we do something?" Kelsey said. "The cops are there, aren't they?" She looked at me and Babs for reassurance.

"Do you know what happened and who it is?" Evan asked. "Should we be worried that there's a killer on the loose?"

I began by giving him the real story. There was no body rolling down the stairs. I mentioned the heat, the carbon monoxide alarm and the condition of the body. Kelsey and Pia looked a little green in the face when I got to the part about the smell.

Evan let out an understanding grunt and started to herd the women out of the street. "Other than the annoyance of the helicopters, I don't think it's our concern." He looked back at me as he went to his car. "I'm sorry you had to see that. It must have been very upsetting."

I accepted his words with another nod, and he got in his car and continued up his driveway to the garage. Kelsey returned to their house as well, and Pia took off down the street in her SUV.

Babs had been very quiet during the whole exchange. When they were gone, she turned to me. "They're not very neighborly. In Iowa City, we always bring over something tasty when someone has troubles. I'm going to take a casserole over to CeeCee's as soon as the cops leave."

Babs couldn't see it, but I made a face imagining how welcome her visit would be. Though if she brought food, CeeCee probably would let her in. "You might want to bring her some more of your brownies. I heard they were a big hit."

Even though she said I didn't have to, I walked her the rest of the way to her son's house, which was a few houses down from Pia's. Like the others, it had a big fence and an electric gate. She punched some numbers into a keypad, and the gate slid open. I followed her in. Since I'd come this far, I might as well go all the way.

Plus, I was curious to see what was behind the fence. I was busy checking out the exterior of the huge beige stucco house and the surrounding yard when I heard Babs making a tsking sound. I followed her gaze and saw two women standing over two toddlers who were being instructed on how to kick a soccer ball.

"I know my son has his own financial management company and his wife is a dermatologist, but really, two nannies? There's one for each kid. I don't know why my son even wanted me to come here." Her open, friendly face appeared distressed. "Those kids are so overprogrammed. I can't believe that my son doesn't want them to have the time for fun and imagination that he had. When he was that age, he could spend hours with a cardboard box." She composed herself. "I have so much time on my hands. Other than the one night when they let me babysit, I might as well not be here."

I put my hand on her shoulder in a supportive gesture. "I don't know if you're interested in crochet, but you're welcome to join the Hookers. I'm not really qualified to teach you how to crochet, but I'm sure one of the others would be happy to do it."

"I know how to knit," she said.

"You might want to keep that to yourself," I said, thinking of how Adele twitched when Babs had mentioned it earlier.

"Okay, then. When do I start?"

"You sort of already have. You volunteered to be a student at Sheila's rehearsal." As I said it, the whole situation came back into focus, and I realized that not only had we not had the rehearsal, but Sheila was probably traumatized by the whole event. I was sorry about what had happened, and I wanted to know who the person was and how they got there, but I had the success of Yarn University to think about.

"Are you busy tonight?" I asked Babs.

CHAPTER 7

WHEN I RETURNED TO GET MY CAR, THE CHANNEL 3 news van was set up in the street in front of CeeCee's, and the anchor, Kimberly Wang Diaz, was adjusting her skirt, getting ready to go live. She saw me and started walking toward me. We'd met numerous times under similar circumstances, and she seemed to think of me as being a crime scene groupie, which was a totally absurd term. It had certainly never been my choice to deal with dead bodies. They just seem to keep showing up. I waved her off, yelling, "No comment," before jumping into my blue green vintage Mercedes. I'd like to say I sped off, but *vintage* is another word for *old*, and the greenmobile, as I called it, had lost some of its zip over the years.

When I finally got to the bookstore, Mrs. Shedd was in the front of the store helping a customer pay for some yarn. As the woman walked out of the store, Mrs. Shedd came over to me. "Oh good, you're finally here. We had to make do without you—the woman that just left signed up for the beginning crochet class and bought her supplies. Just before her a woman came in to buy the supplies for Sheila's class. I'm glad she knew what kid mohair yarn was. I didn't realize how expensive that yarn is." She paused as several customers came in the door and walked past us. "Sheila's class is getting a lot of interest. She's all ready to teach it, right?"

"She'll be fine," I said with a confident smile. Had somebody said something to my boss? I was relieved when Mrs. Shedd seemed okay with my answer. I hadn't told her the real reason the group was meeting at CeeCee's, and I was hoping to keep her in the dark about Sheila's problems with the class until I'd solved them. As far as Mrs. Shedd knew, the group wanted to get together outside of the bookstore to go over our plans for all of the classes.

"I didn't realize you were going to take so long," my boss said. "And with Adele gone, it was difficult."

"I'm sorry," I said, leaving out the reason for our delay. It's not that I wanted to lie. I just thought the truth would make her uncomfortable. But I should have known it would come out anyway. We started to walk toward the information booth, which was the closest thing I had to an office.

"Molly, I'm worried about Yarn University. We have invested quite a bit of money and can't afford for it to be a flop, or even for any single class to be a flop. I don't want unhappy students asking for refunds."

"Don't worry," I reassured her. "It's going to be fine. In fact, we're all getting together here after the bookstore closes to go over things," I said, trying to sound confident and in charge. "We have the event here coming up. All the teachers will show off what each class is going to make."

Mrs. Shedd's face started to relax. "Of course. You do seem on top of things. I knew I was making the right decision when I made you assistant manager."

If only Mrs. Shedd had walked away then. Instead, Adele came in the door and flew across the open space, stopping next to the information booth. She was in full drama mode with her hand to her forehead. "Molly, you're lucky they let you go so quickly. I told them about my fiancé, Eric, but nobody seemed to care, and they kept me there forever, asking me again and again if I knew who that person was."

Adele had worked at the bookstore longer than I had, and we'd initially gotten off to a bad start because I had been hired as the event coordinator and she had expected to be moved up to the position. As a consolation, she'd been put in charge of the children's department, which mostly involved putting on story time. Considering she didn't like kids, it wasn't much of a prize, at first, anyway. But then she realized she could dress up in costumes and do dramatic readings. Since costumes and drama were second nature to Adele, it was as if she'd found her calling. Best of all, the kids loved it.

Mrs. Shedd was staring at me now with her mouth hanging open. "Tell me that the person you're talking about isn't dead and that it wasn't the real reason you two were gone so long."

My silence spoke volumes, and Mrs. Shedd started to shake her head and mutter to herself about how I always seemed to encounter dead people.

"Pamela, I know what you're worried about," Adele began, calling our boss by her first name. "I just want to assure you that there is no reason to worry. If Sheila can't do it, I can always take her place. I've even developed a shortcut to her color effect."

My eyes were wide, and I was waving my hands frantically

behind Mrs. Shedd, trying to stop Adele before she said anything more. Luckily, Adele was more interested in showing off her version of the piece than talking about Sheila's problems. She had pulled out the same blue length of crochet she'd shown us earlier and laid it on the counter of the information booth for Mrs. Shedd to see.

"Adele, it's very nice, but learning Sheila's special method is what's attracting all our sign-ups," our boss said. "If we do Yarn University again, maybe we can have you do a class then." I let my breath out when I realized Mrs. Shedd had missed the comments about Sheila. Adele appeared disgruntled as she put away the strip of crochet. Mrs. Shedd turned back to me.

"Molly, I don't know how you do it, but dead bodies seem to show up in your life way too often. It must make people nervous about spending too much time with you." She sighed. "I shouldn't say this, but you better tell me the details."

Joshua Royal joined us as I was telling the story. Joshua and Mrs. Shedd were partners in more than just the bookstore, though they didn't talk about it, and we all pretended that we didn't know. They were the perfect example of the unfairness of nature. They were both somewhere in their sixties but wore the age so differently. Her blond hair was natural and didn't have a single gray strand, but her body and face had settled into a matronly shape, while Joshua still had a boyish quality to him. It didn't matter that his shaggy hair had some gray and his face had a few lines—somehow they just gave him more character. Returning my attention to the conversation, I noticed a duffel bag at Joshua's feet.

"Don't worry, Pamela," he was saying. "Molly's a great sleuth. She's probably already on it, right, Molly?"

Mrs. Shedd shook her head with concern. "This isn't the time for Molly to be investigating, not when we're about to have Yarn University." She put her hand on Joshua's arm. "I wish you weren't going."

"I'll be back before you know it. Besides, you don't need me for the classes. Molly and the Hookers will do great." There was no talk about where he was going or why, but I knew that it was part of their arrangement that he could take off whenever he got the itch to travel. For years he had traveled the world and been just a silent partner in the bookstore. I hadn't even believed he was real when I was first hired. Mrs. Shedd looked at him sadly.

"Do what you have to do," she said. I noticed that he didn't look at her face for too long, quickly picking up the bag and waving to us all before Mrs. Shedd walked him to the door.

Joshua had actually hit the nail on the head. Between talking about Yarn University and keeping Mrs. Shedd in the dark about Sheila's anxiety issues, I had been thinking about the incident at CeeCee's. I had a lot of questions. Who was the person? How did they end up there? Why had the vest they were wearing looked familiar? Was the cause of death carbon monoxide? Was it an accident? Then that made me wonder again how the person ended up there to have an accident in the first place.

"Earth to Pink," Adele said, waving her hand in front of my face. Yes, she called me by my last name. It had annoyed me in the beginning, but now it was just habit. Adele couldn't help it—she was just difficult. I thought of her as that cousin everybody seemed to have who was always stirring things up but whom you dealt with because they were family. The crazy part is that Adele thought I was her best friend and wanted me to be her maid of honor. Though she had said the correct title for me was matron of honor, which made me sound like I was a hundred years old.

I snapped out of my reverie and got back to the matter at hand. "I need your help," I said. Adele perked right up and of course misunderstood.

"Of course. Yarn University should really be a co-project for us," she said. There was no point in going into why that wasn't true. Mrs. Shedd had put it all on me, just as she had the yarn department, because Adele went bonkers over knitters. You can't have a yarn department or yarn craft classes and exclude knitters. But what I really needed her help with was completely knit-free.

"Sheila never got to do her practice class," I said. "We can't just let it slide. I was thinking we could try again here at the bookstore after we close. I don't think we can count on CeeCee to come, though."

"I'm on it," Adele said, pulling out her cell phone. "I'll get in touch with everybody. It's perfect for me to step in for CeeCee since I really am the leader of the group."

I rolled my eyes. Adele was still dueling CeeCee for the position, but at the moment, I doubted CeeCee cared in the least.

HOURS LATER, AS THE BOOKSTORE'S LAST CUSTOMers were filing out, Rhoda and Elise came in. After waving hello, they went right to the back table, put down their totes, and started laying things out on the table.

Mrs. Shedd was standing with me near the door of the bookstore. She looked back toward the yarn department. "Maybe I should stay and see how everything goes."

"You've had a long day," I said in a concerned tone. "You don't need to stay. I'm sure everything will go fine. Adele and I will lock up." I glanced back at the door with apprehension. Sheila hadn't arrived yet, and I really wanted Mrs.

Shedd gone before our nervous teacher showed up. All it would take was Sheila to start apologizing about her problems and Mrs. Shedd would have her own anxiety attack.

Finally my boss reluctantly left, and I let out a sigh of relief. I let out another when Sheila showed up. "I'm here," she said, sounding nervous but determined. She glanced around at the closed bookstore and finally to the back table. "Is CeeCee coming?"

"Adele left word for her, but considering what happened, I would think not." Her face fell at the news. "But Dinah's coming. I spoke to her myself." I gave Sheila a reassuring pat. "The only no-show is Eduardo. He has something to do with his business." Sheila seemed okay with the news and headed back to join the others.

I had hoped Dinah would arrive early, but I was still hanging by the door waiting for her when to my complete surprise CeeCee showed up, along with Babs, who had wisely brought a tray of brownies. I sent them back to the yarn department and continued to wait for my friend. I'd gotten her voice mail when I called, and I had given her only the most basic information on the events at CeeCee's, hoping to fill her in when she got there. I was glad when I saw her rush past the front window and come inside.

"Sorry I'm late. I miss all the excitement. Really—a body in CeeCee's guest quarters," Dinah said, giving me a fast hug. I started to lead her toward the back.

"I need more time to give Commander an answer," Dinah was saying as we approached our friends, presumably talking about Commander's proposal. "When I was young, I just jumped into things, but now I can't help but think about all the consequences." She stopped just before we reached the table. "And that's the last you'll hear of it tonight. Now it's all about Sheila." Her eyes locked on Babs as she circulated with the brownies. "I miss one get-together and you find a mysterious body and get a new member!"

No surprise, the conversation at the table was all about finding the body, what the cops had asked people and what was going to happen next. There was certainly a connection between chocolate and upset women. The brownies had disappeared at an alarming rate. By the time I finally sat down, there was only one left on the plate. I gestured for Dinah to take it.

"How long do you think the body was there?" Dinah asked me between bites.

"Too long," I answered, making a face. Adele was quick to add her commentary about the horrible smell.

"Eww." Dinah held the brownie out with sudden distaste.

But nothing seemed to affect CeeCee's sweet tooth—she asked Babs if there was a chance there were more brownies in her car. Poor Babs seemed upset that there weren't, and she profusely apologized.

"I would have made more if I'd known. I love having a purpose. Mostly all I do is watch the nannies take care of the kids. The first time I actually got to put them to bed was last Thursday. The nannies had the night off, and my son and daughter-in-law went to a party." Babs looked around and was embarrassed that she had vented so much. "I'm so sorry. It's just that I feel like such a third wheel here. I don't understand why my son was so anxious for me to come and stay with them. Every minute of those kids' lives is programmed with dancing lessons, tennis lessons, reading lessons, swimming lessons. How about a few minutes just to pretend and be kids?"

The members of the group made some consoling noises, but conversation quickly turned back to the events of that afternoon.

"When I told my officer that I was a police fiancée—"

Adele paused and held up her hand to show off her engagement ring to the group, as if there was any chance we hadn't seen it. Her gaze stopped on Babs, and she realized Babs might not know everything about Eric. "He's a motor officer and first responder." At that Adele turned to the whole group. "When my officer realized I was almost a police wife, I got special treatment."

I looked at Dinah, and we shared a disbelieving raise of our eyebrows. Most likely Adele's special treatment was in her imagination. Her officer certainly must have had his work cut out for him when he tried to question her. With her ample build and height, she had a presence that demanded attention. The fact that she was always festooned with a lot of her crochet handiwork made her stand out even more. Her current outfit included a beanie with a large flower and a long denim skirt with white doilies sewn on it—not your everyday wear.

"It was just horrible," CeeCee said in a small voice. "They certainly didn't give me any special treatment." CeeCee was usually perfectly done up, but tonight she looked almost disheveled. Her normally flawlessly coiffed brown hair was askew. She was still wearing the outfit she'd had on earlier, but the events of the day had left their mark. The white shirt seemed wilted and had gotten pulled to the side, and her tan slacks were wrinkled. She sighed heavily.

"How many times did they have to ask me when I was last up in the guest apartment? And did I know who the victim was?" She turned her attention to me. "Most of the questions came from your Barry Greenberg and some other detective. Allen somebody. They were treating me like an outsider in my own house! They looked through everything and in every room. I suppose I should be grateful they didn't dump all the drawers out."

"First of all, he isn't my Barry Greenberg anymore," I said. "And when *was* the last time you were up in the guest apartment?"

CeeCee shook her head vehemently. "I don't know. I think I went up there last week. That's when Tony and I talked about it being a studio." She paused for a moment, and her brow wrinkled. "But I'm sure the shutters were open, because I was thinking that we'd need to enhance the natural light. And the heat certainly wasn't on. And if you're going to ask me about who the victim is, all I can tell you is what I told the police. I don't know."

"Who has access to the place?" Rhoda asked. CeeCee seemed unhappy with the question.

"The cops asked me that, too. There's Rosa, and she lets the pool man in, and the pest control guy. A handyman came by to do something to the garage door." She hesitated. "And, well, Tony does." She had never completely spelled out their relationship, and I had no idea how much time he actually spent there. I was trying to think of a nice way of asking if he lived there, but Rhoda beat me to the punch.

"Then Tony is living with you?" she said with a note of surprise.

CeeCee let out another heavy sigh. "When he lost the job on the soap opera—excuse me, continuing daytime series— he was devastated. I tried to tell him something would come along, but he wouldn't listen. I had no idea his identity was so wrapped up in that one part. I like to think I have never done that. When my sitcom ended, I simply let it be known I was looking for work and that no job was too small. All those guest spots and cameos paid the bills and kept me in the public eye. And then I landed the part of Ophelia, and now I'm in demand again." She fluttered her eyes. "He got it in his head that he wasn't going to wait around for something to come his way. He decided to get some control over his career, so he sold his place and is using the money to finance a web-only series. He's been staying with me." She checked the group for their reaction. Apparently Rhoda appeared a little judgmental. "Oh, so what? We're both adults." CeeCee rolled her eyes. "Can we get down to why we're actually here?"

Sheila had been sitting silently at the table, crocheting with string. It was her own personal tranquilizing system—she wasn't actually making anything; she was just using the repetitive motion to soothe herself. Now all eyes turned on her, and she put down the string and hook.

"If you can't do it, just say the word," Adele said, pulling out the strip of crochet she'd shown off earlier. Hers was made with a single strand of yarn that had color variations, giving it sort of a similar look to Sheila's projects, but the colors weren't as nice and the texture was different.

"C'mon, Sheila," Rhoda said, glancing at her watch. "Just go ahead and do it. You've made lots of these pieces in this style."

The rest of us offered her more encouragement, and Sheila finally went to the head of the table. She swallowed a bunch of times, so Dinah smiled at her and gave her a short pep talk, bringing up all the classes she taught at the community college and the reluctant students. "We're all interested. And so will your students be interested. Think about it. They are so interested in learning from you, they are paying for the privilege."

Instead of reassuring Sheila, that statement had the opposite effect. Her eyes grew big and round, and I could tell her breathing had gotten shallow.

"Show off the finished project first," Rhoda said. She looked to Elise. "We'll show you how." I hadn't noticed with all the commotion, but Rhoda and Elise had set out samples of the projects from their upcoming classes. Elise picked up a scarf done in her favorite vampire style, and Rhoda ruffled through the assorted felted items she had set out before picking up a small multicolored bag and displaying it to the group.

"Say something about your piece when you show the class, dear," CeeCee said to Sheila, trying to sound encouraging.

Adele stepped in. "Don't hold up the finished piece to start with. Just tell them to pick up their yarn and show them what to do with it." Adele followed her own instructions, holding up a skein of yarn and doing the first few stitches of her version of Sheila's pattern.

"That's not very helpful," Rhoda said to Adele. "Don't listen to her." She had turned to Sheila, who was shaking her head and muttering to herself.

"I can't do this," she said in a breathless voice. With that, she turned and ran to the front of the store and out of the building.

CHAPTER 8

"MAYBE YOU SHOULD CONSIDER ALTERNATIVES TO Sheila," Rhoda said. Sheila had left everything behind, including her emergency crochet kit. I had a feeling she had more than one, so I wasn't too concerned. Adele crowded next to Rhoda and not too discreetly pulled out a completed "hug," as Sheila's design was being called. She slipped it over her head and modeled it for the group. The design lived up to its name, hugging her shoulders.

"That's what I was saying," Adele said. "We can't take a chance of her having a meltdown in front of a class."

"Don't be so quick to write her off," Dinah said. "I think that Sheila really wants to do it." I was glad that my friend had stepped in. "We just need to work with her. It has been a rather stressful day for her and the rest of you. She'll come around."

"Amen to that," CeeCee said. She hadn't even taken out her crochet work. "The police have been at my place all day. There's yellow tape around the whole garage now. Imagine, my house, and I can't even go in my own garage. What if I needed a rake or something?"

I looked at the group, and they were all struggling not to smile. CeeCee getting a rake? Would she even know which end you were supposed to use?

"The worst part is, they won't tell me anything. Surely the police know if it was a man or woman. Poor Rosa had to stay late to answer all their questions. And it was very awkward for Tony. All I can say is that I'm glad they took the body away. They pulled an innocuous-looking white van up to the garage and took a gurney down the stairs. It looked like they wrapped the person in a garbage bag."

"It's called a body bag," Dinah corrected. Babs came up and put her arm around CeeCee.

"C'mon, I'll take you home. I'm sure everything is going to work out fine." She went to pick up the empty brownie plate.

"I don't suppose you have any more brownies hidden away somewhere." CeeCee turned to the rest of us. "It's for medicinal purposes only."

"Sorry, no more brownies, but I have something else you might like. We'll stop by my son's house first. I made my famous chocolate cake for them, but it turns out they're all going gluten free now."

It was amazing how CeeCee perked up at the words *chocolate cake*. "Well, ladies, sorry it wasn't a successful rehearsal, but hopefully Dinah is right and we'll manage to work it out," CeeCee said as Babs began to steer her to the door. It looked like Babs had found the purpose she was looking for—taking care of CeeCee. She was so nice and supportive. Iowa City must be a great place to live if it was filled with people like her.

The rest of the group started to gather up their things. Adele took the opportunity to throw in a last-minute pitch. "Since we don't know if Sheila is going to get it together, I think we should keep me in mind for an emergency backup," Adele added. "I can step in on a moment's notice."

"I'd appreciate if you kept all this to yourself," I said. Adele nodded knowingly.

"Don't worry, my lips are sealed. Not a word to Mrs. Shedd." She gave me an awkward hug. "Now that we're doing Yarn University together."

I saw Dinah rolling her eyes and trying not to laugh. Adele always wanted to be in charge. I'm not sure how my comment made her think we were now co-heads, but if it would help, I was all for it. The only thing I really cared about was that Yarn University was a success. Not whether I got sole credit.

Luckily, Adele had figured her duties as co-head were done for the night, and she left with Rhoda and Elise. Dinah had offered to hang around while I closed up, but I saw Commander Blaine standing outside the bookstore waiting for her and urged her to go.

It seemed strange being there alone so late. The café was all dark, and the chairs were on top of the tables. When I looked across the bookstore, I noticed that with most of the lights off, the bookcases made creepy shadows.

"Help, get me out of here," a voice cried out. My immediate reaction was to make a run for the door, but then reality clicked in, and as the voice continued its plaintive cry, I realized it was my phone. I had a reputation for missing most calls on my cell phone. My son Samuel had been convinced it was because I didn't hear it amidst all the similar rings. His solution had been to create a unique "ring," which was him wailing for help in a cartoon character voice. Even with that I still mostly missed it, but the people around me didn't, and I got some pretty weird looks when a voice calling for help seemed to be coming from my purse. It sounded really eerie in the dark bookstore, and I flinched as I grabbed for the slippery phone.

"Sunshine, finally," Mason said when I managed to swipe the screen to answer.

"I tried to call you," I said.

"I know. I got your message, and I tried to call you back numerous times. Do you ever check your messages?"

"Oops." Along with missing the calls, I also usually missed the voice mail notification.

"I was getting worried when it was so late and I couldn't reach you anywhere. I was about to call out the cavalry," he joked. He changed the subject, grumbling about still not being able to drive. "I can't wait to be fully functioning again." I offered my reassurance that it would be soon, but it didn't do much good. Mason hated being dependent. He liked to be the doer. He was the one who had gotten in a helicopter and roared over to Catalina to rescue me when I'd been a prisoner on a boat, had shown up in Palm Springs when Adele and I had gotten in trouble, and came by with hot soup when I had the sniffles. He didn't like being on the other side of it.

"I'm still at the bookstore," I said. He knew about the rehearsal we'd planned for Sheila earlier in the day, but not the later one. There was so much to tell him that I didn't know where to begin.

"Why don't you come over now," he said. "It's probably too late to get any food delivered, but there's lots of stuff in the freezer." It sounded like a good idea. I could tell him about my day in person, and I knew he'd have a sympathetic ear and maybe some ideas. But then I heard voices in the background.

"Dad, Mom and I are going to make some fudge," I heard

Brooklyn say. Jaimee chimed in and said that it was sugar-free, fat-free fudge, because unlike some people Mason knew, she and Brooklyn were concerned about their weight.

I think Mason had tried to cover the phone, but I heard it anyway. "How about a rain check?" I said. "Besides, I have a bunch of animals waiting for me." I tried to make it sound light. Mason had his hands full with the two of them staying there, and I didn't want to make it worse.

"Now maybe you understand why I tried to keep my social life away from my family," he said. "Sunshine, if you won't come over, at least tell me about your day. A body in CeeCee's guest apartment?"

"Then you know," I said, surprised and a little miffed. I'd looked forward to telling him about the whole thing.

"Know about it? Are you kidding? It was the breaking news story on the five o'clock and six o'clock news."

By now I was at the front of the bookstore, and with the light coming in from outside, it seemed a lot less scary. I considered talking while I drove home, but the only way to do that in my vintage car was to have the cell phone set to speaker, sitting on the seat. Well, until it slid off and hit the floor. I decided to finish the call where I was.

"The womenfolk have moved on to the kitchen," he said, and he let out a heavy breath. "Sunshine, I'm sorry about all of this. None of this is how I wanted things to go with us—"

"It's not your fault about the accident," I interrupted. It was bad enough that he'd had to endure all the pain of recovering without feeling guilty. And anyway, it absolutely wasn't his fault. A car had made a left turn in front of him and hit his car with such force it had knocked it on its side. I still had the image of the flipped-over black Mercedes etched in my mind, and just thinking about it made me shudder.

"I'm sorry about Jaimee staying here. It certainly wasn't

my plan to have my ex-wife moving in." He let out a low chuckle at the absurdity of what he'd said. "Brooklyn knows all my buttons. She knows I still feel responsible for her mother. We were married a long time, and Jaimee's family helped us when I was starting out. I promise they'll be out of here as soon as possible. And then we'll go on some fabulous trip and get away from all of this."

There were times I wished Mason didn't have so much character. But at the same time, I loved him for it. I was relieved when he changed the subject back to the mystery body.

"The news media really ate up the story. The entertainment shows were all over it, too. There were helicopter shots and reporters in front of her place." Mason chuckled. "Now you know my embarrassing secret—I've been watching way too much daytime television since I've been stuck at home." It was true I could hear the television in the background. He paused for a moment, and I surveyed the bookstore to make sure I wasn't forgetting to do anything. "I suppose the place was swarming with detectives." He paused, and I knew it was his way of asking if Barry was among them.

"Barry got the case," I said. Was that a concerned grunt I heard coming from Mason? "CeeCee convinced me to call him directly. She didn't want to call 911 and have the place swarming with sirens."

"I see," Mason said. "And I suppose he questioned you?"

"No, he turned me over to some uniform with no sense of humor. He didn't crack a smile when I joked that I thought they ought to have my information on file by now." I could hear the relief in the way Mason released a breath.

"I suppose you already have some thoughts on the case," Mason said, the good cheer returning to his voice.

"It's kind of hard to think anything without knowing who the victim is," I said. "Except for one thing." In all the commotion something had flown from my thoughts, and now it returned.

"I'm waiting with bated breath," Mason said.

"There's something about the vest the victim was wearing." And then I dropped my voice as I tried to remember what it looked like. "It looked really familiar, somehow, but I don't know why."

"You'll figure it out. Probably when you least expect it," he said. "So there's no chance I can get you to reconsider and come over? Even when there's the opportunity to sample some really awful fudge?"

CHAPTER 9

IT WAS A RELIEF TO FINALLY GET HOME. THE ANI-
mals were waiting by the door like a welcoming committee.
I let Felix and Cosmo go outside before trying to coax
Blondie out of her chair. It was too dark for the cats to go
outside, though they didn't seem to share my sentiment and
Mr. Kitty tried to open the door with his paws.

"Sorry, guys," I said, pushing the door tightly shut. I had
rushed home during my so-called break to tend to them, but
I really missed having my son there. It made it a lot easier
when there was someone else to share the animals' care
with. Plus, technically three of them were his.

When the dogs came inside I gave the whole crew an
extra round of treats, but then it was time to take care of me.
In all the commotion I had forgotten to eat, and now my
hunger showed up with a vengeance. Luckily, I was prepared. Knowing how busy my life had been lately, I had
cooked up a big pot of vegetable stew that would last for

days. There were biscuits left over from my morning baking, too. All I had to do was heat everything up.

The stew was just beginning to simmer and fill the kitchen with a delicious scent when the phone rang. I figured it was Mason with some plan to convince me to come over, so I grabbed it before the robot voice announced who the call was from.

"Okay, what is it? Did they tie you up and start force-feeding you that awful-sounding fudge?" I said with a laugh in my voice.

"What?" the voice on the phone said. It was only one word, but enough for me to recognize who it was.

"Barry?" I said. I'm sure I sounded surprised.

"I'm sorry for calling so late. I tried to reach you before on your cell." He made a hopeless sound. In a world where everyone seemed to be walking around staring at the screen on their smartphone like they were some kind of zombie, I mostly ignored mine. I didn't find texts until days after they were sent, and I preferred to be where I was when I was there instead of sending somebody a picture of it. My lack of interest in the phone seemed to rub everyone the wrong way, though, because I wasn't instantly accessible. "It's business," he added quickly. "You know the thing about the first forty-eight hours being crucial to a case. The trail is still fresh. Since you were there this morning when everything went down, I'd like to talk to you."

"Oh," I said, surprised. "You know I talked to the other cop at the scene, right?"

"Right," he said tersely. "That was just to take a statement. I'd really like to talk to you directly."

"When did you have in mind?"

"Would now work?" He asked it like a question, but I

knew Barry well enough to know that he meant we were going to have this conversation now, like it or not.

"I suppose so." I looked around at the kitchen, turned off the stew, and put something over the biscuits to keep them warm. "How long until you get here?"

"Now. I'm out front." I went into the living room and looked out into the dark front yard. The streetlight reflected off the black Crown Vic parked at the curb. He was already cutting across the grass. Lots of cops let themselves go after they left the academy, but not Barry. He lifted weights and did some kind of cardio workout, so that even in his fifties he was trim and could still take off after a suspect and catch them. A moment later there was a soft knock at the door.

Even though the knock was quiet, Felix and Cosmo heard it and scrambled, barking, toward the front door. Once I opened the door, though, Cosmo recognized Barry and greeted him by putting his paws up on his pants leg.

Barry was in work mode now, which meant his face had a "just the facts, ma'am" look about it. But Cosmo's greeting cut right through it, and Barry's expression broke as he leaned down to pet the dog's head. He looked at Felix, who was holding his ground and continuing to bark.

"Who are you?" he asked, as if the dog would identify himself.

"It's a long story," I said, closing the door behind him. Quickly, he stopped petting Cosmo and went back into his cop mode, a mixture of authority and impassiveness.

We stopped in the entrance hall, and he glanced toward the living room. "Where do you want to do this?"

"I was just about to eat something. How about the dining room?" I took his nod as agreement, walked into the room, and turned on the light.

"I always liked that table," he said. I did, too. It was one-of-a-kind, made out of a heavy slab of glass set on a polished tree stump. His gaze moved to the French doors that looked out on the backyard. I realized pretty quickly that he wasn't looking out at the view and had totally missed the floodlights illuminating the orange trees, which were still laden with white blossoms. Barry's gaze had stopped on the door handle of the middle door, or rather where the handle was supposed to be. For now there was just the hole. The actual handle was sitting on the floor in front of the door.

"It fell off last week," I said. "I have to get it fixed." He didn't say anything, but I was pretty sure he was thinking about how when we'd been a couple, he'd taken care of all those little household jobs. In fact, my house had never been in better shape than when I was dating Barry. I hoped he wouldn't notice the switch plate was loose, too. Just as I was thinking about that, he moved one of the dining room chairs and the leg fell off.

I feigned surprise, even though I'd known it was loose for weeks. I pushed it against the wall to steady it and put the leg across the seat. "Don't worry, the other chairs are fine." I pulled one out and sat in it to prove it was true. "This probably isn't in line with your usual procedure, and I don't know if you're allowed to eat on duty, but are you hungry?"

His cop face broke again, and he appeared slightly embarrassed. "More like starved," he said.

"It's nothing fancy, but I can offer you what I'm having."

"Anything is fine. I've had your cooking. It's all good."

"Flattery will get you everywhere," I joked. I pulled out a couple of place mats, set them on the table, and gestured for him to have a seat, but he followed me into the kitchen. I could hear him sniffing the air, and who could blame him?

The comforting scent of the stew and the buttery smell of the biscuits was making my mouth water in anticipation.

"Let me help," he said. When I seemed surprised at the offer, his smile deepened. "Remember, we're supposed to protect and *serve*."

I took him up on the offer, and together we brought in silverware, napkins and the food.

"You might as well start asking me whatever you came here to ask," I said, changing the subject.

"If you don't mind, I'd like to wait a few minutes." He took the napkin and put it in his lap.

"I thought you were in such a hurry to keep going before the trail of clues dried up."

He glanced down at the food in front of him. "If you have to know, I'm so hungry I can't think straight. I had it under control until I smelled the food." I held out the basket of biscuits, and he took one.

"Homemade?" he asked. By the time I answered, he was already eating it. His eyes closed with the pleasure of the taste.

I had set the places so we sat across from each other, and for a few minutes we both just ate. It's probably not good manners to compliment myself, but I love my own food. The broth of the stew was thick and tasty. It was loaded with mushrooms, potatoes, peas, carrots and even small cobs of corn. And the biscuits really did melt in your mouth. I'd added hunks of cheese and tangerines on the side to round things off. It was a simple meal but very satisfying.

Barry finished his bowl and polished off a couple more biscuits, several hunks of cheese and two tangerines, then sat back with a satisfied sigh. "Thank you. I feel human again."

At that, he became cop Barry again, pulling out his notebook and starting to ask me questions.

He opened by asking me why we had all been at CeeCee's this morning. I brought up Yarn University and the upcoming classes and Sheila's problem.

"You're doing that in addition to everything else you do at the bookstore?"

"I'm the assistant manager now," I said. I noticed Barry had stopped taking notes and was looking directly at me as he spoke.

"I hope all those new responsibilities came with a pay raise." He actually sounded concerned.

"It all depends on how Yarn University turns out," I said. "Is this part of your investigation?" He appeared momentarily uncomfortable and poised his pen over his notebook.

"Sorry, I didn't mean to get sidetracked. So, tell me why you all went up to the guest apartment." He paused briefly. "Let me rephrase that. What prompted you all to go up there?" It sounded like an innocent enough question, but I knew none of Barry's questions were innocent, so I answered as briefly as possible.

"CeeCee had this grand plan about making it into a studio—she wants to direct videos of us crocheting to put on YouTube." I don't think he was particularly happy with that, but since I had actually answered his question, there wasn't anyplace for him to go but to move on.

Barry scribbled down some notes. "Who actually discovered the body?" Barry had an even expression, but I knew that he already knew the answer.

I raised my hand, which was stupid because there was nobody else there. "I did." I started to relive the whole thing in my head, trying to remember exactly how it had happened. Barry noticed my eyes shifting back and forth and realized what I was doing. That was the problem with being questioned by someone who knew you too well.

"How about you tell me what's going on in your head." There was just the hint of a smile on his lips. I shrugged and began to talk.

"CeeCee was ahead of me on the stairs, but when we got to the top and she realized there was something wrong, she pushed me ahead of her. She was pretty much out of commission after that. I think it was Rhoda who helped her sit down on the stairs because she seemed faint."

"You know CeeCee pretty well. She's an Oscar-nominated actor. Do you think her shock was genuine?"

"Seriously? You think CeeCee was acting? You didn't see her. She had her head between her knees."

He didn't offer any sort of answer but instead took something out of the zippered case he had with him. "I want to show you a photograph," he said. He set it on the table and pushed it closer to me. "Do you recognize her?"

I looked at it closely. A woman was sitting at a table. A croissant with a birthday candle stuck in it was sitting in front of her. I recognized the background and realized it was taken at Le Grande Fromage. I couldn't help myself and answered his question with a question. "Why are you asking?"

A ripple of frustration crossed Barry's face. "Molly, please just answer the question. We're both on the same side. We want justice for bad guys."

Maybe we were, but we didn't always agree who those bad guys were. Barry tended to believe too strongly in his cop instinct. Once he'd locked on to who he thought had done something, he was like a terrier with a bone—he wouldn't let go. I, on the other hand, tried to keep an open mind as I followed the clues.

"Sure, but I want to know why you want to know. Is she the victim?" I did recognize her, but I was doing my best not to show it in my face until I knew why he wanted to know.

"Okay, I give up. Yes, this is the victim." He gestured toward the picture again. I tried to match up the face with what I'd seen in CeeCee's guest apartment. The only part of the photo that matched was the rust-colored hair. "So, do you know her?" he repeated.

I nodded, and Barry rolled his head with frustration when I didn't expound on that. "What about the cause of death? Was I right about it being carbon monoxide? Do you think it was accidental or something else?"

"I don't have to tell you that," he said. "Can't you pretend that you don't know me and I'm just a detective who stopped by to ask you some questions, and maybe you're a little nervous and anxious to cooperate since you found the body and I might think you're a suspect?"

"Aha, a suspect! There aren't suspects in accidents. You must think it *is* foul play."

Barry put up his hands in capitulation. "We don't know what it is yet. It's up to the coroner to decide. If you want all the gross details, when the body was moved, they found vomit that had alcohol and pill residue in it. Her face was cherry red, which I'm sure you probably already know is a sign of carbon monoxide poisoning. And when we checked the vent, it was clogged with a bunch of twigs. Now will you tell me what you know?"

When I hesitated, he pulled out his trump card. "You know what can happen to people who withhold evidence." In spite of himself, his lips curved into a small smile. We both knew it was an idle threat and there was no way he was going to arrest me.

"There's no reason to hide it," I said. "I didn't recognize her at first. She's not a friend—more like an acquaintance. I'd say hi when I saw her, but that was pretty much it. Actually, I haven't seen her in a while, so I have no idea what was going on in her life."

"Do you suppose you could give me her name?" Barry asked.

"C'mon. I'm sure you know it by now." He gave me a look and urged me on. "Okay, her name is Delaney Tanner," I said finally. There was some dead air after that.

"And what else can you tell me about her?"

I shrugged. "Our paths used to cross a lot, but not lately." I decided that was enough information to give him, but in my mind's eye I had an image of standing in line with Delaney and our kids on the first day of kindergarten. We were never really friends. She was much more interested in being part of the "in" crowd than I was, though it seemed like she was always just shy of truly belonging there. It was funny how I used to see her all the time at school functions and now it had been years since I'd run into her.

"What's her connection to CeeCee?" he asked.

His question made sense, and frankly, I was wondering about it myself. "Why don't you ask CeeCee directly?" I said, and Barry grumbled. "How did you figure out who the victim was?"

Barry shook his head. "I know what you're doing. You're trying to pick my brain for your future investigations. Uh-uh. I'm not giving away any trade secrets."

"What did you do, match her up with a missing person's report?" I asked. I could tell by Barry's expression I was right. I glanced at the photo. "And that picture was in the file."

"You must have some idea how CeeCee could have been connected with the victim."

"I don't. Really. I have no idea what Delaney has been up to lately. Even when I knew her in the past, it was minimal."

"Are you sure you're not holding anything back?" Barry said, scrutinizing my eyes.

"That is all I know, honest. How about a cup of tea?" He

seemed to accept that I didn't know anything else and agreed to the tea. I cleared the table and then spent some time in the kitchen putting the dishes in the dishwasher before making the tea and finding some cookies to put on a plate. When I brought in the tray of tea things, Barry was just sliding back in his seat. He began to pack up his notebook and the photograph as I set down the steaming mug of Earl Grey tea in front of him. The fragrance of the oil of bergamot perfumed the air, and I set the plate of cookies between us.

"How's Mason?" he asked as he picked up the cup.

His question made me feel uncomfortable. I tried to be noncommittal and said he was improving and hoped to be back at work soon.

"I'm just kind of surprised that he isn't recuperating here. I stayed here when I got shot," he said. It was true—Barry had stayed at my place because he couldn't deal with stairs for a while. We hadn't even been together at the time. I'd done it out of friendship. I could see it did seem like I'd abandoned Mason.

"He's got plenty of help. One of his daughters moved in with him." I wanted to leave it at that, but Barry was a very good detective, and he immediately picked up that there was something more. I might be good at keeping details of a crime scene from him, but when it came to personal stuff, it was a whole other story.

"There's an 'and' in there," he said, locking his gaze on my face.

"Well, she isn't exactly a big fan of my relationship with Mason," I said finally.

"There's still more, isn't there?" he prodded.

"Okay, his ex-wife is staying there, too." Barry's eyes opened wider and he laughed.

"Now I get it. That's the funny thing about kids in a

divorce—they want their parents to get back together, no matter how old they are. I went through it with Jeffrey when he first came to live with me." Barry's gaze softened. "He stopped pushing it so hard after he met you." Barry stopped talking abruptly, and I had the feeling that Jeffrey might now be trying to get me and Barry back together. I certainly had a soft spot for Barry's son.

He polished off a couple of cookies and drank down the last of the tea. As he set the cup on the table, he said, "That will do it for now." There was a heavy emphasis on the word *now*. He blew out his breath and shook his head as he looked directly at me. "I know you didn't tell me everything you know. We'll talk again soon."

It was only after he left that I noticed the door handle was back on the French door, the chair was back to all four legs, and even the switch plate was secure.

CHAPTER 10

I WAS WIRED WHEN BARRY LEFT, AND ANXIOUS TO brainstorm with someone now that I knew who the victim was. I still couldn't get over the revelation that it was someone I knew. It was too late to call Dinah. Even though she claimed it was never too late to call her, I knew she was probably asleep. Ah, but there was Mason. Since the accident he'd had insomnia. I figured he was probably watching television and would be glad to have something else to occupy his mind.

I called his cell, not wanting to disturb the house. As soon as the phone was answered, I blurted out, "I found out who the victim is."

"Who is this?" a perturbed female voice said. Brooklyn and her mother sounded a lot alike, so I wasn't sure who it was. "It's too late to be calling," she continued. I sensed she was about to hang up, but Mason apparently managed to get the phone from her.

"Sunshine, it's you, isn't it?" He sounded annoyed, not at

me, but at whoever he'd grabbed the phone from. Apparently, he'd walked away from the phone for a moment, and it was his daughter who'd answered the call. "Brooklyn, I'm fine. You can go on to bed now," he said, talking away from the phone. She didn't go quietly, though—I could hear her telling him he shouldn't let me get him all worked up. Then she reminded him she'd left him some hot milk to help him sleep.

"Finally," he said, and I gathered she'd left the room. "Hot milk, my daughter bossing me around and treating me like an old man—" I imagined that he had thrown up his hands in frustration. "Please, oh please, don't ask me how I'm feeling or if I've taken some pill."

"No problem," I said. "I called to brainstorm. I found out who the victim is."

"And?" he said.

"Her name is Delaney Tanner. She's lived in Tarzana for years and years—"

I was surprised when Mason interrupted me. "You just found out, this late? Who told you?" He sounded worried. I didn't really want to tell him about Barry's visit, but I wasn't about to lie, either.

"Since I'm the one who actually found the body, the cops wanted to talk to me again."

"So a couple of uniforms came by almost at midnight and asked you a bunch of questions?" He seemed even more perturbed. "You should have told them you wanted your lawyer present—me."

"It wasn't a couple of uniforms. It was Barry," I said.

I heard Mason make an angry sigh. "The same goes for him. Don't talk to him unless I'm there."

"It was fine. I just gave him a few facts. I got more than I gave. I found out the victim was Delaney. All he found out was that I sort of knew her a long time ago."

"I suppose he wanted to know if there was a connection between her and CeeCee. If he didn't, I do."

"I have no idea if or how she knew CeeCee. But somebody there must have known her, or how else would she have gotten inside?" I explained the electric gates and intercom.

"I suppose CeeCee has an attorney, but in case she needs one, I could hobble over there," he said with a chuckle. I was relieved that he was back to his good-humored self. "Sunshine, it isn't that I don't trust you with the detective. I just don't want to see him bothering you at all hours on his quest for justice."

"I was awake anyway." I didn't mention the food or the tea. I did my best to make it sound like we'd stood in the doorway talking. And I certainly wouldn't have wanted Mason to be there. The last thing I wanted to do was to have the two of them vying to see who was top dog. "I think it's easier for me to deal with him directly." I took a breath before continuing. "That is, as long as he doesn't start looking at me as his prime suspect," I said, trying to lighten the moment.

"What's your next step?" Mason asked.

"What makes you think I have a next step?" I countered. I was glad when I heard him chuckle.

"We all know that you've probably already started trying to connect the dots in this case."

"To be honest, until I knew who the victim was, I had no idea what to do."

"But now you do?" he said. It was such a relief to hear him sound like his old self. It seemed whenever I called, Brooklyn was somewhere in the background, making it difficult for him to talk. Now there was the addition of Jaimee. I was glad that for once it was just the two of us talking with no audience.

"Actually, that's why I called. I thought we could shoot ideas back and forth."

"Of course," he said. "There's nothing I'd like to do more." He stopped, and I heard him chuckle. "Well, there is, but due to my mobility issues at the moment, it isn't on the table." Cosmo jumped next to me on the couch. "Why don't you come over? I can let you in without the ladies finding out. We could at least cuddle while we talk."

It sounded appealing, but by then the long, long day had kicked in, and I wondered if I'd even be able to get off the couch. "Rain check," I said. "And we better talk fast. I'm fading quickly."

Mason suggested talking to CeeCee and whoever else was regularly in the house. "That would be the housekeeper and Tony Bonnard," I said.

"Really?" Mason said in a gossipy voice. "He's living there?"

"CeeCee said it was just temporary. He's trying to put together a web-only show, now that he's off the soap."

"I knew that," Mason said. "And every other Hollywood tidbit. I need to stop watching all this television. It's so much better to talk about something real."

I was quiet for a moment, and he asked if I was still there. I'd gotten distracted because the image of the body on the ground had come back in my mind, and I was thinking about the vest. "Sorry," I said. I mentioned the vest and the fact that something about it seemed familiar.

"I'm afraid I can't help you with that," he said. I yawned, and he heard it. "Sunshine, maybe I can't sleep, but you certainly need yours. We'll talk tomorrow and do some more brainstorming." He signed off with his usual "love you."

"Me, too," I said before clicking off.

I didn't dare sit longer or I would have fallen asleep. I undressed quickly and fell into bed. I was drifting off to sleep as I felt my assorted animals join me, all in their usual spots.

* * *

I WOKE UP THE NEXT MORNING WITH THE VAGUE
memory of some very odd dreams. First, I'd been investing
in a yarn company, and then a line of sheep had walked
through the scene. There were some dancing crochet hooks
that tripped over one another and fell down, then a pair of
knitting needles popped up in a triumphant manner.

"Knitting needles winning," I said aloud and swung my
feet over the side of the bed to get up. "I better not mention
this dream to Adele." Felix put his head up when I spoke.
He seemed less concerned with what I had to say than with
the prospect of being let outside. He was off and running
across the house before I had put on my slippers.

I was still thinking about the dream, trying to figure out
what it meant while I drove to the bookstore. I guess I should
be grateful I dreamed about dancing crochet hooks rather
than dead bodies.

On my way into the bookstore, reality hit, and I wondered
if any of our group would show up for our regular get-
together. I was totally shocked when I'd barely walked in
the front door of the bookstore and I saw CeeCee hanging
out by the poster promoting Yarn University.

People often came up to CeeCee at the bookstore and
wanted an autograph or a photo, and she never, ever refused,
so she always took special care to look nice when she came
here.

But this morning, she was dressed to be ignored. CeeCee
was smart enough not to don a big hat and sunglasses if she
wanted to be invisible, but this was the first time I'd ever seen
her in jeans—and these weren't designer ones, either. She had
a hoodie over the washed-out jeans and a bandana tied over
her hair. She made eye contact with me and pointed toward

the yarn department in the back. Instead of walking straight to it, she stuck to the side of the store, practically in the shadow.

I let her get a head start before taking the direct route, so we arrived in the yarn department at the same time. She flopped into a chair and leaned back in exhaustion. "I had to get out of there," she said, making a vague gesture, probably toward her home. "The cops are relentless. They were back at the crack of dawn to question us again, and this time they had the identity of the victim."

"Then you don't know Delaney Tanner?" I said when I joined her at the table. I wanted to ask her if Barry was part of the questioning committee, thinking of how late he'd left my place. But I didn't want to mention his visit, so I didn't say anything.

"No. The name didn't mean anything to me or Tony." CeeCee had done a poor job of securing the bandana, and it slid off. I'd never seen her hair look so disheveled before.

"What about her face? They did show you a photo, didn't they?" I asked.

CeeCee seemed tired of the questions. "Dear, I glanced at it, and she didn't look familiar. Tony did the same and had the same response. They wanted to question Rosa, and they got very upset when I explained that after she'd stayed so late, I had to give her time off this morning." CeeCee shook her head in distress. "I thought Detective Greenberg was going to put out an APB for her."

So, Barry was part of the questioning team. I wanted to ask her if he looked tired, but I mentally told myself to snap out of it. Whether or not he had circles under his eyes was not my concern. Surprisingly, CeeCee actually had brought a bag with her current project, and now she pulled out the yellow baby blanket she was making. There was a state law that a mother could surrender her newborn at a fire station with no questions asked. CeeCee wanted to give baby blankets to the local fire station so they'd have something when someone left them with a baby. She absently began crocheting as she continued her tale of woe.

"The worst was how they're grilling Tony. They wanted to know exactly what our relationship was and if he was living at my place. They even asked what financial arrangement we had. He's already embarrassed about his circumstances." Her eyes went skyward. I considered asking just what those circumstances were, but it didn't seem like a good time since she was already so upset.

"I wonder how long Delaney was up there," I said. It felt very strange to add her name to the body I'd seen. CeeCee responded with an uncomfortable grunt.

"They certainly weren't giving me any information. They were trying to pull it out of me. They kept asking me about last Thursday. Who was at my place? Who did I let in? And to be honest, dear, I'd rather not think about it. I just want this whole thing to be over with." She got to the end of a row and, with barely a pause, did a turning chain and started on the next row.

"What did you tell them?" I asked.

"That none of us let that woman in," CeeCee said. She set down the crochet as she suddenly had a realization. "I suppose that means they know she died on Thursday. That means she was up there all weekend." CeeCee shuddered. "Imagine if Tony or I had gone up there alone? I'm just glad you were there when we found her."

Her comment made me uneasy. I had heard over and over how killers tried to arrange for someone else to find their victim, or at least to have someone with them when the body was found. Hadn't Tony encouraged her to take us up there to see the "studio"?

CeeCee picked up her work again and began to crochet. I could see that she was beginning to relax. "It feels so much better to be here, talking to you. Dear, please work your magic and figure this out. Nobody has said it yet, but I saw the way those detectives were looking at me. Even Barry. I'm one step away from being their number one suspect."

I had a bad feeling she might be right.

Rhoda arrived at the table and dropped her tote bag before pulling out a chair. "Elise isn't coming. And Eduardo has something going on at his store." She did a double take when she saw CeeCee, and she pulled me aside. "What happened? Did they take her down to the station and keep her overnight? She looks terrible."

Dinah arrived a moment later. "What have I missed?"

CeeCee waved a tired hand at me. "You tell them, dear." I was up to the part where we'd figured out that the time of death was the previous Thursday, based on what the cops had said, when Babs showed up. She had come prepared and had a bag with yarn and crochet tools.

"Oh, that's you," she said, trying but failing to hide her surprise at CeeCee's appearance. She gingerly patted her on the shoulder and turned to the rest of us. "I hope it's okay if I join you all today. You have no idea how much I miss this kind of companionship." I explained that I was just bringing Dinah and Rhoda up to speed on what was going on at CeeCee's.

Babs listened intently as I continued. She gasped when I mentioned that CeeCee was concerned about being considered a suspect.

"Nobody can possibly think you'd hurt somebody," she told CeeCee. "Don't worry, I'll take care of you." She glanced over CeeCee's appearance and let out a few tsks. "First things first. Let's get you fixed up." She helped CeeCee up and took her off to the bathroom.

With them gone, Dinah, Rhoda, and I began to talk. Rhoda was the first to speak. "No matter what CeeCee says, there is one thing that is absolutely true. One way or another that woman ended up in the guest apartment."

"And I bet the cops think she was invited. With the locked gates CeeCee has now, there's no way she just wandered in," Dinah said.

"She was alive when she got there," I said. I didn't want to mention the gory details of the vomit and pills and was glad when nobody asked why I was so sure. The image of Delaney's body flashed in my mind again, and I thought of the vest. "The vest she was wearing seemed oddly familiar," I told them. "It has to be something about the yarn." I looked at the cubbies of yarn, which had swatches in both knit and crochet hanging off them.

"You probably just have yarn on the brain," Rhoda said, watching as I checked out a couple of the swatches.

I let go of the swatch of some variegated worsted-weight yarn in shades of brown. "You're probably right."

"Molly," Mrs. Shedd said, coming into the yarn department with a young woman. Our arrangement was that I could sit with the crochet group as long as I took care of any customer who needed help.

"I thought your name was Polly," the new person said, looking around the yarn department. "I'm Erin Willis. Actually, I'm Erin Willis Allen. You probably don't remember that your son Peter took me to prom." I noticed the young woman's belly, and it came back to me that Kelsey Willis had been interested in having a crochet-themed baby shower. But remember that my son took her to the prom? More like I didn't know. My older son was big on leaving me out of the loop—then and now. Her parents must have gotten all the photo ops. I just remembered something about having to get him a corsage.

"Nice to see you," I said with a friendly smile. Now that I had gotten a better look at her, she and Kelsey really did look more like sisters than mother and daughter. Erin had the same sharp features and the same shade of blond hair, which I doubted either of them was born with.

"Molly will tell you all about our events," my boss said. I noticed that she didn't leave when she turned Erin over to me.

"I really didn't have much time to tell your mother what we do for a shower," I said. I went over to the cabinet below the cubbies of yarn, brought out a container, and set it on the table. Mrs. Shedd made approving noises as I explained that we would teach the guests to crochet and each of them would make a small square in the colors the host chose. "After the event, we'll join the squares into a baby blanket and give it to you," I said.

"It certainly would be different than what my girlfriends have done," Erin said. I smiled and continued explaining our usual procedure for showers, before showing her a sample of the gift bag each guest would receive. "This is just a basic one, with a crochet hook, a small ball of yarn, and a sheet with directions on basic crochet stitches in a paper shopping bag. But we can make the gift bags as elaborate as you want, including more yarn or things like scissors and tape measures." I brought out samples of paper and canvas project bags, explaining they could be personalized.

"We'll want everything super deluxe," she said. She asked about refreshments, and I explained that we used the café. I was trying to play it cool, but inside I was jumping up and down. "Super deluxe" was music to my ears. "What about sort of a tea thing?" she suggested. "You know, scones, finger sandwiches, pretty little pastries."

"That's a wonderful idea," I said. I was going to mention that a "tea thing" usually included tea, but I let it go. Whatever drinks she wanted would be fine.

Mrs. Shedd was all smiles and added her approval to the high tea plan. "My mother wants it to be unique," Erin said. "Something that everyone else will want to copy."

"Perfect. Shall we write it up?" I said, taking out an order form.

Erin seemed to hesitate, then turned resolute. "I like the plan. So, yes, write it up." I saw Mrs. Shedd give me a thumbs-up, although she wilted a little when Erin said her mother would bring in the deposit. It was too easy to back out when you didn't have any skin in the game.

I made conversation as I filled in the form. "Your father works for Wolf, doesn't he?" It was really more of a statement than a question. The whole name of the company was Wolf Film Studio, but everybody just called it Wolf. I didn't know what his exact title was, but I knew he was a high-level executive.

But Erin seemed distracted and ignored the comment in favor of tapping the table with her elaborately decorated nails. They were done in glossy pink stripes, with a pearl embedded in one nail. She noticed me staring at them and seemed almost annoyed. I suppose because my nails were so clearly not manicured.

"It was nice seeing your mother and Pia the other day," I said. "They seem like they're joined at the hip." I went back to my writing, relieved her expression had lightened up.

"She does live almost next door. They've been best friends for as long as I can remember. My mom is the one who got Pia through her divorce."

"I didn't know Pia was divorced," I said, trying to keep the conversation going. Actually, I didn't know much about Pia at all. "Are you friends with her kids?" I'd said "kids" because I didn't know how many there were, or if they were boys or girls, though by now they were all grown up.

Erin made that face like I'd just asked a totally absurd question. "Her boys are a couple of years younger than me. And they stuck with their father after the divorce."

Suddenly, the bell on the bookstore door jangled and Adele rushed in. She fairly screeched to a stop when she got to our table.

"You won't believe what I just heard from Eric," she announced. As usual, Adele was done up to be noticed. She had taken a spring green boiled wool jacket and covered it with different crocheted flowers, all done in shades of pink. It looked like she was wearing a garden, and while it was a little over the top, it was stunning at the same time. She noticed Erin and held up her hand, wiggling her ring finger so that the small diamond caught the light and shimmered. "Eric's my fiancé," she added quickly. "He told me who the victim is." Adele put her hand to her forehead in a gesture of woe. Then, knowing she had all of our attention, she paused to heighten the suspense before she continued. "It was a woman, and her name is—or maybe I should say was, though I suppose it's still her name, even if she's dead."

By now Mrs. Shedd was getting impatient with Adele. "Just tell us who it is," my boss said.

Dinah and I traded glances and silently agreed to let Adele have her moment and not let on that we already knew who it was.

But Adele didn't like being told what to do by anyone, not even our boss, and let out an unhappy sigh. "I was just trying to be accurate in what tense I used. I'll use the present tense. Her name is Delaney Tanner."

Mrs. Shedd appeared shocked. "That's who they found in CeeCee Collins's guest apartment?" She'd suddenly gone very pale.

She seemed about to say more, but Adele slid in first and

explained. "Delaney used to work here." Adele turned to me. "It was before your time." I thought Adele was going to say what a great employee Delaney had been, but Adele being Adele, she instead critiqued the job Delaney had done. "Her job was to help with customers, but it seemed to me she was trying to be too cozy with them. I think she put people on the spot, asking overly personal questions when she was supposed to be suggesting a book they might like."

Mrs. Shedd seemed uncomfortable. "I wasn't going to say anything, but now that Adele mentioned it, I was relieved when Delaney said she was leaving. I really don't like to have to let people go, but I noticed that customers seemed to be avoiding her."

Erin was standing next to me, listening to it all. "I know that name," she said in a stunned voice. "I have to tell my mother." She pulled out her cell phone and stepped away from us for a moment. A minute later, she then rejoined us.

"Her daughter Marcy was in my class." Erin's thoughts seemed to drift off, and she started to mutter to herself that they'd lost touch after high school. "She always talked about going to some Ivy League college, but I heard she ended up having to go to Beasley Community College because her father died."

"Then your mother knew Delaney?"

Erin shrugged. "Not really, just that she was Marcy's mother." She started to gather herself up to leave. She shook her head and said, "Poor Marcy. She's like an orphan now. It makes you want to go home and hug your family." She looked at the form I'd been filling out and held out her hand. Once I gave her the copy, she left.

Dinah watched her go. I could tell my friend was perturbed at Erin's condescending tone when she mentioned the community college where Dinah taught. A moment later, Babs returned with CeeCee. Somehow, by rolling up the jeans and adjusting the hoodie, adding some makeup and combing CeeCee's hair, she'd made her look almost stylish. Her final touch had been to tie the bandana around CeeCee's neck.

CeeCee's appearance may have been more put together, but she was still upset. "Dear, I think I'm going to need some medicinal chocolate." Babs seemed thrilled at the idea of doing anything for CeeCee and rushed off to the café.

Rhoda had packed up her things. "Nothing personal, but I came here hoping to get some peace and all there's been is drama." She began to push away from the table. "And we haven't even talked about Sheila." I cringed as Mrs. Shedd's head shot up, and Rhoda walked away with a disgruntled shake of her head.

"Is there a problem with Sheila?" Mrs. Shedd said, interrupting. "I thought you had everything worked out."

CHAPTER 11

IT HAD TAKEN SOME DOING, BUT I'D MANAGED TO calm down Mrs. Shedd's concern about Sheila and keep Adele from repeating that she could always step in. I really did believe that once Sheila actually got through one rehearsal, she would be fine to teach her class. Appearing satisfied that everything was under control, Mrs. Shedd had gone off to help some customers who were hanging by the information booth, and Adele had gone back to the children's area to prepare for story time.

"You're such a dear," CeeCee said to Babs when she returned from the café with two double chocolate cookie bars. CeeCee grabbed them like they were life preservers and took a big bite. "That's so much better already," she said between chews. As she finished the first bar and moved on to the second, she looked at Rhoda's empty chair. "What's going on with her? She's never grumbled like that before. She's always the one who seems to take everything in stride."

Dinah and I both shrugged. "Next time we get together, we ought to ask her if everything is all right," I said.

CeeCee popped the last of the chocolate bars in her mouth and got up. "Now I can handle going home." Babs was out of her chair and next to CeeCee before I could blink.

"If you want, I can drive behind you to make sure you get home okay," Babs said. "Then just give me a couple of hours and I'll bring over a pan of brownies."

"Thank you, dear," CeeCee said. "I always say chocolate is the best medicine."

With them gone, the get-together was officially over. Dinah stayed at the table and took out some papers she needed to grade while I cleared everything up from the group. I straightened the yarn bins and, most importantly, put Erin's shower on our calendar. After a while, Dinah and I decided to go grab some lunch and were headed to the door when Mrs. Shedd stopped me.

"Mr. Royal usually takes care of this, but with him gone I think you, as assistant manager, should handle it." She held up a zippered pouch of cash and checks. "Could you please deposit this at the Bank of Tarzana?"

I wasn't sure how to feel as I took the bulging pouch—honored that she trusted me with the money, or nervous to have to walk around with it. Most people used credit cards, but there was still some cash business and a few checks.

"Nobody would think we were carrying a couple thousand in cash, would they?" I said to Dinah as we walked to my car.

Dinah looked us both up and down before laughing. "Only if they were psychic." Even so, I drove the most direct route and parked right next to the bank. The parking lot was busy, but nobody gave us a second look as we walked to the entrance.

I dealt with another bank for my personal finances, and

I hadn't been inside the Bank of Tarzana for years. "What ever happened to imposing buildings with arches and columns and gold lettering on the window?" I asked as we went inside. The Bank of Tarzana was shaped like a shoe box. The inside was as bland as the exterior, though I didn't have much of a chance to notice. We were barely in the door before we were greeted like long-lost relatives by a man in an ill-fitting blue suit. He wanted to know how our day was going, offered us bottled water and cookies, and finally asked the purpose of our visit.

"A deposit," I said, turning down his offer of drinks and snacks and going right for the line waiting for tellers. Being that it was lunchtime, it was long, and I was glad I had Dinah to keep me company. She immediately started talking about her situation with Commander.

"I wonder what he'd do if I said no." My friend adjusted her long purple scarf and looked to me for an answer. I didn't want to say anything, but if he was really set on getting married and she didn't want to, it was possible he would call everything off between them. Personally, I couldn't understand that. If you loved somebody enough to want to marry them, wouldn't you want to stay with them even if you didn't get married?

"Maybe you should tell him your concerns about getting married," I said.

My friend shook her head at the thought. "How can I tell him that as much as I like to see him, I'm glad when he goes home? I wish I could be caught up in the fairy-tale idea of happily ever after, but I'm past that illusion."

"I see your point. It would be hard to tell him any of that." As the line edged forward, I noticed something strange. There was a wreath made out of laurel leaves with black ribbons hanging in front of one of the teller windows, and all the tellers were wearing black armbands. The man in the bad suit cruised by the line to assure us all that we'd be helped soon, and I stopped him to ask about it.

"What's with the wreath and armbands?"

His too-friendly smile faded, and he leaned close. "We've had a terrible tragedy. One of our tellers died, and it's a very strange situation. Nobody knows exactly what happened to her. Personally I thought we should be more low-key about it, but the manager wanted to show that we care for our customers and our employees."

I had a bad feeling. "Was her name Delaney Tanner?" I asked.

The man seemed surprised. "Then you know her. She was one of our most outstanding tellers. She treated our customers like they were old friends."

I didn't say anything, but I was thinking that some of the customers probably *were* Delaney's old friends.

My turn came, and I stepped up to a teller and unzipped the pouch, taking out the stack of bills, checks and deposit slip.

"Oh, this is for the bookstore," the teller said, making a surprised face. She pointed down toward a teller window with a separate line. "That's for our merchant accounts."

"I'm sorry, this is my first time doing this." I started to retract the money, but she said she'd take care of the deposit this time.

"Is there anything else I have to do?" I took the blue pouch and began to zip it closed.

"That's it as long as it's under $10,000." She pointed out a cup full of lollipops. "Have some candy while I count it. She loaded part of the cash into a machine, and I took the opportunity to ask her about Delaney. "If you had come here last week you would have been dealing with her," the teller said. I realized the wreath was hanging near the business account window. "The manager calls it customer service, but to me, she seemed a little too talkative. But that's the style of the banks now. We give you water and roll out a red carpet. We have candy and stickers for the kids. How about we just wait on the people in a timely fashion and not make this into a circus?"

"Well said," Dinah said with a nod of approval. The teller put the rest of the bills into the machine.

"Those are Delaney's daughters. Poor girls came in to pick up her things," the teller continued. Dinah and I turned as two young women came out from an office. The counting machine stopped, and the teller completed the deposit and handed me a slip. "You're good to go. Have a fabulous day."

The two young women had been talking to someone whom I supposed was the bank manager. They both had the same rust-colored hair as their mother. I watched them for a moment, remembering how they'd looked as third and fourth graders at the school holiday assembly. It seemed strange to see Marcy and Rachel all grown up. Dinah nudged me. "I know one of them. I didn't put the name together when the young woman arranging for the shower mentioned that one of Delaney's daughters had gone to Beasley. Marcy Tanner was my student a while ago. I remember her because I didn't have to remind her to act like a college student. She wrote some really good papers. I don't remember the exact details, but it seemed like the family went through some kind of trauma."

"We should offer our condolences," I said as Dinah and I crossed the bank and caught up with them before they reached the door.

Dinah didn't need to introduce herself. Marcy Tanner recognized her immediately, though both she and Rachel gave me a blank look until I mentioned my sons' names.

"We're so sorry about your mother," I said. I was at a loss

as to what to say to them next, so I just kept blabbing, and the next thing I knew, I'd invited them to join us for lunch. They both agreed readily, which surprised me. It took Dinah and me a moment to come up with a place to go. Under the circumstances, a loud café didn't seem like the right setting. "I know just the place," I said finally.

Los Encinos State Park was one of my favorite locales. It was made up of a natural spring that fed a small lake surrounded by a couple of acres of grounds. There was an old ranch house and some other buildings that had been turned into a sort of museum. Recently, a restaurant on the edge of the place had been redone, and part of it was incorporated in the park. When we regrouped a few minutes later outside the park, I led the way to the outdoor patio that overlooked the water, which was filled with ducks and geese, and we were given a table.

We used to take my boys to the "duck pond," as we called it, all the time when they were small. I assumed Delaney's daughters had gone there, too. I thought it might be a soothing spot for them. I didn't plan to grill them, but if some useful information came up, I wasn't going to turn it down. I didn't have to say anything to Dinah, because she knew how I operated.

For a few minutes we just enjoyed the surroundings and placed our orders. I liked breakfast no matter the time of day and picked out an omelet. When the waiter left, there was an awkward moment of quiet while we all sipped our water. I finally broke the silence by saying I hadn't seen their mother for years. I didn't mention that I'd actually seen her the day before. That was all it took for both girls to start talking.

"I don't think anybody appreciated what our mother did," Marcy said. "Our father died when Rachel and I were in high school. It turned out he'd cashed in whatever life insurance he had, and we were left with nothing but his debts. My mother had to sell our house, and we moved into an apartment, but she never complained about anything and just did what she had to do. She hadn't had a real job for years, but she took whatever she could get. We all got jobs." Marcy looked to me. "You must know how friendly my mother was. She made relationships when she worked at the cleaners, which led her to get a job at a jeweler's."

I mentioned that I knew Delaney had worked at Shedd & Royal. "That was really a second job," Rachel said. "But it led to her becoming a teller at the bank. Our mother worked so hard to keep things going after our father died. She really liked working at the bank, though. She hinted recently that it was going to get even better, like maybe she was going to get a promotion." Rachel was beginning to tear up. "I just wish I had told her how much I appreciated everything she did."

I offered her a sympathetic pat as I thought about how my situation had been so different. I was devastated when Charlie died, but he had taken care of everything and left me very comfortable in the financial department. I felt a twinge, thinking just like Rachel that I wished I could say thank you.

The waiter brought the food, and the conversation stopped momentarily. Dinah had stayed silent up until now, but as the waiter left she jumped in.

"It sounds like your mother had things to look forward to," she said.

"I know why you're saying that, Mrs. Lyons," Marcy said. "Our mother was not depressed. She'd come through a hard time, but she was making the most of things. She liked her job at the bank. She was always talking about her customers. I was surprised at all she knew about them, but then she was smart and really friendly. And, no, neither of us have any idea what she was doing in CeeCee Collins's guest apartment. I don't think she even knew CeeCee Collins, though my mother was very discreet. She talked about customers but never named names."

"We had to go over all of it with some detective," Rachel said. "It had to have been some kind of accident." The waiter refilled our water glasses. When he left, Rachel continued. "I know she had some plans that night, but she didn't tell me what they were. I've been racking my brain, trying to remember any little detail. I just remember she seemed happy, not depressed."

There was something else on my mind, but I wasn't sure how to say it so they would understand that I wasn't just being nosy but was trying to help find out what happened. Finally, I just said it. "Was your mother seeing anyone?"

Rachel and Marcy traded looks, and finally Rachel spoke. "We wanted her to meet someone and tried to get her to sign up for online dating, but she wouldn't do it. She said if she met someone it would have to be the old-fashioned way. I don't think she was seeing anyone, but if she was, she didn't tell us."

The conversation died off after that, and we concentrated on our food. The Tanner sisters finished first and set their napkins on the table. "Thank you so much for this, but we have to go," Marcy said. "There are details we have to take care of." She let out a heavy sigh. Dinah and I stood when they got up, and they hugged both of us.

"Thank you again. You have no idea how nice this was. You let us talk. It's been nothing but questions from the cops or us having to try and tell other people that it's okay, when it's anything but."

Rachel turned to me. "I know your reputation as some

kind of amateur detective. Please let me know if you find out anything about what really happened."

After they left, Dinah and I spent a few minutes walking on the grounds of the park. We'd bought some feed from a dispenser and were dropping handfuls to the ducks that clamored at our feet. "What did you think of their answer to that last question?" I asked. "Do you think Delaney would have been seeing someone and not told them?"

Dinah took a moment to think. "The best way for me to judge is by what I've told my kids about any men in my life." Dinah was long divorced, and her kids were grown and lived out of state. "They don't know about Commander," she said finally. "The way I look at it is, if we get engaged, I'll tell them."

"So you're saying you think that Delaney could have been seeing someone but didn't tell them."

"She could have been waiting to see if it was going to go anywhere." Dinah threw the last of the grain to the ducks.

"But that doesn't help us figure out what she was doing in CeeCee's guest apartment. I don't think CeeCee is lying when she says she doesn't know."

"What about Tony?" Dinah said. "Do you think he has something going on the side? And if so, would he do anything as crass as actually meet that someone on CeeCee's property?" I watched a mother with two toddlers go by. The toddlers had almost the same walk as the pair of ducks in front of them.

"I hope not." I glanced at my cell phone to check the time and saw that a reminder had come up. "Oh no. How could I have forgotten about tonight?" Dinah had a blank look, and it was clear she'd forgotten as well.

"The promo for Yarn U. The idea is that all the teachers will show off what they are going to teach, including you.

How could I have forgotten? I'm supposed to be the assistant manager, and I forgot something as important as this!"

Dinah stepped in. "You've had a few things on your mind. We all have. After what happened at CeeCee's, it's a wonder you remember anything." She put her hand on my shoulder. "Okay, now take a deep breath and then let it out. It's not too late. We just have to make a few calls."

What would I do without my best friend?

CHAPTER 12

It turned out that only Dinah and I had forgotten about the Yarn U Preview that night. Well, CeeCee had, too, but under the circumstances, I didn't think that counted. I told her not to worry about it. Her class was going to be a onetime thing showing how to make items for charity. It was going to be free, at her insistence, and I was sure it would be full. Despite her earlier fussiness, Rhoda said she would be there, and Elise was coming and bringing samples of the projects for her class as well as some kits in case someone didn't want to sign up for a class but still wanted to make something vampire style. Eduardo was full of apologies about missing all the group things lately, but he promised to attend with samples of his lacy crochet work. Adele already had all of her things at the bookstore. And luckily, Dinah had all her pieces in her tote bag.

I saved contacting Sheila until last, but I was completely surprised when she seemed okay with showing off a sample of the hug. Though she did make sure that all she had to do was stand there and let her work speak for itself. What a relief. I had somehow managed to pull off the reminders without giving anyone an inkling that I'd forgotten. I didn't even think Mrs. Shedd realized it as I went around the store, putting up signs on the posters for Yarn U directing people to the yarn department.

The rest of the setup was easy. I just had to move the chairs away from the long table in the yarn department and put out cards with the class names and instructors, along with lots of sign-up sheets. And then it was home to take care of the animals.

"OH, YOU'RE HERE," I YELPED IN SURPRISE AS I came through my kitchen door. My son Peter was standing at the counter, eating a bowl of the vegetable stew. He set down the spoon momentarily.

"Sorry if I scared you. I left messages everywhere that I was stopping by. You still don't look at texts, do you?" I didn't think he expected an answer.

"I'm guessing you heard about the excitement." I slipped off my jacket and set it down.

"An unknown body is found in a celebrity's guest quarters by a crochet group—yes, I heard about it, and I saw you running away from the news crew. Actually, it was my assistant who said, 'Isn't that your mother running away from the reporter?' Mother, not again. Do you know how embarrassing it is to have my assistant point out that my mother found another dead body? He made all kinds of jokes calling you Hercule Pink, Molly Marple, and Sherlock Hooks." Apparently Peter's assistant knew about my crocheting.

There was reproach in his voice. Peter dearly wanted me

to keep a low profile—or maybe no profile. He was a TV agent and very concerned about his image. He'd been ambitious from the time he was a kid and had a lemonade stand that offered iced, blended drinks.

"It's not an unknown body anymore," was the only thing I could think of to say.

"I know who it is." He said it in a dismissive manner, as if he didn't want to talk about the fact that he had gone to school with Delaney's daughter. "You should be more careful. I know you and your friends go sticking your noses where they don't belong."

I told him not to worry, that me and my friends were Teflon when it came to trouble. He didn't see the humor in it and went back to eating the stew.

"Why don't you sit down and eat?" I said, doing my best Vanna White impression to show off the built-in kitchen table.

"No time." He tilted the bowl and got the last of the broth onto his spoon. Peter disapproved of just about everything I did, so in the hopes of avoiding him going through the laundry list of everything I was doing wrong, I changed the subject.

"I saw an old friend of yours. Erin Willis. She has another name now, and I can't remember what it is, but she reminded me that you two went to prom together. She's going to have a baby, and her mother wants to do the baby shower at the bookstore." He had his back to me, and I couldn't see his brown eyes, but I had the feeling they were glazing over. Now that I thought about it, it occurred to me that Peter had probably asked her more because of who her father was than any great love between them. "You must see Evan Willis all the time. Isn't one of the shows you packaged with Wolf Films?"

When he turned, he had that look that kids give their parents—basically a how-can-you-be-so-clueless look.

"Mother, Evan Willis hasn't been at Wolf Films for a few years. And when he was, it had nothing to do with my work."

"I suppose they gave him some kind of production deal when he left," I said, trying to prove that I wasn't as clueless as he thought. Peter shook his head in distress at what I'd just said. I guessed that meant I was beyond clueless.

"No, he didn't get a production deal. Last I heard he was out of the business."

"He must be doing something that pays well. They still have the house with the tennis court, and Erin Willis didn't even ask the price of the crochet shower. She just said they wanted the deluxe package."

Peter just shook his head again as he put his bowl in the dishwasher and slipped his suit jacket back on. I opened the door and let the herd of animals go outside. Even Blondie came across the house to join them. I followed them outside to supervise the cats, and a moment later Peter joined me.

As much as I'd tried to avoid it, I got the laundry list of everything I was doing wrong. It started with me dating a homicide detective, even though that was ancient history now, and went into how I shouldn't be letting my other son live with me or have all these animals. His final point was I should downsize and relocate to some condo settlement meant for older people. Then he surprised me by giving me an awkward hug. The best I could guess was that it was because there was no one around. "The stew was good. Thank you." More surprise. Peter couldn't be accused of overusing those two words.

"How's it going with Mason?" That question was not a surprise. Peter had introduced me to Mason and had been hoping we'd get together all along. Mason was a powerful attorney with a lot of celebrity clients who could be helpful to Peter's career, but mainly I think he hoped Mason would keep me out of trouble.

Cosmo and Felix were excited at having company and were sitting on Peter's feet, looking up. Peter let out a sigh and then looked back at me, shaking his head in reproach.

"You do realize that having this many pets limits your options for moving."

I remember thinking that when I grew up I'd be able to do whatever I wanted. What I hadn't considered was what it was like to have adult children. Samuel, my younger son, wasn't a problem. He seemed pretty nonjudgmental about whatever I did, though maybe he thought that was part of the deal when moving back home. It was a different story with Peter. He'd been unhappy with my life choices since I'd become a widow and probably even before.

I think at the bottom of it all, Peter was unhappy with his name and blamed me. When he was born all I could think of was Peter the Great, and it hadn't occurred to me that he would end up with the initials PP.

"I stopped by to pick up my golf clubs," Peter said. I'd seen them leaning against the wall in the entrance hall. He must realize that if I ever followed his advice and relocated to a smaller place, he would no longer be able to store his skis, kayak, golf clubs, collection of bats and who knows what else here.

He looked at me. "I suppose you know what happened." He didn't have to say more. I knew he was alluding to Delaney Tanner.

"No, I don't," I said as Peter followed me inside. He let out a sigh of relief until I added, "At least not yet."

"Not *yet*? Oh no, Mother, not again." Poor Peter.

IT WAS DINNERTIME WHEN I RETURNED TO THE bookstore. I waited on a few customers, and then the Hookers started to arrive. Whatever was bothering Rhoda seemed to have subsided, because she appeared upbeat as she methodically arranged her items on her section of the table. She had said more than once she wanted to do everything she could to make her felting class a success, but it wasn't completely altruistic—it had been Mrs. Shedd's idea to pay the teachers a piece of each student's tuition for that class instead of a flat fee for teaching.

Elise arrived next, pulling a small cart. The disconnect between her appearance and her personality still always came as a surprise. She looked like a strong breeze could carry her away but she was all about business and had brought a large assortment of her kits. To further get the message across, she was wearing a crocheted black-and-white striped tunic with a bloodred tassel. The white was for vampires' pale skin, the black for their clothes, and the red—well, that was obvious. I didn't have to look closely to know that the tunic was done in half double crochet stitches, or as she referred to them, vampire fangs.

Eduardo Linnares would have stood out even if he weren't the only male in the group. A former book cover model, he was tall and incredibly good-looking in a romance novel sort of way—long black hair drawn into a low ponytail, strong jaw, even features and a killer smile. He had left the leather pants and billowy shirts behind and now wore well-tailored slacks and sports jackets. The only leather was the tote he carried. It still amazed me how his large hands were able to manipulate a tiny steel hook and crochet thread to create dainty Irish crochet pieces. His grandmother had taught him well.

Dinah found her spot on the end. Her class was on easy and quick crochet. Since she was a community college instructor, teaching was second nature to her and she seemed the most relaxed of the bunch.

Adele waited to make an entrance. I'm sure she would

have preferred to parade in when everyone was there, but my guess is she got impatient waiting for Sheila, or maybe she thought Sheila wasn't going to show. Since Adele's class was beginning crochet and the project was a basic scarf, she didn't have much to put out. To make up for it, she was dressed like a crochet sample book. She wore a black cocoonlike shrug and had attached brightly colored swatches in all different crochet stitches. To highlight the special qualities of crochet, she wore a wide-brimmed hat she'd crocheted in yellow raffia. The hat band was covered in crocheted flowers that were all different colors and designs.

I had arranged to have Sheila next to Dinah, but our tense crocheter's spot was still empty. People were beginning to wander into the yarn department, and I had to take on my job as greeter and pitch person for the classes. Mrs. Shedd was watching from a distance.

I was relieved when Sheila came rushing across the bookstore carrying a large tote. I'd had my doubts that she would show after last night.

"Sorry, I got stuck at the store," she said quickly as she passed. I saw that Dinah immediately started helping Sheila set out several versions of the hug. All of them had been done with three strands of yarn in blues, greens and lavenders, but she'd used different combinations of the colors in each of them. They made a beautiful hazy display. I think Adele was crushed when all the people at the table gravitated toward Sheila.

I held my breath waiting to see what Sheila would do, but it turned out it was a waste of worry. She did fine, probably because all she had to do was hand out sign-up sheets and accept compliments. No teaching involved.

There was a steady trickle of people coming through, and I registered quite a few new students. We started a waiting list for Sheila's class, and it was suggested we just add another class for her. I groaned internally—now there were two classes I'd have to worry about her teaching.

A whoop of excitement came from the table, and when I looked, Adele had come around the front and was greeting two people. It was hard to miss Eric Humphries, her fiancé. He was very tall with a barrel chest—imposing-looking was an understatement. At least he wasn't in his motor officer uniform. The woman with him was Mother Humphries, as Adele kept calling her, which might explain why the older woman wasn't in favor of the union. Adele had let us know that her future mother-in-law was visiting from San Diego, again, and making things difficult for Adele.

I went to stand near the table to get an idea of how people were reacting. A small, intense-looking woman moved down to Rhoda's display. Very smartly, Rhoda had put out a skein of variegated yarn, a crocheted swatch of that yarn and a crocheted swatch that had been felted, along with the pouch bag that was the project for her class.

It was amazing to see the difference in how the colors looked on the skein, the first swatch and the felted swatch. I stared at the first two for a long time, and it stirred something in my mind while I listened as Rhoda explained the felting process. Basically the item to be felted was swished around in very hot water, which caused the fibers to twist together. The end result was a solid piece with no hint of the stitches that had made it.

The woman seemed interested and picked up the felted piece to examine it as I was about to offer her a sign-up form. "Can you use any yarn?" the woman asked.

"Sure, so long as it's wool, and not the washable kind."

"Wool?" the woman squealed, dropping the swatch like it was flaming. She began scratching her hand frantically. "I'm allergic to wool. One touch is all it takes."

I heard Adele say something about an emergency and that Eric was a trained first responder, and the next thing I knew, the large man was towering over the woman, who seemed to be itching even more frantically.

"Can you breathe?" he asked. "Do you need an EpiPen? I know how to do a tracheotomy with a pen. Don't worry, you're going to make it." He turned to the crowd around the table. "Get back, everyone! We have a woman in crisis here."

He ordered our group to clear the table of their displays, and then he picked up the woman and laid her on it while she continued to scratch at her hand, trying to tell him something.

Adele was acting as his assistant and handed him his phone, presumably to call for help. The crowd might have moved back, but I stayed close to the table to see what was going on. The woman seemed overcome, but I had a feeling it was more from all the attention than her allergic reaction. "I just need some antihistamine cream. It's in my purse," she said to Eric, then to me. Eric hadn't seemed to have heard and pulled out a pen.

While Eric felt for the pulse on her neck, I got the purse, found the cream, and slipped it to her. A moment later, she pushed back his hand and sat up. Then she stood and announced to all that she was okay.

"My fiancé saved her! Isn't my Cutchykins wonderful?" Adele said proudly. The crowd hesitated a moment, then gave him a round of applause. Meanwhile, the woman slipped out the side door. I crumpled up the sign-up sheet I'd had for her. I didn't think we could count on her being a student.

CHAPTER 13

I HAD FINALLY THOUGHT TO LOOK AT MY PHONE AS I was clearing up after the end of the preview. We'd gotten quite a few sign-ups, so I considered it a success. As I scrolled through the messages, I noticed one from Mason saying he couldn't wait to see me and that he had a surprise for me. I finished up quickly and headed for his place. I was really curious about the surprise. It couldn't be too much with his ex and daughter around. It was dark when I parked in front of his house. I still felt funny about using the key he'd given me, so I rang the bell. Instantly Spike began to bark and I could track Mason's progress to the door by the increase in volume of the yipping.

"Sunshine, you're here, at last," Mason said with a happy grin when he opened the door. "Come in." He made a flourish with his hand as he scooted back, giving a couple of tugs on the bell on the scooter handle. "Hooray, Molly is here."

I walked and he pushed himself on the scooter as we

went down the hall to the den. Spike was running along, trying to stay in the middle of things. I told him about the Yarn U Preview, and he laughed when I got to the end.

"It sounds like first responder Eric was having an adrenaline rush. That poor woman."

"I have to admit that I got a little nervous myself when I saw him take out the pen, since he'd just talked about tracheotomies. But it turned out he was just going to write down her heart rate."

"I wish I could have been there. I wish I could have been anywhere." He looked skyward with frustration. "I hate being stuck here."

"You mentioned having a surprise," I said, trying to change the subject. It seemed like a better thing to say than my usual, *Don't worry, you'll be back on both feet soon.* "Where is it?" I asked, looking around.

"You'll see," he said. We'd reached the room that faced the yard and pool, and there was no burst of confetti or a net of balloons falling down. Everything looked the same as usual. The TV was on, and Spike had already reclaimed his seat on the arm of the leather sofa. Just to be sure I hadn't missed anything, I gave the room another once-over and then shrugged.

"I give up. I don't see anything different."

Mason chuckled. "You're looking at it the wrong way. It's not what is here; it's what is not here." My brow furrowed, and I checked out the room again, wondering what was missing.

"Never mind guessing. I'll tell you. The surprise is we have the place to ourselves. I gave Jaimee an invite I had to a charity dinner. Jaimee heard that some of the people from *The Housewives of Mulholland Drive* were going to be there, and she talked Brooklyn into being her date."

He had a merry expression as he glanced around his house. "It's like we're teenagers and our parents are away. We can get into all kinds of trouble. Although we could have gotten into much more if you'd gotten here earlier," he teased.

A new show started on the TV and captured Mason's attention. "Do you want to watch it?" I asked. He seemed mesmerized by the screen.

Mason seemed distressed. "It isn't the pain meds I have a problem with. I'm addicted to these shows! They're all glorified soap operas that forever leave you hanging. This one is about a PI whose life is a mess. He's gone over to the dark side." Mason sat down on the sofa, continuing to explain the program to me.

"The PI started working for some guy, laundering money. You'd think the writers would be more creative than having them launder money by owning a bunch of coin-operated laundry centers."

Mason watched for a few more minutes then shut off the TV. "I'm recording it. I can watch it later when I don't have you here all to myself."

He patted the spot next to him on the couch. "All I can do is say how sorry I am that things are the way they are. I can't believe I bent your ear about a stupid television show when you're in the middle of a real mystery. How about we order an Indian feast and then you tell me everything?"

It sounded like a good plan to me. I let Mason do the ordering, and in no time there was a man at the door with bags of fragrant food. It had been an eternity since lunch, and I was starved.

Mason had been scooting around too much, and I knew that the pain was always worse at night, so I insisted he sit on the couch while I brought out the food. There was a mountain of tandoori chicken and vegetables in orange masala sauce; spicy spinach with cubes of mild cheese; rice with peas, raisins and cashews; and a circle of bread called paratha that had buttery layers. We made it into a mini buffet on the coffee table. Mason insisted on filling his own plate.

"Where to begin?" I said between bites. "You know I found out the identity of the victim." I didn't mention it was because Barry showed me a photo. "The cops are all over CeeCee now, asking her what Delaney Tanner was doing in her guest apartment. CeeCee is insisting she doesn't know the woman, but it seems like everyone else does. I know her from way back when the boys were in school, and I found out she used to work at the bookstore. Then, when I went to make the bookstore's deposit at the bank, it turned out Delaney was a teller there."

Mason listened with interest as I mentioned meeting Delaney's daughters and how they'd insisted she wasn't depressed and told the cops so.

"It sounds like they still haven't decided if it was suicide or foul play," he said.

"It also could have been some kind of accident. The real question is who invited her to the guest quarters. I'd like to talk to Tony and the housekeeper, Rosa. One of them had to let her in."

"Is Tony living there?" Mason said.

"CeeCee isn't broadcasting it, but he is. I think it is just temporary."

"Maybe someone left one of the gates open and this woman was some kind of stalker and slipped in," Mason offered. "And maybe in spite of what her daughters said, she was depressed and she was looking for somewhere to die. She had pills and booze with her and stuffed something in the heater vent and got ready to say good-bye. She chose CeeCee's because it would get a lot of attention and she would be the somebody in death she hadn't been in life."

"You need to get back to work. You are definitely watching too much television."

"Tell me about it," he said with a melancholy smile. Mason sopped up some of the masala sauce with a piece of the paratha bread and fed it to me. "Or it could have been an accident. She was drunk and on pills and wandered in there and was cold and turned on the heat."

"There's something that doesn't fit," I said. But when he asked what, I had to tell him I didn't know.

Even with all his casts and sore spots, we'd managed to cuddle quite close together, and he sighed with pleasure. "This is how it's supposed to be." He leaned forward and set his plate on the coffee table and then moved even closer, so that our cheeks were touching. "We could adjourn to the other room," he said.

A door slammed in the distance, and Spike instantly awoke from his nap. He took a guard dog stance on the couch cushion and began to bark. Mason and I reacted like two naughty teenagers and instantly pulled apart. A moment later, Jaimee marched into the den, giving off a prickly vibe.

"Ha! So those Housewife people thought there was no drama in my life," she said. She took one look at us on the couch and squeezed into the space between us. Spike gave her a token bark before taking off for another part of the house.

"Where's Brooklyn?" Mason asked.

"She went into the other room to change," Jaimee said.

"I'm sure you're very tired from your evening out. . . ." Mason said. He let it trail off, hoping she would get up, but either he was too subtle or she simply chose to ignore it. All her attention seemed to be on the remains of our takeout on the table.

She pulled off a piece of the tandoori chicken and nibbled

on it. "The dinner was inedible," she said, as if it was Mason's fault. "Don't you want to know what happened?"

"Not really," Mason said with a grin. "But I bet you're going to tell us anyway." He put a little emphasis on the *us* since Jaimee seemed to be doing a good job of totally ignoring my presence.

I had been to enough of these charity dinners to be able to picture the setting. It would have been at a ballroom in one of the nice Beverly Hills hotels, filled with round tables. There were always celebrities there since they got publicity for the event and were a draw for guests. There was usually a silent auction with things like walk-on parts on sitcoms or scripts signed by the cast of a current hit show, items with studio logos and donations that were advertisements for assorted businesses. I'm sure there was an open bar, a lot of networking and, as she'd said, an inedible dinner, followed by some entertainment.

Jaimee wiped her fingers on an extra napkin. She let out a sigh. "Todd was there." This was the point where she acknowledged that I was there by making sure I understood that he was her ex-boyfriend, who was much younger than she was and an athlete, and that she had broken up with him. "He made a big scene right in front of the Housewives' table, saying that he wanted me to give him a chance to make things right with us. He said he wanted to see how the work on my house was progressing."

"Maybe you should give him another chance," Mason said. "It sounds like he really wants to win you back." I knew Mason was hoping she'd take his suggestion immediately.

"He's going to have to do a lot more than that for me to give him another chance. Ha! I said I wasn't born yesterday and that I knew it was all about him wanting to get back his stuff. I bought most of it and I told him that all his equipment was my property and that I had it in storage with the rest of the things from my house." She seemed pleased with the last part and pulled out her cell phone to lay it on the table. "I wouldn't be surprised if the Housewives people called me tonight and wanted me back on the show. Maybe they'll even want us to recreate the moment."

"If you want drama," Mason said, "Molly was in the group that found the body at CeeCee Collins's house. We were just talking about what we think happened."

It was pretty clear Jaimee couldn't care less, and I was already gathering my things. Mason saw what I was doing and tried to get me to stay, but a moment later Brooklyn came in the room, dressed in loose-fitting white pants and a kimono-style top.

"I'm going to get your meds, Dad. Then we can do some tai chi." She glanced in my direction. "It helps him sleep." I offered to help. "Thanks," she said halfheartedly, "but we have a whole ritual." Her eyes went toward the hall leading to the door, and her message came through loud and clear. I was the odd man out.

Mason pulled himself off the sofa and rode the scooter along with me to the door. He winced a few times. "The pain gets worse at night." He looked back to the ruckus going on in the den and turned to face me. "It seems to be important for my daughter to handle things. She hasn't said anything to me, but I think she was looking for a reason to leave San Diego. You know how they say you never retire from being a mother? Well, the same is true for being a father, at least for me."

How could I possibly find fault with that? We went outside, finally getting some privacy, and he gave me a good night kiss that promised things to come.

CHAPTER 14

I DREAMED ABOUT YARN AGAIN. NO SURPRISE. THIS time I was crocheting. I couldn't remember the details, just that it felt like a fever dream. The yarn was full of bumps and thorns, and the stitches kept coming out wrong. At one point I think I picked up the ball of yarn, threw it in the air, and hit it with a bat, sending it sailing off into space, but it kept coming back, and each time the ball of yarn was bigger. I was relieved to wake up, though I was twisted in the sheet. I fell out of bed trying to untwist myself.

I rushed through my morning chores, already thinking about what I had to take care of at the bookstore. I certainly wanted to call Kelsey Willis and confirm everything about her daughter's shower. I remembered I'd given her a card and then she'd given me one in return. I hadn't paid attention to it at the time because I didn't really expect her to book her daughter's shower at the bookstore. I'd never been so happy to be wrong. If it went well, we were sure to get other business. I definitely wanted to stay on top of it.

I searched the house and couldn't find it. I was just about to see if one of the dogs had carried it off somewhere when it came back to me—it was still at CeeCee's. I had managed to get the cops to give me the purse I'd left in the dining room, but I'd forgotten all about the tote.

It was probably still sitting on the floor in CeeCee's dining room. I thought about calling CeeCee, but it seemed easiest to just swing by. I handed out treats to the animal crowd at my feet and rushed out the door. The air smelled cold and damp but also incredibly sweet from the orange blossoms on the row of trees in the yard.

I would have liked to linger and relish how green the yard was and the way the sun sparkled in the dewdrops hanging from the leaves, but I needed to get my tote bag and get on to the bookstore.

I parked in front of CeeCee's and was glad to see there were no cop cars or news vans. I rang the intercom, and Rosa answered. I asked if CeeCee was there.

"No," Rosa said curtly. I thought she was going to shut off the intercom.

"Wait," I said quickly. "I left something the other day, and I wanted to pick it up."

Rosa seemed to hesitate, but I really wanted to get the bag with the card. We went back and forth a few times, and she finally buzzed the gate open. As soon as I got inside, I couldn't help it—my eye went right to the garage and the stairway. A piece of yellow tape still hung from the railing, and I gathered it had been released by the cops.

When I'd walked through it before, I had always just taken in the yard as a whole. I'd noticed there was a small forest of trees, but my perception of the rest of it was just green with no details. Now I saw that it had been landscaped to make the outside world seem almost nonexistent. There were trees arranged along the sides of the lot, and the space between them was filled with bushes. Flowers had been added to give bursts of color. When I'd walked around the outside of the property with Babs, I'd noticed there was a wall of green created solely out of bushes and ivy that was separate from what I was seeing. So much more attractive than seeing the fence that surrounded the property.

Rosa had the door open, and the two Yorkies ran outside, barking. She corralled them, and we all went inside. I'd never been there when CeeCee wasn't home before, and it seemed very quiet. I had said to Mason that I wanted to talk to the housekeeper, and it seemed like I was going to get my moment. I figured she knew all the inside information, what skeletons were in the closet and where the bodies were buried, to borrow a couple of figures of speech. Not that it would be easy to pry it out of her. My impression of Rosa was that she was rather stoic, but then if you wanted to keep your job as a celebrity's housekeeper, it was better not to be too chatty.

"Where did you leave the tote bag?" she said, standing so that I couldn't move beyond the entrance hall. I pointed toward the dining room, and she stepped aside to let me walk in. She seemed a little nervous, and I sensed she wanted me out of there as fast as possible.

"It must be different having Tony living here. More work for you. I suppose he wanted you to get the guest quarters cleaned up."

"No. It is okay. Mr. Tony didn't want me to deal with the guest apartment, before or after." Her voice faltered on *after*, and I knew she meant after the other day.

"After?" I said with a question in my voice. "Do you mean like clean up after the crime scene?"

"Yes. He said he would take care of it all. He wants the vent replaced right away so there won't be the chance of another accident." She paused and seemed to be considering her words.

"I know Miss CeeCee can't even make a cup of tea for herself, but she is a very kind person. When she found out how long it took me to take the bus to and from here, she gave me a car to use." I thought she was finished, but then she added, "I worry for her with Mr. Tony. I think maybe she is too kind to him."

I wanted to ask what she meant and get into whether she had any ideas how Delaney had gotten in, but she made it very clear she was done talking and led me into the dining room. "Please," she said, gesturing for me to check the room. Of course, the purple tote was on the floor just where I'd left it. Rosa ushered me right back outside and closed the door.

Maybe Tony wasn't the Prince Charming we all thought he was.

I waited until it was quiet in the information booth at the bookstore before I took out Kelsey's card. You better believe this time I looked to see what it said. It listed her name and title—executive VP—and the company was Willis Industries, Inc. It appeared she'd started a new chapter in her life, too. When I called to go over the choices her daughter had made for the shower, I asked her what Willis Industries, Inc., did.

"I don't see why you need to know that to put on a shower," she said with a little edge in her voice.

"No problem. I was just making conversation. As long as

you pay for the shower, whatever you do is okay with us." I punctuated it with a friendly laugh. She didn't join in. Now it came back to me. She had never had much of a sense of humor, and certainly had none about herself.

Mrs. Shedd overheard my end of the conversation and figured out who I was talking with. "Molly, we don't want to rile the customers. She didn't cancel, did she?"

I assured my boss that Kelsey was still on for the shower, and then I moved on to other tasks. I had been gone so much over the past couple of days that I worked straight through until the evening. I stopped by Mason's on the way home. His other daughter, Thursday, was over, and she answered the door. I had a much better relationship with her than with Brooklyn, but still, when I realized they were all having dinner together, I begged off. There was no way I wasn't going to feel like an intruder.

I called Dinah when I got home and laid it all out to her.

"And here I thought you two had just the relationship I wanted," she said when I filled her in.

I mentioned that I had stopped over at CeeCee's and talked to Rosa. "She didn't say much, but if you read between the lines, it's very interesting."

"Okay, you got me curious. Are you up for company? We can sit and crochet and forget about the problems of the men in our lives. Let's talk about murder instead," she said with a cheery laugh.

I'd barely changed into a pair of sweats and a T-shirt when I heard a soft knock at my kitchen door. The menagerie heard it, too, and raced me to the door. The cats were silent, but Felix and Cosmo seemed to be having a contest over who could be the louder watchdog.

I opened the door, and before I could stop their escape, the whole crew ran into the dark yard.

"Sorry, I would have stopped them, but they were too fast for me," Dinah said, coming inside. She dropped her tote bag on the table.

"The dogs aren't the problem," I said, peering out into the darkness past the patio illuminated by the floodlights. "It's the cats." The two of them had rushed out to the back of the yard and were already out of sight. My backyard was wide but not too deep, ending in a row of redwood trees with ivy and bushes between. I knew there was a fence behind all the foliage, but it was ancient. It had been there long before we moved in, and I had no idea of its condition and often worried there might be a hole somewhere. Mr. Kitty ran past me and went back into the house, but I could hear rustling in the bushes along the back of the yard. Cat was quite the huntress, and I could only imagine what she was doing in the undergrowth. Or finding, I thought with a shudder. I shined my flashlight along the redwood trees and saw some of the ivy moving.

"I have to get her out of there," I said, running across the grass. I followed the sound and then plunged into the ground cover. I grabbed her at the base of the fence. I had never really seen it before, since it was virtually covered by the bushes and ivy. Chain-link fence certainly lasted, though it probably had gotten shorter with the thick ivy vines weighing it down.

While I was back there, I shined the flashlight into the foliage. "I'm not sure I like that," I said when Dinah had joined me. It was almost impossible to see with all the growth, but the flashlight had illuminated a gate in the old fence. The property behind mine was on a cul-de-sac, and I didn't know the people.

"I don't think you have to worry about them using it," Dinah said, giving it a push. It seemed to be rusted in place.

"Didn't you find a similar gate on the fence that runs along the side of your property?" my friend asked. I thought for a moment and realized she was right.

"That gate doesn't matter anymore. The neighbor next door put up a wood fence on his side that blocks it." Cat was beginning to squirm at being held, and any moment she would start using her claws to break away, so I quickly carried her across the yard and brought her inside. "You didn't know that gate was there, and they probably don't, either," Dinah said, following me inside.

I put Cat on the floor, and she went off looking for Mr. Kitty. A moment later Felix and Cosmo came to the door and wanted to come in, too. I kept looking through the window toward the back of the yard. It had stirred something in my mind.

"Are you up for an adventure?" I asked, grabbing my keys.

"Are you kidding? I live for our adventures. Where are we going? What's up?" Dinah said.

"I just want to check out a hunch," I said. We got into the greenmobile. By now it was late enough that there was no traffic on the back road I took. I drove right past the front of CeeCee's and kept going around the side of her property until I got to the street at the back of it. I pulled the car to the curb, and we got out.

The temperature had dropped into the low fifties, and there was a bite to the air. The street seemed dark and deserted, but then again, all the houses were on the other side of the street hidden behind high fences and mature foliage. The only light came from some fixtures on the gates.

Our footsteps were absorbed by the asphalt as we walked along the back of CeeCee's property. The light on the gate across the street illuminated the wall of bushes. There was no sidewalk, just a strip of dirt with ivy covering it, and instead of a concrete curb, there was a raised layer of asphalt. I kept shining my flashlight on the greenery, looking for some kind of opening as we walked the whole length of it.

"I see where you're headed," Dinah said. "You think there's a gate somewhere in the fence, like at your place. Wouldn't the cops have looked for one?"

"Maybe not. If there is one, I don't think CeeCee knows about it. If, according to Rosa, she can't make a cup of tea for herself, I doubt she knows much about her fencing."

"Speaking of Rosa, what did you find out?" Dinah asked.

"Mostly that she's a loyal employee who is protective of CeeCee and not a big fan of Tony, though she didn't offer any details. It seemed a little suspicious to me that he wanted to take care of everything with the guest apartment."

We had reached the place where CeeCee's property ended and the neighboring lot began. "I could be wrong about a gate," I said.

"I hate to bring this up, but you found the gate at your place by looking at the fence. It might be more helpful if we went in." She stuck her hand in the greenery. "It looks like a wall, but these are bushes."

"Wait a second. I have an idea." I trained the flashlight on the strip of ivy growing between the street and the bushes. Then I spotted it. "There's an indentation in the asphalt curb, like this was a driveway once," I said, getting excited. I turned toward the wall of green and began to examine it more closely. Dinah was right. The planting only looked like a wall, and I noticed a slender opening. I slipped in and once I was behind the tall bushes saw that despite the fanciness of CeeCee's place, the fence was just ancient chain-link covered in ivy. The flashlight reflected off two metal poles sticking up out of the ground that clearly belonged to a gate—a rather large gate. "This must have been a back entrance," I called in a loud whisper to Dinah, who was still outside the green wall. "C'mon," I beckoned.

"The flashlight looks really weird coming through the bushes," she said when she joined me. I gave the gate a push, expecting the resistance I'd had with the gate at my place. But this one moved easily, as if it had been used recently. All I had to do was move back the thin vines of ivy that covered it and push it open. I slipped inside, and Dinah was close behind.

"Where are we?" I said in a soft voice. The large trees with their spreading branches made the area seem even darker. I shined the flashlight around, trying to orient myself. The ground was covered with patches of ivy and some bald spots. Nothing like the beautiful landscaping of the rest of CeeCee's. My light hit a row of tall bushes, and I heard a soft swishing sound coming from the area to one side. "That's the pool, which is right behind the house." My flashlight illuminated a wall and, as I pointed it upward, windows from a second story. "That's the garage and the upstairs apartment. This must be sort of a no-man's-land. I wonder if CeeCee even knows it's here."

Dinah made a move to go around the end of the bushes into the pool area, but I stopped her. "What if CeeCee looks out her window and sees people skulking around her yard?"

Dinah nodded with recognition. "She'd probably freak out before she had a chance to see it was us." She glanced down at the dark ground nervously. "Let's get out of here. Who knows what's wandering around in this ivy."

It seemed a like a good idea. All the darkness and the fact that we were walking around right near where a death had recently occurred started to get to me. I grabbed Dinah's arm and tried to see where the way out was. A disembodied voice made us both jump. "Please get me out of here," the voice cried out.

"It's my phone," I said, trying to get it before it repeated. Instead it slipped through my fingers and fell into the ivy as the voice kept on urging me to answer it.

I managed to fish it out of the ivy without encountering anything creepy and swiped the screen to answer it before the voice could cry out again.

"Molly, are you there?" There was a pause. "Sunshine, say something."

"I'm here, Mason," I said in a low voice as I finally got the phone to my ear.

"Why did you leave without even coming in?" he said. "Thursday was looking forward to talking about yarn with you."

"I can't talk now. Dinah and I found something important at CeeCee's, but we need to get out of here."

He said something, but it was drowned out by a loud thwack coming from overhead. Just as it registered that it was a helicopter, Dinah and I were bathed in a bright spotlight.

I grabbed her hand, and we began to run.

CHAPTER 15

DID WE REALLY THINK WE COULD OUTRUN THE cops? Did we really *think*, was the real question. In a word, no. We flew out of the bushes and onto the street. A police cruiser had just pulled to the curb. The doors flew open, and two young officers came after us. By the end of the block, they'd snagged us. They had barely broken a sweat, but both Dinah and I were breathless.

You'd have thought we had just robbed a bank or something. The helicopter kept circling while more cop cars arrived. They blocked the street, leaving their headlights on to illuminate the area. A sergeant arrived and started asking a lot of questions, trying to sort things out. The trouble was, he was talking to everybody but Dinah and me.

All the commotion had brought the neighbors into the street, and I could see the lights from their cell phones as they tried to capture the moment.

"If you could just call CeeCee Collins," I said, grabbing

the floor. "She can vouch that it was okay for us to be on her property."

While I was talking, one of the uniforms was shaking his head. "We checked the house. The housekeeper said she's not vouching for anyone and nobody is supposed to be wandering around."

"But you have to tell her it was me," I said. The cops ignored what I said and started talking amongst themselves. "He's the one who called," one of the cops said, indicating a man with a dog standing off to the side. He was outside the bright glare of the headlights, and I had to squint to make out that the man was Evan Willis and the dog was a Jack Russell terrier.

Evan didn't wait for the sergeant to ask for his story; he just started talking. "I was out walking my dog when I saw two people loitering on the street. Then they disappeared into the bushes. It looked pretty suspicious to me, particularly after a dead woman showed up on the property. And you know how celebrities get stalkers."

"You know me," I said. "Molly Pink." He looked at me blankly. "I'm working with your wife and daughter on her baby shower." He looked at the cops and shrugged. "It's Polly," I said finally.

"Oh," he said at last. "You're the one from the other day."

"You seem very observant, the way you noticed us hanging around," I said. I heard Dinah let out a little gasp as I took the opportunity to bring up the night Delaney died. "Maybe you noticed something suspicious last Thursday night, too."

I guess I caught them all off guard, because it seemed like all the cops' mouths fell open. The sergeant stepped closer to me, probably to stop me from talking, but Evan answered first.

"I have already been over that with the police. We had a party that night, so I wasn't paying any attention to what was going on out here." He made a broad gesture toward CeeCee's property.

"Was Delaney Tanner one of your guests?" I asked. Out of the corner of my eye I noticed the sergeant gesturing toward a couple of uniforms, who were taking out their handcuffs.

Evan seemed taken aback by my question, and it took him a moment to answer. "The name doesn't ring a bell," he said in a dismissive tone. The sergeant seemed exasperated and told the two cops to cuff us. "I think we'll just take this down to the station."

Just as the cuffs clicked shut, the crowd parted as someone demanded to be let through. Mason used his foot to propel the scooter through the opening, with Brooklyn trailing behind him. The scooter and the tai chi outfit he was wearing apparently caught the cops by surprise, because they let him through.

"Molly, don't say another word." He eyed the bunch of cops. "I'm their attorney."

I heard a groan go through the cops as he asked what their plans were for us.

The Channel 3 news van arrived a moment later, and Kimberly Wang Diaz pushed her way into the crowd, asking every cop for a statement.

I hung my head when I saw Barry step through the crowd, too. He went right past Kimberly Wang Diaz and caught a glimpse of Mason on his scooter. A look of exasperation flashed on his face for a moment, then he was all business as he joined his associates. He was obviously off duty, and I had the feeling he might have been sleeping. No suit this time—instead he wore jeans that were soft with age. I saw a dark T-shirt showing under his leather jacket. His badge was pinned to his pants pocket, and the edge of his gun peeked out from the open jacket. I suppose years of being awakened out of sleep to hunt down clues had trained him to skip groggy and go right to alert.

His gaze washed over me and down to my now cuffed hands. There was a flicker in his dark eyes and just the slightest tilt to his head that seemed to say, *What have you done this time?*

Mason started to repeat his comments about being our attorney, but Barry stopped him and walked over to the sergeant. "I think I can help straighten this out. What exactly happened?" The cops wouldn't let Dinah, me or Mason speak, and they told their version of what had happened, which was basically that we'd snuck into CeeCee's yard and were either stalkers or connected to the body that had been found there. But any way you looked at it, we were up to no good.

I was shocked when Barry asked for my cell phone. He had to help himself, since my hands were tied up at the moment. He scrolled through the numbers and did what the cops should have done to start with. He called CeeCee, who wasn't home and had no idea what was going on. When she heard about what had happened, she said whatever we'd done at her place was okay with her. Or at least that was my best guess at what she said from hearing his end of the conversation. He slipped the phone back into my pocket and pulled the sergeant aside.

A few moments later the sergeant turned to the crowd. "Show's over, folks. You can all go home." The cops uncuffed us, and the sergeant headed back to his car, grumbling that the first batch of cops should have done more than just go to the door of the house. Kimberly tried to make the most of the moment and asked me if we'd actually been investigating the recent death.

"We all know what a nose for murder you have," she said, trying to interject some personality into her report. Barry was standing close by, obviously listening for my answer.

I just mumbled that I had no comment. Disgruntled, she and her cameraman packed up to go. I went over to Barry. "Thank you for straightening everything out."

"And now you owe me one," he said in a low voice. Before I could react, he walked away. The cops went back to their cars, and the street cleared of the neighbors.

"I was hoping I could play the white knight," Mason said, making a sad face. "But I'm happy I could even make the effort. I am sure you have a lot to tell me. How about we all go out for coffee and discuss?"

Dinah begged off. "It's been a long day for me, and I need to touch base with Commander." She leaned close to me. "It's terrible, but I've been avoiding even talking to him. I'm afraid he's going to push me for an answer. And I'm worried what he'll do if he doesn't like the one I give him." She said she'd drive my car back to my place, where she'd left hers.

Brooklyn had been hanging in the background, but now she stepped forward. "Dad, it's late and you should really go home." Mason's smile faded.

"I appreciate your concern, and I hate to be a bother to you. That's why I wanted to hire a driver until I was done with this." He adjusted his position on the scooter. "We can drop you off at home, and Molly can drive the SUV," he said. He gave the bell on the scooter a playful ring.

"That's okay," Brooklyn said. "I'll drive. Then we can take Molly home after." Dinah threw me a meaningful glance as I gave her the keys to my car. It was so awkward, I really wanted to beg off, too, but Mason was the most exuberant I'd seen him since the accident, and if he wanted to go out for coffee and hear about things, I was willing to put up with Brooklyn's attitude.

"Shall we?" I said, taking the lead toward the Mercedes SUV that was Mason's current ride. I wanted to help load the scooter in the back, but Brooklyn insisted on doing it, and had me sit in the backseat.

Our choices were limited, due to the hour, and we ended up at the twenty-four-hour IHOP. We had the place to ourselves, and the waitress didn't bat an eye when Mason parked his scooter next to the booth and slid in. Nor did she seem surprised to see him wearing his tai chi outfit. Brooklyn seemed to be going along under protest and took out her phone and started playing with it. I was sorry it hadn't been Thursday who'd driven him, but apparently she had an early day and had already gone home.

Mason made a production of ordering something for us to share, creating a dish that wasn't on the menu. He seemed thrilled to be out in the world. He'd come up with a concoction of pancakes smothered in fried bananas and soaked with melted butter that turned out to be sinfully delicious. All the excitement had caused me to build up quite an appetite. The coffee cut into the rich sweetness of the pancakes and complemented the flavor. Mason savored every moment and was thrilled that I was enjoying the food.

"Now, do you want to tell me the whole story?" His broad face lit up with an excited grin, and as always, a lock of his dark hair had fallen across his forehead. "It's so good to be out late at night, doing the detective thing with you."

Brooklyn's face was still glued to her phone, and she seemed immersed in texting. I thought she was just ignoring us, but then she started muttering about Jaimee. Mason reached across the table and squeezed my hand, I think as reassurance, and then asked his daughter what the problem was.

"Mother said that Todd sent her flowers and then called her tonight. Doesn't he get that it's over?"

"He seems to be trying to make amends for whatever she

thinks he did wrong. Who knows, they could work it out," Mason said. He saw that his daughter wasn't looking, and he winked at me and gave my hand another squeeze before letting it go. "You were going to tell me what you found out."

I began by explaining what we had been doing at CeeCee's. "Finding that gate was really important," I said. "That means that CeeCee wouldn't have had to know that Delaney was even there. She could have come in on her own."

"But, Sunshine, why would Delaney have been sneaking into CeeCee's guest apartment?" Mason stopped to think for a moment. "Well, the obvious reason would be that she was meeting someone." He put a lot of emphasis on *someone*, and I got the drift.

"You mean you think Tony could have been having a fling with her on the side?"

Mason cocked his head and put up his hands. "Not all men are as nice as me," he said with a grin.

"I can't bring it up to CeeCee," I said. "Unless I know for sure that it's true."

Mason nodded and said he could see my point. "What sort of work did Delaney do? Maybe if you could find out if their paths crossed," he offered.

"She worked at the Bank of Tarzana," I said. Brooklyn had lost interest in her phone and was picking at the plate of food in front of her. She looked at her watch with concern.

"Dad, it's really late. You shouldn't tire yourself."

I was shocked to find myself agreeing with her. Mason was still healing.

THERE WAS ALMOST NO TRAFFIC, AND IT ONLY TOOK a few minutes to get to my house. Mason opened the passenger door of the SUV, and I leaned over to say good night.

We did an awkward arm dance as he attempted to hug me. With his daughter in the driver's seat, it was too uncomfortable for there to be anything more.

My greeting committee of Cosmo and Felix was full of reproach for my being gone so long, and they had knocked over the trash to make sure I knew it. I let them out in the yard and went across the house to rouse Blondie and coax her out for the last time of the night. The cats came in the kitchen and saw the mound of coffee grounds and vegetable peelings all over the kitchen floor and did an about-face. I was about to tackle the mess when the phone rang, startling me and giving me a whole new adrenaline rush just when I'd been starting to recover from the fuss with the cops.

"Hello," I said with a bit of worry in my voice.

"Molly, it's me, Bar—I mean, Detective Greenberg," he said. Without even a hint of apology about the hour, he continued. "Remember I said you owed me? I want to collect. Could we talk now?"

"Now? Already? It's midnight." I had looked at the clock and rounded it off to the nearest hour.

"Yes, it needs to be now while everything is *fresh* in your mind." The way he emphasized *fresh*, I was pretty sure he was referring to how he'd recently kept me and Dinah from having to go down to the station.

Figuring I might as well get it over with, I said it was okay, stifling a yawn. I really needed to find a way to stop burning the candle at both ends. The knock at the front door was almost immediate, and I realized that once again he'd called from out front. The timing of his call made me wonder if he'd been out there waiting until I got home.

I let him in, and he followed me as I went through the kitchen to open the door for the dogs. As we passed through, he saw the mess on the floor.

"The dogs?" he asked, and I nodded in answer. I heard him let out a sigh. He hadn't asked which one had done it, and I wasn't going to name names, but Cosmo—who was technically his—had a rep for knocking over the garbage.

By the time the dogs came in, Barry had already retrieved a fresh trash bag and started cleaning up the mess. Cosmo rushed up to him and put his paws on Barry's leg in greeting.

Barry shook his head. "You'd think he'd feel at least a little guilty," Barry said, stroking the dog's head in spite of himself. Then he tried to give the dog a serious scowl. "Cosmo, we need to talk about this."

Barry was as clueless about dog training as he had been about being a father, though now that his son had been living with him for a while he was getting better at it.

It was against my nature not to be hospitable, even if I was pretty sure he was here to grill me for information and it was practically the middle of the night. "I was just going to have some tea. Would you like some?"

"Yes," he said quickly as he finished cleaning up the last of the coffee grounds.

"I was going to have chamomile. It's good when you're wired. Does that work for you?"

"A shot of scotch works, too. Chamomile tea sounds a little wimpy."

"If you want scotch . . ." I made a move to go check the dining room. Charlie had always kept a stocked bar, and it was all still there. Barry stood up from his cleanup work abruptly.

"I'd be happy to try the tea."

A few minutes later we each carried a mug of steaming tea into the living room.

"Thank you for bailing Dinah and me out," I said.

Barry let out a mirthless laugh. "Hold off on the gratitude. I was really thinking of all the time and paperwork a trip to station would have generated. And it would have ended with the same result: the two of you being let go." I checked his expression to see if he was joking, but he was all serious cop.

"Okay, then I'm taking my thank-you back," I said, teasing.

"But you still owe me," he said, ignoring my joke.

"How do you want to be paid?" I asked, all serious myself this time.

"I think you know." He waited until I'd positioned myself at the end of the leather couch, and he took a seat at the other end of it. "Information—and all of it." Barry was trying to be stern and full of authority, even though Cosmo jumped on the sofa and flopped across his lap.

"You can stop with the authority voice," I said, setting out coasters for the mugs of tea. "It just seems ridiculous since we have a history."

He blinked a few times, as if he was processing what I said, and then he let out a sigh. He looked tired and wary. "Are you playing the 'we're friends' card to get out of talking?"

"Oh please, Barry, give me more credit than that. I don't need a 'card' to get out of talking."

"You've changed since you started hanging out with Fields," he said.

"Changed? How?" I asked.

He took his time answering. Barry was never rash. "I'm not sure what it is, but you never would have said that whole thing about not needing a card before. You might have thought it, you might have even answered my questions with questions, but you wouldn't have been so up front about it." He picked up the mug and looked down at the greenish liquid.

"Maybe it's from hanging around Mason, but it could be because I'm the assistant manager at the bookstore now and it's made me tougher."

"Right. You did mention that before." He set the mug down, and I watched all the friendliness leave his face as he went back to cop mode. "Let's just forget we know each other and get on with this."

"Sure," I said.

"So then, Mrs. Pink, tell me what you and your associate, Mrs. Lyons, were doing wandering around in CeeCee Collins's yard."

"Mrs. Pink? Mrs. Lyons? Are you kidding? Even with your authority face, I still know it's you."

"Are you deliberately trying to make this difficult?" he asked.

"I don't think so. But this whole setup feels very strange. Doesn't it feel strange to you, considering our past?"

Barry said no too quickly. "Just tell me what you two were up to."

"Nothing. We were just checking out the yard."

Barry made a disgruntled groan. "You know I'm not going to buy that. I know you two were looking for something. Save us both a lot of time and just tell me."

"I probably should take the fifth. You could use the information against me."

"I promise I won't if you tell me right now, Molly." I hesitated a moment, and he shook his head with consternation. "Thank heavens most people I interrogate aren't as difficult as you." I thought I saw just the faintest hint of a smile.

"Fine. You want to know what we were doing?" I gave him the whole story, starting with being in my yard and finding an old gate along the back of it, and how it made me wonder about CeeCee's.

Barry interrupted. "You should put some kind of a lock on it. Otherwise someone could just wander into your yard."

"I don't think so. You didn't see the condition of it. Anyway, it made me think there might be a forgotten gate at CeeCee's." I told him how I'd found the remnant of a driveway and used it to locate the hidden entryway. Was it my imagination or did Barry look uncomfortable? Probably because he realized his guys had missed it. "The one in my yard was old and rusted and wouldn't open. The one in CeeCee's yard moved freely, like someone had used it frequently. I'm sure you see how this opens up new possibilities of how Delaney Tanner ended up in the guest quarters—just in case you were focusing on CeeCee as some kind of suspect. Delaney could have even come in on her own."

He scribbled something down on his notepad.

"Don't be too upset your crack team missed it. The fence is hidden by greenery on the inside and outside," I said. "The way I see it, you now owe me since I handed over such a big piece of information." Barry actually laughed.

"Okay, but next time you have some kind of hunch, call me. What do you want to know?"

"What was it—an accident, suicide or foul play? And what was the cause of death?"

"It's still inconclusive. And it looks like the cause of death was probably carbon monoxide poisoning."

"Then I was right," I said with a note of triumph in my voice.

"Yes," he said, almost choking on the word.

"It might be inconclusive, but you must have some cop gut hunch about what happened," I said in a friendly voice.

He cocked an eyebrow as he looked at me. "Maybe I do, but I'm not sharing. That's it. We're even now." He picked up his mug of tea to show he was done talking. We sat there drinking in silence for a few minutes, and I felt calmed by the quiet. I remember setting down the mug and leaning back against the soft leather cushion. The next thing I knew I was opening my eyes and sun was streaming in through the shutters on the front window. Barry had fallen asleep, too. Cosmo was still on his lap, snoring little dog snores. Worse, Barry was leaning against me.

My movements startled him awake. He sat forward, immediately alert, taking in his surroundings. He coughed a few times and said, "That tea is like knockout drops. I should have taken the scotch. Drinking on duty is not nearly as bad as falling asleep on duty."

I shrugged it off. "How about some coffee?"

CHAPTER 16

"WHAT HAPPENED LAST NIGHT?" DINAH ASKED when she found me in the yarn department late that morning. I cringed, wondering if she'd developed mind-reading abilities. Much as I tried to put it out of my mind, Barry's visit kept popping up. Then I realized she was talking about what happened after she'd left me with Mason and Brooklyn. I struggled, trying to remember what we had talked about, but I didn't really have to worry about answering. Dinah seemed preoccupied and started shaking her head in some kind of internal disbelief before blurting out, "I almost said yes."

"What?" I said, stopping my work. Boxes of yarn were at my feet, as I'd been loading misty blue mohair into a bin. Once the classes started, I expected a lot of that kind of yarn to move, since it was the mainstay of Sheila's designs. There were a few women who I recognized as regular customers gathered at the table. I laughed inwardly, glad that Adele was off in the kids' department, because the women were all knitting. They were lost in their clicking needles and conversation and paid no attention to us.

"You didn't, though?" I asked warily, glad to ignore her original question about the previous night's activities.

Dinah usually looked well put together, accenting whatever she was wearing with a couple of long scarves, but this morning it appeared that she had been preoccupied when she got dressed, and there wasn't even one scarf to add a splash of color to her black pantsuit.

"I'm due for a break," I said. "Let's get some coffee and you can tell me all about it. And I'll tell you about last night. Just a hint: I got some more info from Barry."

Dinah's eyes lit up as I shoved the yarn back in the box. "Wow! I think I'd rather talk about your stuff," she said.

"Let's go to Le Grande Fromage. I want to check the supply of flyers." It was probably wishful thinking, but I imagined the stacks of papers I'd left in the stores down the street had trickled down to a few last pages. I dropped a new stack in my canvas tote.

Dinah and I made small talk as we left the bookstore. It seemed her students had reached a new low—one of them had tried to turn in his essay as a text.

"He couldn't understand why I wouldn't accept it," she said. "What kind of precedent would that set? You should have seen it." She stopped long enough to pull out her smartphone. "Actually, you can see it." She scrolled through a mass of words in the dialog box.

"How can you tell where a paragraph starts?" I asked.

"Exactly. And half the words are in some shortened version."

"What did you do?" I asked.

"The only thing I could do! I texted him back an F." Dinah threw up her hands. "These students!"

"Let's go in," I said as we passed the display window of Luxe, the lifestyle store next to the bookstore.

"Is it the flyers you want to check, or Sheila?" Dinah said.

"Maybe both." I pushed open the door. I called it a lifestyle store because they sold a little bit of everything, the one common element being that it was all stylish. It smelled wonderful from a mixture of the soaps scented with things like rose geranium and lemon, along with the exotic spices and teas they sold. There wasn't a lot of any one thing, and the stock was always changing. The only constant was there was always a display of different pieces made by Sheila out where customers could touch them.

Sheila looked up from behind the counter when we walked in. She was writing up a receipt for a customer and gave us a smile. She was more or less the manager of the place.

We hung by the corner near a selection of interesting pottery. "Isn't it amazing how she can have no problem dealing with customers in here and yet practically have a panic attack when it comes to teaching something that has to be second nature to her?" I said.

"It's not the same. Just like last night, when people were admiring the finished projects she had on display. Teaching is a whole other thing."

"Maybe if I give her a pep talk." I noticed the stack of flyers I had strategically placed near the display of the pieces of her work she had for sale was down to the last few. Sheila finished up with the customer and waved us over.

"I bet the class we added for you is going to be full," I said as we approached the counter and I pointed out the dwindling supply of flyers. The face she showed off to the customers faded into a distraught expression.

"I have to tell you the truth—I got rid of almost the whole stack. I know I should be happy that our customers were so

excited they could learn how to make a piece in my style."
She stopped and took a deep breath. "But I'm afraid I can't
do it. Don't you think it's some kind of omen that when we
met at CeeCee's to rehearse the class we found a dead body?"

"One has nothing to do with the other," I said, trying to
sound airy and light. "Delaney Tanner had nothing to do with
any of us. I'm the only one of the group who even knows her."

Sheila looked worried. "Every time I think about teaching, I just have an image of that woman lying there."

"We need to try it again. This time, no interruptions," I
said. "You'll see; you'll do fine." Sheila didn't seem sold. I
put down some more flyers and got her to promise that she
would leave them out for people to take.

"You almost sounded like you believed it," Dinah said
when we got back outside.

"I do. When Sheila starts talking about the yarn and how
she mixes it, she'll forget about her nerves. I think this class
is going to be a game changer for her. She'll never be the
same after."

"I hope you're right," Dinah said as we continued down
the street.

"I hope I am, too." We'd reached the corner. "Finally,
they're open." I pulled open the door of the nail salon and
walked in.

A young woman with long brown hair was reading a
book behind a small desk that seemed to serve as reception
and cashier. I glanced toward the back. It looked very
state-of-the-art with comfortable-looking lime green chairs,
which were all empty.

The young woman stuck a bookmark in what she was
reading and looked up. "Mrs. Lyons?" she exclaimed in
surprise when she saw Dinah. It took my friend a moment
before her face lit in recognition.

"You're in my 2 P.M. English 101 class. Third seat in the right-hand row," Dinah said. "That would mean your last name probably starts with a *B*." Dinah's eyes moved back and forth, and I imagined that she was trying to remember her class list. "Emily Bergman, right?"

"Yes, that's me." She held up the book she was reading. Dinah got all excited when she saw it was one of the extra books she had told the class about. Dinah mostly dealt with students who were trying to avoid studying, so anyone who did extra work stood out—way out.

"Your students are everywhere," I said, reminding her that one of Delaney's daughters was a student as well.

After they exchanged some small talk about the class and Emily told Dinah how much she was enjoying it, the girl looked at us. "If you're here to get a mani or a pedi you'll have to come back. We're not technically open yet." The girl shook her head. "That's what they want me to call them, but it sounds weird to me. I'd rather say the whole thing— manicure and pedicure."

"We're not here for our nails," I said and held up the flyers. "I work at the bookstore down the street. You might not know this, but all the store owners around here help one another." I gave her a few examples, like how we let our customers know when the jewelry store had a sale or when Le Grande Fromage had a coupon deal. "We're holding something called Yarn University, starting next week. We're still taking sign-ups." I showed her the copy. "So, can I leave some?"

Emily seemed uncertain. "Maybe you should talk to the owner. He's in the back." She gestured toward the area past all the lime green chairs.

Dinah stepped in. "Emily, there's no reason to bother him. We'll just leave some, and if there's a problem, you can toss them."

"Thanks," I said to Dinah when we were back on the street. "That was a much quicker way to handle things. And if we asked the owner, he might object, but if they're just there, he probably won't notice." I laughed to myself. "Not that it really matters. How many people really go in there? I've heard of a soft opening, but that place is taking it to an extreme."

Dinah smiled. "Well, then Emily will have that much more time for the extra reading list."

"Now, it's on to what I really want to hear about. You almost saying yes." We had reached Le Grande Fromage and went into the airy café. The place smelled of buttery croissants and espresso. We joined the late-morning line at the counter.

"Well," Dinah said, letting out a sigh, "Commander insisted on coming over when I got home last night. He said he just wanted to see me." We did an *awww* together at the sweetness of his gesture before she continued. "He's the absolute opposite of all the other men in my life. They always had one foot out the door." She smiled. "Soon followed by the other foot."

The line moved up a little, and more people came in behind us. I instinctively turned to survey who had come in. Tony Bonnard was at the end of the line. He didn't see me, as he was too busy looking down at the screen on his phone.

Tony was one of those men who actually got better-looking as he got older. He had some character lines, but his chin was still strong-looking, and his blue eyes had a sparkle. The silvery white hair stood out more than his dark hair ever had. It was no wonder he'd been a star for so long on the soap opera.

Dinah was on a roll, and I didn't want to interrupt her and point out the new arrival. "He's so straightforward in how he feels. No games, no eyeing other women. He looked so hopeful when he came over and he asked if I'd decided."

She stopped talking abruptly and got a faraway look in her eyes. I was sure she was reliving the moment. There hadn't been a lot of real romance in Dinah's life. She deserved to savor it.

"Sorry," she said, realizing she'd drifted off. "I just couldn't say the words. It was too final." She looked down. "I hate to admit this, but I was glad when he left and everything felt normal."

For a moment I flashed back on Barry in my living room. It had felt anything but normal to wake up and find him leaning against me. I'd given him coffee, but I think we'd both wanted him to leave as quickly as possible.

It was our turn, and we ordered our food and took the last of the round tables. Tony had moved up in line, not realizing we were there, but now Dinah had seen him as well. "I'd sure like to talk to him," I said.

By that time, Tony had placed his order and turned, looking for a table. "I think I can make your wish come true." Dinah caught his eye and gestured toward the empty chair at our table.

"Thanks for the invitation. It looks like a full house," he said as he sat down and put his order number on the table.

Before I had a chance to say a word, he'd started to talk. "What was the fuss about last night? Rosa said the cops came to the door. Then CeeCee got a call about you being in the yard. We were out at a social event and CeeCee got all upset. She said the call reminded her of everything that had happened." Our food was delivered, and it took a moment to figure out what went where. Tony's arrived a minute later, but he ignored it as he continued. "The obvious question is what were you doing in the yard and how did you get in?"

"Probably the same way Delaney Tanner did." I took a drink of my coffee.

"You're not going to leave me hanging, right?" he said with a flirty grin. He was known for his charmingly crooked smile, which was the only feature on his face that wasn't perfect.

He pulled off a small piece of his croissant and slathered some jam on it before neatly taking a bite. There was something elegant in how he ate, but then again, he was an actor. He probably practiced eating for the camera. He'd ordered a cappuccino and managed to sip it without ending up with a foam moustache.

I began with the story about my yard and how it made me wonder about CeeCee's and finished by saying that the gate seemed to open pretty easily.

"It let us into the back area behind the garage," I said.

His smile faded. "Maybe it's lucky we weren't home when you were sneaking around back there. Who knows what could have happened? I have a gun, and I'm a really good shot. I learned a long time ago when westerns were popular. Having the skill made it easier to get cast, even if it was for Cowboy Number 4." His smile returned.

"I think we're all glad you weren't home then," I said. It was bad enough we'd had to dodge the neighbors, without bullets besides. "Then you didn't know about the gate?"

"No," he said quickly. "The only time I've gone in that back area was to fetch CeeCee's dogs. I don't know why they go back there."

"What about CeeCee? Would she know about the gate?" Dinah asked.

This time Tony laughed. "CeeCee lives in the house, but when it comes to taking care of things, she depends on Rosa. She had no idea the vent to the heater was so dangerous."

"But you're handling things now?" I asked.

He gave me another crooked smile. "I don't claim to be

all that handy, but I do know who to call," he said. "Though I will manage to put a lock on that back gate myself."

I thought about what he'd said before about the gun. "But you didn't notice anyone sneaking around in the yard back there last Thursday?"

"The truth is, you can't really see back there from the house, and I wasn't home anyway. Evan Willis had a shindig. I know he doesn't work for the studio anymore, but I was hoping to chat with him about maybe investing in my web series."

"Then of course Evan must have seen you," I said. The comment seemed to completely change Tony's demeanor.

"Are you trying to see if I have an alibi?" There was no smile this time, crooked or otherwise.

CHAPTER 17

BABS WAS HANGING AROUND THE TABLE IN THE yarn department when I got back to the bookstore. Dinah had gone off to Beasley to teach her class. Neither Dinah nor I was too happy with our conversation with Tony. Had he mentioned having a gun to discourage me from any further sleuthing? Babs seemed rather nervous, but her face lit up when she saw me approaching. She started talking before I reached the table.

"That was some excitement last night. I tried to find out what was going on, but the police officers kept telling us to go home. I saw you and your friend Dinah. It looked like you were in the thick of it. Was there another problem at CeeCee's house?" she asked.

Babs had a friendly face, like she had spent most of her life with a smile. I had seen her enough times now to realize that fashion was certainly not at the top of her priority list. Her brown hair was done in a short style, and it was obvious she didn't spend a lot of time with a blow-dryer. Her clothes were sensible and not jazzed up with scarves or jewelry, other than a pair of gold hoops on her ears. Makeup seemed to be limited to a dab of lipstick. She glanced toward the kids' department, where Adele was in the midst of doing one of her dramatic readings.

She seemed to have forgotten that she'd asked a question. "This is the only place my son will let me take the kids. He'd never let me do it if he knew that adults are banished from story time." She looked around the yarn department with a sigh. "I was hoping some of the group would be here." Babs clearly needed to be around people and to have some kind of purpose.

"I'm the only one here right now. I wish I could sit down and crochet, but I have to finish putting away the stock." The words were barely out of my mouth before Babs was next to me, offering to help. It seemed almost therapeutic for her, so I let her join me.

"It was all a misunderstanding with the cops," I said, referring to her question about the night before. I told her Dinah and I had found a back gate to CeeCee's. "One of the neighbors saw our flashlight and called the cops."

"It looked like they had you in handcuffs," she said, leaning in for more details.

"Only temporarily." I pushed some skeins of forest green yarn to the side of the cubby so I could fit in a batch of turquoise-colored yarn. "Did you know there was a gate on that part of CeeCee's yard?" I asked.

She shrugged and said she didn't. "I know more about the people in the area than their property." I stopped to think for a moment and suddenly came up with a win-win situation. She needed something to do, and I needed some information.

"I wonder if you could do a little detective work for me."

"I'd be glad to," she said before even knowing what it was. "Whatever it is, it's better than standing around watching my grandkids be hovered over by the nannies." She finished with another box and turned to me. "Does it have to do with the woman we found at CeeCee's house? I would be glad to do anything to help straighten that out. I heard the police believe she's somehow involved, and I'm sure it isn't true."

So the word on the street was that CeeCee had something to do with Delaney's death. I was afraid of that, but then without knowing about the back gate, I could see where people might think that. "I'd like to know who knew about that gate at CeeCee's," I said.

Babs was listening intently. "I can do that. I'll do it this afternoon and report back later."

Mrs. Shedd drifted into the department and gave Babs a puzzled look. "I know I made you assistant manager, but any new hires still need to go through me."

I stepped away and let Babs continue filling up a cubby with orbs of lavender yarn. "She's a volunteer helper," I said, and Mrs. Shedd relaxed—a little, anyway.

"Have you gotten the deposit for the extravagant baby shower?" my boss asked.

"No," I said, and Mrs. Shedd gave me a knowing look. Filling out paperwork didn't mean anything. Until we had a nonrefundable deposit, it was too easy for the client to change their mind. I promised to work on it later in the afternoon.

"You do remember we're having an author event later." She picked up on the momentary blank look on my face. "Molly, I know you said you could handle all this, but are you sure? I'm depending on you to make sure Yarn University is a success. It will certainly help support the yarn department. And the crochet parties are definitely bringing in extra revenue. But we need to take care of our core business of selling books."

"I'm on it," I said as the details came into my mind. "I'll do the setup later," I said. When I went back to the yarn department, Babs had unloaded the boxes and straightened up the other cubbies. Kids were beginning to come out of story time. Babs grabbed her things and started toward them, and I followed along on my way to the information booth.

"Until this afternoon," she said to me. "Aren't you supposed to say something like ten-four?" I guess I wasn't the only one who liked to play Nancy Drew.

THERE WERE POSTERS AROUND THE BOOKSTORE advertising the event—I'd just gotten immune to seeing them. I quickly refreshed myself on the details before beginning the setup. There were boxes of books to put out, along with an assortment of natural body products. I had just cut open the first box when Mrs. Shedd found me. She was carrying the blue zippered pouch, and it seemed to be bulging. "We took in a lot of cash this morning, and I don't like to keep it around. Would you take it to the bank now?" She said it like a request, but I knew it was a command. As she had said before, it went with my new title of assistant manager. I suppose I should have been happy that she trusted me with the cash, but it still made me nervous. There had to be a reason a lot of stores used a service with an armored car and men with guns to pick up the cash. I made some lame remark about wishing I had an armored car with a guard, and she shook her head.

"Just put the pouch in that tote bag full of yarn and nobody will even suspect you're carrying a large amount of cash." Her attention was already back on the main part of the store, checking to see that all the customers who needed help were getting it. She saw a lone person looking lost in the travel department and, with a cluck of her tongue that no one had helped him, left to offer her assistance.

I retrieved my tote and stuffed the pouch in it as I walked toward the front of the store. Adele was at the checkout counter. She handed our cashier a stack of children's books and thanked the customer for their business. It amazed me that nobody seemed bothered that Adele was still in her story time outfit. I'm not sure what book she'd read this time, but she had on a purple velvet cape and was holding a wand with a star on the end of it. She topped the outfit with a silver crocheted crown.

"Where are you going?" she asked as I walked by. I considered what to say. She was still not over the fact that I had been hired to be event coordinator when she thought she should have been given the position. I imagined she was even more upset now that I was assistant manager—she didn't realize that most of what came with the title was more work. But before I could think of another answer to give, Adele had already figured out I was off on some business for Mrs. Shedd. I could tell she was about to get pouty, so I told her the truth.

"She's sending you off alone with a bag of cash?" Adele seemed genuinely concerned, though I wasn't quite sure if she was questioning Mrs. Shedd's trust in me or actually worried that I might get mugged. Adele was a handful, but at the same time she had decided I was her best friend in the world—she called us French toast sisters because I had invited her for brunch once.

"Pink, you better let me come with you. Eric showed me some self-defense moves." To demonstrate, she jumped back and assumed a stance with both of her arms out in front of her, hands balled into fists. For once, I was actually glad that she wanted to get into the middle of what I was doing.

"Okay," I said. The word was barely out of my mouth when she had her bag and had already told Mrs. Shedd that I needed some backup to help deliver the cash. I think Mrs. Shedd had long since decided just to go along with whatever Adele said, especially because the kids' department was flourishing under her direction. All her drama and costumes were a hit with the kids, and they got their parents to buy a lot of books.

The sky was gray as we walked outside, and there was a cold, wet feeling to the air. A true winter's day in Southern California. Adele pulled the purple cape around herself for warmth and stuck close to me as we walked down the street and around the corner to the parking lot. Her head was constantly moving as she surveyed the area for any danger, making the silver crown wobble.

She rode shotgun and jumped out of the greenmobile as soon as I'd parked in the Bank of Tarzana parking lot. There were lots of people coming and going to the bank, and Adele seemed to be viewing each of them as a threat. I can only imagine how they viewed her.

Evan Willis came out of the bank, dressed in track pants and a blue jacket, with his gym bag slung on his shoulder. He stopped to talk to a similarly dressed man who was just heading into the bank. I only got a glimpse of the other man's bland good looks. Was it Pia's husband? As Evan Willis started down the steps, I caught his eye. I nodded my head in the start of a greeting, which I intended to follow with a verbal hello, but he abruptly looked away. I was sure he'd seen me. Then I realized that it was a reproach for the previous night. He'd probably mentally branded me as a trouble-maker. What if his wife felt the same?

I thought of Mrs. Shedd's question about the deposit for the shower. As soon as I got back I was going to contact Kelsey and do damage control.

Adele was taking her role as bodyguard very seriously and stuck to me like her purple cape was made of Velcro as we threaded through the people coming and going and went inside.

The greeter practically curtseyed when we came in and barely did a double take at Adele's outfit. Then I realized why—the local kids' dentist, who called himself Dr. Supertooth and wore a Superman-like costume, was already in the line. This time I knew to go to the special line and steered my caped and crowned associate toward it.

When it was my turn I stepped up to the window and slipped the pouch under the divider. I heard Adele let out a satisfied sigh. "Eric would be so proud of how I got you here safely."

"What?" the teller said.

"It's nothing. We're just relieved to have gotten here without a problem to drop off the cash," I said. By then she had opened the pouch and was separating the bundle of cash from the checks.

"I don't know if this will make you feel better, but we have people coming in with lots more cash than this, and they just walk in by themselves," the teller said. "I just handled one of those transactions. I think the deposit was for nine thousand dollars."

Adele was still sticking close, even though I'd turned over the money. "What kind of business did he have?" she asked the teller.

The teller didn't seem happy with the question. "I know we're supposed to be friendly, but I think it's more important to be discreet. I don't think you'd like me telling someone else how small the deposit from the bookstore was."

As she took the bills and put them in a counting machine, she continued talking. "I'm new to handling the business accounts, but that's just what I think."

It didn't register at first, but her comment made me think about something. "Did Delaney Tanner used to handle the business accounts?" The teller seemed surprised and a little uncomfortable with my question.

"Yes, this was her regular spot. I want you to know that I'm nothing like her. The way she went on about some actor who came in . . . She said he used to be in a soap opera."

"He was in the business line?" I asked.

The woman caught herself. "I shouldn't say anything. I thought Delaney was wrong for talking about the customers. Actually, the bank wants us to call them clients."

"Did she say anything else about him?" I asked, suddenly very interested.

"I guess there's no harm in me telling you since it really didn't have to do with the bank. She said he was going to let her be an extra in some series he's doing. Did you know her?" She took the stack of bills out and put in some more to be counted. "No one will tell us what really happened to her. I'm sure it was an accident or suicide." She looked at me with a furrowed brow. "It couldn't have had anything to do with the bank, right?"

I felt bad for the woman and could understand her concern since she'd taken over Delaney's position. "I actually was the one who found her," I said. The woman's eyes widened so much I thought her eyeballs were going to pop out. "I'm trying to figure out what happened."

"You're the one," the teller said. "I've heard about you! You're like the Sherlock Holmes of Tarzana."

"Not exactly," I said, blushing. "It's just that I seem to be somehow connected to people who have died around here."

Our transaction was done, but the teller kept talking. She offered us bottles of water and lollipops from the jar on her counter, but eventually several people had gotten into the merchant line and the teller realized she had to let us go. As we walked away, she said something I didn't quite hear. Did she say Molly or Manny?

Adele and I retraced our steps and were back in the bookstore in no time. I knew it was going to turn into a big deal, but I thanked Adele for accompanying me. She surprised me by throwing her arms around me, which caused her silver crown to tilt, and said, "That's what French toast sisters do for each other."

CHAPTER 18

WAS THERE ANY DOUBT THAT DELANEY HAD BEEN talking about Tony Bonnard? Not that I had time to think about it. As soon as I got back to the bookstore, I was on the phone with Kelsey Willis doing damage control.

It was a touchy business. My goal was to not lose the shower business and get her deposit, but without making it seem like I thought she might be backing out. I got her on her cell phone, and she sounded like she was in a restaurant. The whole point was to try to get her to come into the bookstore as soon as possible.

It took a minute for her to understand who I was—finally, I had to say it was Polly.

"Oh, it's you," she said. "I was going to call you." I had the sinking feeling that I knew what was going to come next. She was going to cancel.

What I did was rude, but under the circumstances, necessary. I cut her off and started to talk. "I know we talked on the phone before about your daughter's choices for the shower, but I'd really like to show you what we offer." I hesitated about adding, *And then you can drop off the deposit.*

"You showed everything to Erin, right?" she said.

"I did, but I figured since you were paying for it, you should really see what you're getting." That apparently struck a nerve.

"Of course, you're right. I should really see what she gave the go-ahead for."

We agreed on a time that afternoon, and I tried to casually bring up that she might want to drop off the deposit at the same time. She didn't respond.

I WENT BACK TO SETTING UP IN THE EVENT AREA. There were already signs around the bookstore and in the window announcing "An Evening with Esmaya." Her event was to promote her book, *The Average Joe's Guide to Meditation*, and a line of natural skin care products she was connected to. I knew from the copyright that her real name was Lynn Adler. I hadn't met her yet. Mrs. Shedd had set it up because she had been convinced that Esmaya would draw a crowd to the bookstore.

The way the sky was clouding up and the air smelled like rain, I wasn't so sure about the turnout. I set out a bunch of chairs and put together a display at the front with a table for her books and another table for all the body products. I'd smelled them, and they all had a nice, unisex citrus scent.

I was just finishing up when Mrs. Shedd pointed two blond women in my direction. I should have figured that Kelsey wouldn't come alone. But then, Pia was the one who suggested she have the shower at the bookstore to start with.

I stopped what I was doing and led them over to the yarn

department and started to explain that was where we held all the crochet events.

Kelsey didn't say anything. She just watched as I brought out the party bag samples and a finished baby blanket, explaining how everyone made a small square. There was definitely something on her mind. And I was afraid I knew what it was.

"I'm sorry about last night," I said. Kelsey looked up from the selection of party bags.

"There was certainly a lot of commotion—the helicopter, the cops, the crowd in front of our house." She seemed like she felt put-upon by the whole thing. "Evan said he saw two people creeping around in the bushes. And after what happened at CeeCee's, he thought we were next." I heard Pia let out a gasp at the thought before Kelsey continued. "He didn't realize it was you and your friend when he called the cops."

"Oh," I said, thinking an apology was going to come next. I should have known better. People like Kelsey didn't apologize.

"Then we heard you were some kind of amateur detective. So, you were investigating?" she said with a condescending laugh. She leaned a little closer, like she was going to say something important. "If I were you, I'd give up the gumshoe work and concentrate on Erin's shower. I'm sure you understand that our having her shower here could open the door to a lot of business for you."

I wasn't sure if that was some kind of veiled threat or if she was just acting like she always used to in the PTA—holding on to the upper hand by bossing me around. Whatever it was, I instantly gave up my plan to ask her about their party guests the night of Delaney's death. "So which of the party bags do you like?" I asked with a pleasant smile, as if I didn't mind being reprimanded by her.

Kelsey looked up at Pia with a satisfied smile, thinking she'd gotten her way. "I know which one I like, but which one would you choose?" she asked Pia. Pia pointed out the one I considered top-of-the-line, and Kelsey nodded in agreement before saying, "Great minds think alike. That's the one we'll go with." We went over the rest of the details, and except for some minor changes, she agreed with her daughter's choices.

"Okay, then that's settled." Kelsey stood up.

"We just need the deposit," I said, trying to keep it sounding casual. I was relieved when she agreed. "We can handle it up front." I waited until they both had gathered their things and we headed out of the yarn department. We were waylaid when Kelsey paused to check out my Esmaya display. She picked up a tube of body lotion, and I was about to explain the upcoming event to her when my breath stopped.

Babs had just walked in the front door, and she was looking around the store. I knew what she was looking for—me. She'd said she would come back with the information I'd requested.

I couldn't let her meet up with Kelsey and Pia. Not after Kelsey's suggestion that I stay out of sleuthing. I could just imagine what Babs would say about how she was helping me with my detective work. She might even take it further and start asking Kelsey questions.

Babs saw me and waved frantically as she started to walk toward us.

What was I going to do? Just when it seemed hopeless, I heard Pia say, "I can't stand that woman. I don't want to hear any more of her neighborly nonsense." Pia looked around frantically. "Let's use that side door."

Kelsey nodded in agreement and shoved a bunch of bills

in my hand. "Take out whatever the lotion costs and use the rest as the deposit," she said, fairly running for the door. The side door they'd spotted was actually an emergency exit, and an alarm went off as the door opened, but it was a small price to pay.

Babs caught up with me as I was trying to reset the door. "I got your information," she said in an excited voice. "It turns out everyone knew about the gate. Even with those bushes around her place, balls from the neighboring houses ended up in the yard."

"That was fast work," I said, grateful Kelsey and Pia weren't there to hear it.

"It was easy. I asked someone who was familiar with the whole area." It must have shown in my face that I was a little disappointed, because Babs asked me what was wrong.

"I'm still trying to figure out how Delaney ended up in the guest quarters. I thought if only a few people or, best of all, only one person knew about that gate, it would narrow it down. But if everybody but CeeCee was aware of the gate, it isn't much help." As we moved away from the emergency exit, Babs looked back at the door.

"I don't understand why they left that way. I thought for sure they saw me." Babs seemed genuinely perplexed.

IT WAS DARK OUTSIDE WHEN I WENT TO THE EVENT area, ready to act as host. The cloudy skies had given way to a light rain, and the big window facing Ventura Boulevard had gotten fogged up from the warmth inside. Mrs. Shedd had left for the day, and there were a couple of part-time clerks there to help with sales.

By now other people had started to come in. I figured a

lot of them were Esmaya's friends, as they all seemed to have an ethereal thing going.

Esmaya arrived at last. Decked out in a long, pale blue dress with a floaty purple layer over it, she definitely looked the part. She had lots of bracelets, a silk scarf wound around her neck and hoop earrings that had feathers hanging off the bottom. When I looked closer, I realized they were actually tiny dream catchers. Usually the authors stood off behind a bookcase somewhere until I did their grand introduction, but Esmaya stayed right in the front, surveying the people as they came in. I hadn't tried to get the Hookers to come, so I was relieved to see the chairs beginning to fill, and not totally surprised when I saw Babs had come back to the bookstore and had taken a seat in the back. It only took a moment before she came up to me and offered her help.

"I think I have everything under control, but thank you," I said. She went back to her seat, and Adele came out of the kids' area and stood to the side of the chairs. Adele had been fussing that Esmaya's book had made no mention of crochet as an aid to meditation. I could just picture Adele jumping up and raising her hand when Esmaya took questions.

Most of the seats were full, and I stepped to the front to begin the introduction. I'd barely gotten out the welcome to the crowd when I was interrupted.

"Excuse me," Kelsey Willis said, coming right up to the front. I was surprised to see her back at the bookstore so soon. Pia Sawyer was in tow, and they were dressed in similar Burberry rain gear. "I have to return this lotion." Kelsey held it out accusingly toward me. "It has lanolin in it."

Esmaya stepped right in. She took the tube of cream back and handed her another one. "You want the vegan version, then." She turned to the crowd and explained that lanolin came from sheep.

Kelsey seemed surprised that the exchange had gone so easily, but Pia's interest had apparently been piqued. She walked over to the display table of books and picked one up. "Meditation, huh?" she said. "It's the hot thing right now." I had to keep myself from adding that though it seemed to be trendy at the moment, it had actually been around forever. Pia held up her hand, admiring her mint green nails next to the green cover of the book. "It kind of goes with our mani-pedis," the taller blond said to Kelsey. "It's sort of a spa thing. Maybe we should stay."

"I don't think so," Kelsey said, gesturing with her arm toward the crowd. Babs was waving wildly and pointing to the two seats next to her.

The way things turned out, I was glad they had left.

I returned to the front of the crowd and finished my introduction. Esmaya began her program. "The first thing we do is purify the space." She had a big wad of something pungent-smelling in her hand.

"Is that marijuana?" Adele called out.

I got the feeling Esmaya had been asked that before. "No, it's sage and perfectly legal."

She held it up and lit it with a lighter, and it began to smoke. She waved her free hand and urged everyone out of their seats and had them form a line behind her. Then, she led the line around the perimeter of the bookstore, waving the smoking wad of dried plants.

"Pink, you better stop her," Adele said, catching up with me. "I'm telling you—" The rest of what she said was drowned out by a loud wail as lights around the bookstore began to flash off and on.

"I tried to tell you," Adele said. "Mr. Royal installed a new super-sensitive smoke detector system, and it automatically calls the fire department."

"Oh no," I said, grabbing my phone to call and try to stop the fire department. But apparently, once the call went in, nothing could stop it. The fire department was only a few blocks away, and within seconds I heard the whine of their sirens. Meanwhile, the lights kept flashing and the alarm continued to go off.

To make it worse, I saw that the way the windows were steamed up, it could appear the place was filled with smoke. All the engines pulled right in front of the bookstore, and the firefighters came in wearing their full gear, holding axes and a hose. Esmaya waved the smoking sage toward them, I guess in an effort to purify them, but of course all they saw was something burning. One of the firefighters grabbed it, threw it on the ground, and let loose with a fire extinguisher while another went to turn off the alarm.

"I'm so sorry," I said to the captain. This wasn't the first time one of our author events had led to their arrival. Babs had pushed to the front of the crowd.

"I'm from Iowa City, and we know how to treat our brave firefighters." She turned to me. "We need to do something special for them."

I did feel terrible for dragging them out on a false alarm, so we got our barista, Bob, to make them all special drinks and offer them his creation of the day, coincidentally called Hunka Hunka Burning Love Cookie Bars.

After the firefighters left, things went a lot smoother, although Adele did make a fuss, saying Esmaya should have something in her book about crochet being an aid to meditation. The author played some soothing music and was able to get everybody to join in a group meditation. She did a whole spiel on the creams after that and sold quite a few tubes despite one of the audience members bringing up that even all-natural ingredients could be a problem for some people.

Babs came up to me at the end, and I thought she was going to congratulate me on how well the event went, even in the face of the fire alarm incident. Instead, she said, "I can't believe Kelsey and Pia didn't see me again. I'd almost think they were trying to avoid me."

CHAPTER 19

"I SHOULD HAVE BEEN THERE," DINAH SAID WHEN I finished telling her about the meditation event the night before.

"I was surprised that Sheila didn't show up. She always comes when there's something about being calm," I said. "I'm afraid she's avoiding things." We were sitting at the table in the yarn department of the bookstore. It was late afternoon, and it was nice to see that the days were getting longer. "The real test is if she shows up for this meeting."

We called meetings at this time our Happy Hour. Some people had drinks and snacks to relax; we crocheted. Dinah already had a ball of bulky tan yarn on the table, and she showed me the beginnings of a scarf. "It's for Commander," she said.

"Then you have decided to say yes." I touched the yarn, and it was amazingly soft. When she didn't answer, I turned to her. "If you're making him a scarf, you have to expect that he'll be around when you finish it."

Dinah was usually very upbeat, but she put her head down. "I didn't think about that. Oh dear . . ." She let out a long sigh. "Can we talk about something else? Any news about how Delaney ended up at CeeCee's?"

I had forgotten to bring a project to work on. Luckily, I had the one I always carried in my purse. I was using purple worsted-weight wool yarn, and for now I was just making a long strip. Eventually I was going to sew the ends together and make it into an infinity scarf. My hook started moving as I began talking. With everything going on, this was the first chance I'd had to evaluate the pieces of news that had come in recently. "Let me see," I said, mentally going back to the last time Dinah and I had talked. "Did I tell you they still aren't sure whether her death was an accident, suicide or murder?"

"No," Dinah said, surprised. "Who told you?" I realized I hadn't gotten to tell her about Barry's last visit. I quickly recounted how he'd come by to collect on his favor for getting us out of the clutches of his fellow officers. I even told her the part about him falling asleep.

"I don't suppose you mentioned that to Mason," she said, and I shook my head. "Is that all Barry told you?"

"He did begrudgingly tell me that I was right—the cause of death was carbon monoxide poisoning." As I was talking, other tidbits from the past couple of days popped into my mind. "There's more. How could it all have slipped past me? It's about Tony—Rosa said something that makes me think he's taking advantage of CeeCee's good heart." I glanced around to see if there was anyone listening. "And there's even more. Remember how Tony said he didn't know Delaney? Well, the teller at the bank told me that Delaney was very friendly with an actor who had been in a soap and that he'd said she could be an extra in a show he was doing."

Dinah stopped in mid-stitch. "Wow. It had to have been Tony she was talking to."

I had a sinking feeling as I thought of something else. "Remember Rosa said that he didn't want her to take care of cleaning up the guest quarters before we found the body, or when the cops released it."

"When you put that together with the new information, it doesn't sound good for him," Dinah said.

"But it's mostly based on what other people have said. Maybe there are other explanations. And the teller said Delaney was too friendly with the customers. She had access to a lot of information. Maybe someone realized she knew too much?" I stopped to think for a moment. "Mr. Royal must have dealt with her when he brought in the bookstore's deposits before I got the job. Plus, he must have known her since she worked at the bookstore for a while." I took a deep breath and went back to crocheting. "Now that we know she could have come in that back gate, it opens up the possibilities. Babs told me everyone around there knew about the gate. Something about the local kids retrieving balls that had landed in CeeCee's yard."

"Did you ask Babs if her son and daughter-in-law are customers of the Bank of Tarzana?"

"You don't think that they could be involved," I said, trying to remember what I knew about them.

"Didn't Babs say her son has his own financial management business?" Dinah said. A long strand of variegated yarn had gotten stuck to the purple yarn I was crocheting with. I went to pull it and stared at the way the colors changed before I dropped it into my bag. When I looked up, I saw that Babs and Adele were walking toward us, and I gestured like

I was zipping my lips as I looked at Dinah. She laughed and nodded in silent agreement.

As soon as they got to the table, Adele opened a crochet magazine and showed Babs things she intended to make for her wedding. "I'm working on my bouquet now." Adele fished around in her bag and brought out something wrapped in tissue paper. It was some crocheted pink roses. Babs was fascinated.

"I thought you might bring CeeCee," I said as Babs chose a seat near Adele.

"The poor dear can't get out of her place. The newspeople are set up in front again and go chasing after anybody who comes out of the house. I suggested she go out through that back gate you found, but she said the police have it roped off now and are looking around. The only good news is that the police are done with the guest quarters and Tony has arranged for that dangerous old vent to be taken care of tomorrow."

"That's terrible," I said. "What about Tony? Is he stuck there, too?"

"CeeCee said he had to go out. Something about getting things together for the web show. I suppose he isn't as nice as CeeCee and probably just stepped on the gas hard and got through the reporters and paparazzi."

Eduardo came in just as Babs was finishing. They hadn't been introduced yet, so I did the honors. I saw her mouth fall open. "Wait until my girlfriend finds out I met you," she said. He smiled good-naturedly as she gushed, naming the titles of some of the many romance novels of which he'd graced the covers. She knew every product he'd been a spokesperson for, too.

"These days he runs the Crown Apothecary," Adele said, explaining that it was basically a super-fancy drugstore. I think Eduardo liked the fuss Babs made over him. She really cranked it up when he took out his crochet work. I had to laugh when she gave up her seat next to Adele and moved into one next to Eduardo. A moment later, she was snapping a selfie of them. "I'm sending it to everyone."

He let out a sigh of relief as he began working with the fine white thread. "Some people have a cocktail; I make a doily," he said with a wink. His Irish grandmother had taught him how to crochet when he was a boy, and by now, I imagined he could do it with his eyes closed.

I couldn't even see the tiny ring of stitches that started off his work, but by the time Rhoda had arrived, there were already multiple lacy rows around it.

"Hi all," Rhoda said in her New York accent. She seemed like the kind of person who had both feet firmly planted on the ground and could come through anything unfazed, so I was surprised when she appeared a little done in as she set her large tote on the table and took the chair next to Eduardo.

She looked around the table. "Where's CeeCee?" Babs gave her the same story she'd given us, and Rhoda sighed when she heard that Tony had gone out and left her. "I suppose the show must go on." She took out a blanket she was working on but also the felted pieces she'd had at the preview the other night. Seeing how the crochet stitches had disappeared into a solid fabric still amazed me.

"I thought I'd show my class a bunch of samples, even though they're all going to be making a pouch purse," Rhoda said. Babs admired the array of pieces and went to pick up a purse done in multicolors. Rhoda's hand intervened. "If you're sensitive to wool, don't touch it. We don't want a replay of the other night."

"Oh, nothing bothers me," Babs said.

I looked toward the door. "I hope Sheila comes. I was

thinking maybe we could get her to do an impromptu rehearsal of her class in front of us." I picked up one of Rhoda's samples. "I'm glad to see that there are no problems with your class."

"Actually, there is one little problem," Rhoda said. "It's best to use a washing machine to felt things, and I was hoping to take the class to that Laundromat on Victory Boulevard and have everybody felt at once, but the place is never open. I think we're going to have to do it with pails of hot water here."

"A Laundromat that's never open? Sounds like the only thing they're laundering is money," Eduardo said.

"Really?" Rhoda said. "So that's why you think it's never open?"

"Nah, it was just my lame attempt at making a joke."

Elise had come in at the end of the conversation. "Laundering money? Do you mean actually washing it?" she said in her chirpy voice. She appeared frazzled as she put down her tote bag and grabbed a chair.

"No, there's no actual washing of the money," Eduardo said. "It's just a front. Nobody knows if the money really comes from people washing their clothes, or something else. But you could launder money through any kind of retail business." He glanced around the interior of the store. "Even a place like this, or for that matter, the Crown Apothecary."

It was just like that show Mason had been watching. Now I understood. There was something about deposits under ten thousand dollars being taken without question.

"Is CeeCee coming?" Elise asked as she took out a lap robe she was making to donate to a retirement home. We had talked her into doing it in more colorful yarn than her usual vampire style of black, white and red, but she'd insisted on doing it in half double crochet, or as she called it, fangs.

Babs continued as spokesperson and repeated her story. Elise seemed confused. "Is she staying there because she wants to or is it that the cops won't let her leave?"

I was thinking that through when Sheila finally showed up. She tried to slip in quietly and take a seat, so I was glad when Rhoda stepped in and suggested the impromptu class. "Just get up in front of us and start talking."

"I wish it was that easy," Sheila said. "But every time I start thinking about doing a run-through, all I can think about is finding that woman at CeeCee's."

I could certainly sympathize. As Sheila was talking, I was reliving the moment when I'd seen the figure sprawled on the floor. The rust-colored hair and the colorful vest. The vest that had looked somehow familiar. It was driving me crazy that I couldn't figure out the connection.

"I don't know how to get past it," Sheila said, turning to me. Her eyes got round. "What's wrong, Molly? You look like you saw a ghost."

"I did, sort of." I explained seeing the image of Delaney as Sheila was talking. "There was something I noticed and then forgot about." They all continued working on their projects, looking at me as I reached into my bag and pulled out the length of variegated yarn I had found stuck to my work and held it up. "Something about the vest Delaney was wearing seemed familiar, but I didn't know why until now. It was made out of this yarn."

"Okay," Adele said warily. "What's your point?" She actually stopped crocheting the pink rose she was working on as she waited for my answer.

"You don't remember this yarn, do you?" I looked over at the group. Babs seemed to be having trouble with the practice swatch she was working on and had turned to Adele. Eduardo's fingers kept moving as he gave me a shrug. Rhoda looked up from putting the felted pieces back in her bag and held up her hands to indicate she didn't recognize it. Elise just shook her head. Dinah was the only one who actually said no out loud. "Do you remember the yarn exchange we had a while ago?" I asked. Everyone but Babs nodded, though she looked like she wanted to nod to be part of the group.

"Do you remember the yarn I put in?" I got a lot of blank faces, but then Dinah asked to examine the strand I was holding.

"Now I remember it. You loved all the colors but not the kinks in it." Dinah took the other end of the yarn and pointed out how the yarn was twisted and had bumps. "You said you'd had a hard time crocheting with it and you thought it might work better for knitting."

Adele got her storm cloud face. "Nonsense, you can crochet with any yarn. It's the crocheter, not the yarn."

"So, then you were the one who took it?" I asked. Adele shook her head.

"No. I was just making a comment."

"The point is," I said rather sharply to Adele in reference to her earlier question, "Delaney was wearing a vest made out of that yarn."

"Don't you mean the same kind of yarn?" Rhoda said.

"No, it had to be that yarn. I bought it at a yarn show. It had been hand spun from the woman's sheep and then hand painted. I bought the whole stock of it. There is no same kind of yarn." I looked over the group. "How did Delaney end up with a vest made out of my yarn?"

"I get it, Pink, you want to know who took the yarn in the exchange." Rhoda looked around at the group. "C'mon people, fess up!" Everybody shook their heads. "Well, there you go. It wasn't any of us." Stumped, we all returned to our projects, and I racked my brain to think of a possible explanation.

"Oh look, it's raining," Rhoda said, gesturing at the window. Usually it was either dry or we got a deluge, but this time it had kept to a soft rain. "Glad I'm prepared." Rhoda pulled on her rain jacket and dropped her project into her tote bag. "Got to go home and cook," she said. There were some jokes about wanting to go to her house for dinner. She rolled her eyes. "Join the crowd," she said with a tired smile.

"Oh!" Dinah said in surprise when she looked toward the front of the bookstore. Commander Blaine was standing in front of the window, dressed for a flood and holding Dinah's raincoat and an extra umbrella. It was impossible not to see the love in his eyes when he looked at her. I think she was aware of it, too, because she swallowed hard and then looked away, clearly uncomfortable. My poor friend was having such a hard time accepting a good thing. I still thought that if Commander didn't get impatient and insist on an answer, there was a good chance she would say yes.

Finally, it was just me and Adele looking out the window as the traffic crawled along Ventura Boulevard. It didn't rain that much here, but everyone freaked out when it did. Even though it was just twilight, the streetlights came on and reflected in the wet pavement.

"There's Eric," Adele said as a police motorcycle went by and slowed. She seemed a little befuddled. "Pink, you're my best friend and you're going to be the maid of honor at my wedding. I need to tell you something. You know how I keep saying that Eric and I haven't set a date yet because we're not sure what kind of wedding we want? It's not exactly the truth. Every time I try to talk to Eric about picking a date, he somehow changes the subject."

I didn't know what else to do, so I hugged her and assured her that everything would be okay. Like I really knew? In any case, it seemed to make her feel better, and she rushed to the front of the store to greet Eric as he came inside.

I started to clear off the table. The strand of yarn was still sitting there. They had all denied taking it at the yarn exchange. But nobody had mentioned the obvious. If it wasn't any of them, it had to be the one person who wasn't there—CeeCee.

CHAPTER 20

Unlike Rhoda, I wasn't prepared for rain. I never even thought to leave an umbrella at the bookstore for days like this. I made a run for it to my car and was nicely damp by the time I shut the door.

I would certainly be glad when Samuel came home. It was hard not having help to look after the herd of animals. I had to dart home during my workday and then stop home after work before any other plans.

The crew was waiting by the door when I got home. Well, everyone but Blondie, who was doing her Greta Garbo routine as usual. I had to rouse her out of her spot and get her across the house. The dogs didn't seem to care about the rain, and it was too dark for the cats to go out anyway. I fed them all and gave them some attention before heading out again. This time with a raincoat.

I looked forward to the day when Mason was operating

at full tilt and we could once again go out and do things, but for now the only option was to go to his place.

The rambling ranch-style house was built of dark brown wood and seemed almost to melt into the night, making the lights coming from the windows appear like they were floating. The light reflected in the small puddles on the walkway as I made my way to the front door.

I was brimming with news to tell Mason. I couldn't wait to hear what he thought about everything. I already had the key out, and I was definitely going to use it this time. After all, he had given it to me to use. Who cared what Jaimee or Brooklyn would say or think if they realized I had it?

I put the key in the lock and opened the door. I waited for disaster to strike or for Brooklyn to appear and ask what I was doing there, but when nothing happened, I went inside. I still felt I should announce my arrival and called out down the hall. Mason came scooting toward the door with Spike running alongside.

"Sunshine, you're here. And you're all wet," he said, his face breaking into a big smile. Spike checked over my shoes, as usual, since I carried the scent of all my animals. I deposited my coat on the coat tree near the entrance before leaning in to hug Mason. "Thank you again for last night," I said. He let out a disappointed sigh.

"I'd be much happier if you were thanking me for another reason," he said with a naughty grin. "But I'm glad I could at least show up, even if Barry really did the actual rescue."

"But I knew you had my back," I said. "I have so much to tell you." I started to lead the way to the den. Mason seemed to be trying to tell me something, but I was so wound up, I had already started to spill my story as we walked. Well, I walked; he scooted.

"The cops were back at CeeCee's," I said, "looking around that back area. I wonder if they looked at all before. CeeCee didn't show up at the group today. Supposedly with the cops and the newspeople, she couldn't get out of her house." I stopped to shake my head in dismay. "I told you about the dead woman's vest looking familiar." I started to explain the whole yarn exchange but finally just cut to the chase. "I think CeeCee might have made that vest." Mason was listening, enjoying every second of the drama. "And I heard that Tony was keeping everybody away from the guest quarters both before we found Delaney and after the cops released it. It turns out he was in a big hurry to change the vent, too. Probably so it won't happen again." I stopped and realized I was spitting out facts out of order. "Sorry, I didn't mention that the cause of death was carbon monoxide poisoning because the vent was stuffed up with twigs."

"And you found that all out from?" he asked, his expression fading into concern.

"Assorted people," I began. "Some of it came from CeeCee's housekeeper, Rosa, some from Babs, the neighborly woman from Iowa City, and the carbon monoxide thing Barry told me," I said, not mentioning when or where I'd found out that last tidbit of information.

"Are you sure he isn't trying to win you back by giving you information about the woman's death?"

"No, absolutely not. It's more like he's using the fact that he knows me to pump me for information."

It was slow going to the den. Every time one of us said something, we stopped to talk. I started moving again, but Mason grabbed my arm.

"There's something I have to tell you." He dropped his voice to a whisper and then pointed to the big room ahead. "We'll have a nice evening together, because Jaimee and

Brooklyn are off shopping somewhere." There was something in his voice that made me sense a big *but* coming. And then there it was: "But first I have to take care of something." He leaned into me and squeezed my shoulder. "It's really some*one* I have to take care of."

"Okay," I said, curious as to who the someone was. I suppose I was afraid it was a woman, so I was surprised when I saw the man sitting on the soft leather couch.

The TV was on, but the frame was frozen, as if something had interrupted Mason while he was watching it. It was the same show he'd been watching the last time.

The man turned in our direction as we came in the room. "Molly, this is Todd," Mason said, indicating the man. He looked sort of familiar, but I was at a loss to place him. Mason picked up on my confusion and leaned close to me. "Jaimee's ex," he whispered. "But I'm trying to remedy it." I gave the man a second look. He was younger than Jaimee by a good fifteen years. I couldn't imagine being with someone that much younger. I guessed he was tall, though it was hard to tell since he was sitting down. He had the symmetrical good looks of a model, and his ivory polo shirt brought out his tan. It tickled me that he had the collar turned up. I guess it was supposed to look like it just ended up that way, but it was so clearly arranged.

I noticed that Mason didn't give Todd any explanation as to who I was other than to sit down, pull me down next to him, and put his arm around me. "Todd came looking for Jaimee. Since she's not here, Todd and I have been talking about their breakup." He turned to Todd. "Now, you were telling me that Jaimee just announced she was breaking up with you with no warning," Mason said.

Todd nodded with a look of consternation. "She didn't say anything about why. I came over and the locks had been changed, and when I rang the bell, she said we were done. She wouldn't even let me get my stuff."

"You mean the stuff I bought for you," said a female voice, startling all of us. Jaimee sashayed in, dropping a handful of shopping bags with high-end store names on the floor before she continued. "Do you have any idea how expensive those handmade tennis rackets were? And how many people are given tennis balls made with their name on them? Though I don't know why you kept everything in those dull bags."

"Some of the stuff was mine. Did you go through all of them?" Todd asked, definitely perturbed.

Oh man, did I want to get out of there. I didn't want to hear about their problems, and I certainly didn't want to be in the middle of this. I edged down the sofa, but Mason held on to me. I got it. He wanted me there for moral support.

"Hardly," Jaimee said. "I have better things to do with my time. I just unzipped a couple and saw the balls and rackets. Technically, I guess the bags are yours. They're not at the house anymore. Everything is in a storage unit. If it means so much to you, when I get everything out of storage, I'll go through everything and ship back what is yours."

"I don't really care about the things. What I care about is that you won't give me another chance."

"Then you're admitting I was right! There is someone else, and that's why you were always so busy and didn't want me to stay at your place."

Mason stepped in and spoke to his ex-wife. "Can't you see that Todd really wants another chance?"

"I do," Todd said. "We could start all over again." He got up and stepped close to Jaimee. "Remember how I used to give you lessons? I'd stand behind you and we'd practice your swing. We could start again tomorrow. The court up there is functional, right?"

I thought Jaimee was going to go for it. Todd moved his hand, and for some reason I thought he was going to scratch his arm, but instead he began to run his fingers along her arm in a seductive way. He leaned in so close to her that his breath must have been tickling her ear.

"No," she said, stepping away. "It's time for you to go." She ushered him to the door.

Mason looked at me and shook his head, unhappy that his plan hadn't worked. Jaimee returned a moment later.

"If that guy wants you back so bad," Mason said, "why not give him another chance?"

"It'll take more than the offer of another tennis lesson. How about admitting what he did and apologizing, and then pleading for me to forgive him? Then I'd consider getting back with him."

"Why didn't you tell him that was what you wanted?" Mason said.

"He should be able to figure it out himself." Jaimee sounded angry.

"What's going on?" Brooklyn asked, coming into the room. "I saw Todd going out the door. What was he doing here?" She didn't admit to it, but I guessed she'd been standing around the corner, eavesdropping.

"He wants your mother to give him another chance. And I was trying to help them work it out."

Brooklyn threw me a hostile stare, and I got the message—she didn't want to talk in front of me. I excused myself and went into the kitchen, supposedly to get a drink. Of course, I could hear everything that was going on.

"Why are you trying to get them back together? I'm glad

they're broken up." Jaimee tried to say something, but Brooklyn continued. "What's wrong with you, Dad? You used to keep your women out of our lives. That's it, isn't it? You want to get rid of Mother and me so you can scoot off into the sunset with that woman."

Whew. So I was *that woman* now, when she knew my name perfectly well. I waited to see who would speak next, and Jaimee jumped into the fray. "Mason, having her around is too taxing in your condition. If you want, I'll tell her you need to get some rest."

I had edged closer to the door to better hear his answer, but instead of responding, Mason rolled into the kitchen on the scooter. "You heard, didn't you?"

I mumbled something noncommittal.

"I am so sorry," he said. "Now maybe you understand why I kept you and my family separate. I'll get Jaimee back together with that boyfriend of hers, and then she'll be gone. Then, once I'm driving again, it will be time for Brooklyn to leave."

I saw his shoulders drop. "And face whatever she is running away from." Our eyes met, and he gave my cheek an affectionate brush. "I wasn't born yesterday. The way she showed up insisting on taking care of me, when that isn't her nature—something's up." He put his arms around me, and I stuck my foot in front of the wheels of the scooter so it wouldn't start to roll. "All I can say is how sorry I am for you to be caught in the middle of this."

I both loved and hated that Mason was so responsible for his family. I was just settling into the hug when Jaimee came in, waving a take-out menu.

"Brooklyn and I are ordering some food. Do you want something?" There wasn't the slightest doubt that her question was only aimed at Mason.

CHAPTER 21

"ARE YOU SURE THIS IS SUCH A GOOD IDEA?" DINAH said the next night as I pulled out the bin of supplies for Sheila's practice class. It was just about time for the bookstore to close, and the yarn department was deserted.

"Sheila needs to get that image of Delaney out of her head." I made sure the top on the bin was secure, put my bag on it, and got ready to go. It had taken a bit of doing, but I had gotten the group to agree to gather for Sheila's practice class. I had even rushed home and baked more biscuits. "I think this is going to work." We started to walk to the front. "At least I hope so. We're running out of time."

Sheila was waiting outside the front door of the bookstore when Dinah and I came out.

Her round face seemed racked with tension as she tried to smile. It always struck me as odd that while Sheila crocheted things with such lush colors and had a background in costume design, when it came to her own wardrobe, she always went for bland. Sheila hadn't even added a scarf or cowl for color with her beige jacket. Underneath, the navy blue pants and sweater over a white shirt looked kind of like a school uniform. Not that I was in a position to talk. I'm sure people said the same about my standard khaki pants and shirt.

"Thank you for doing this," she said. She seemed determined and tense at the same time. "I'm sorry for being so difficult." It had taken a bit of doing to get Sheila to agree to go back to the scene of the problem.

Adele bustled out the door a moment later. "I'll take Sheila," she said. "I can give her a pep talk on the way over." I hesitated, wondering what kind of pep talk Adele would give our shy crocheter. I had my doubts that Adele could understand how Sheila felt, since she was fearless when it came to being in front of a group. If anything, she loved the spotlight.

Thankfully, it hadn't taken much persuading to get CeeCee to agree to my plan. Having the cops all over her place the day before had only made her more uncomfortable in her own surroundings. She hadn't been up to the guest quarters since we'd first found Delaney.

Luckily, I'd had the genius idea of contacting Esmaya to see if she did private purifying rituals. When she heard it had to do with CeeCee Collins and a crime scene, she agreed immediately and said she'd do the premium spiritual counseling package.

Dinah and I drove together, and a short time later, I parked the greenmobile in front of CeeCee's. I was relieved to see there were no news crews or photographers hanging out in front anymore. Adele pulled her Matrix up behind me. The lanterns on top of the pillars on either side of CeeCee's front gate illuminated the area. "Uh-oh," I said, seeing Sheila rush out of the passenger seat with a stunned expression.

I grabbed Adele and pulled her aside. "What did you tell her?"

Adele seem unfazed by Sheila's expression or my question and shrugged as she spoke. "I just told her the thing I've always heard if you have a problem with public speaking. You just imagine everyone in their birthday suits."

No wonder Sheila had looked stunned. Did she really want to imagine all that naked skin? "Uh, I think you're supposed to picture them in their underwear," I offered.

"I like my version better," Adele said. No surprise.

"I'm here," Babs said as she walked into the circle of light. "Thanks for including me. I told my girlfriend in Iowa City that I was hanging out with celebrities and had become a Hooker." She laughed at her own joke.

The Buick carrying Rhoda and Elise pulled up a moment later. Eduardo had had to beg off, as he had some kind of event going on at the Apothecary. Esmaya zipped up in a Smart Car just behind them. I wasn't totally sure about her skills as a spiritual counselor, but she sure dressed the part. She wore a long white caftan with a necklace of carved wooden pieces. Her honey blond hair was twisted up and held in place by some leather thongs. She carried a tote made out of thick, dry grasses.

"Is her hair twinkling?" Dinah asked.

"I don't think so," I said, but then I looked again and saw that Dinah wasn't seeing things. I stepped closer for a better look.

"They're LED lights," the spiritual counselor said. "Don't they add a nice touch of magic?"

CeeCee buzzed the gate open, and we all trooped in. CeeCee was standing outside waiting, and I could hear Tallulah and Marlene barking from inside. CeeCee seemed unusually tense and grabbed my arm. "I certainly hope your plan works for all of us. I haven't been able to bring myself to go up there since it happened." Rosa came outside and stopped next to her employer, eyeing all of us.

"Is there anything you need?" the housekeeper asked. CeeCee seemed preoccupied and shook her head.

It was the first time I'd ever come over and CeeCee hadn't asked what treats I'd brought. I was going to mention the biscuits, but CeeCee was impatient to get to the guest apartment. I was glad that there was a hanging string of lights on the patio next to the house. They brightened up the whole area.

Unsurprisingly, CeeCee had Esmaya and me go up the stairway first. I opened the door but felt a little apprehensive as I got ready to flip the light switch. I was automatically holding my nose, remembering the smell of death from last time. I was relieved when the recessed lighting in the ceiling illuminated the whole room and nobody was lying there. The only reminder that anything had gone on there was a piece of yellow tape on the doorknob.

CeeCee was right behind me. "Tony cleaned up everything after the cops left." I started to breathe through my nose again and noted the faint scent of Murphy's Oil Soap. A long folding table had been set up with folding chairs around it. A few other chairs had been spaced around the room. As I stepped inside I noticed the air was warm and stopped in my tracks.

"It's okay," CeeCee said, giving me a slight push. "Tony arranged for the heater vent to be changed." I took her at her word and went inside and set the basket of biscuits on the counter next to a brown box. "Should I move this?" I asked CeeCee.

"I don't know what it is," CeeCee said, nervously backing away from it. Babs came forward and opened the flap of the box.

"What is it?" I asked, pulling back the flap on the other side of the box. There seemed to be pipes, a lot of leaves and twigs, and something bright and fuzzy. Babs closed the flap on her side and then closed the one on mine.

"The workmen must have left it. Where I come from, they always leave the old stuff so you can see what they did."

"I don't care," CeeCee said in an impatient voice. "Let's just get going on this." We all moved to the center of the room. "Where's Tony?" she asked. "He was going to come for moral support."

"Here I am, honey," Tony said in a bright voice as he entered the room. "I just wanted to make sure you know there's nothing to worry about. The battery in the carbon monoxide detector has been changed." He pointed out something hanging on the wall. "The green light means it's working."

"He's sure chipper," Dinah said in a low voice meant just for me to hear.

"And he's an actor," I said. "Who knows what's real?"

I stood back and let Esmaya take over. She looked around the big room and did some ethereal-ish moves with her arms. "Ah yes, I can feel the bad energy lingering in here." She moved her arms around some more. "When I'm done it will all be gone."

She put down her tote, took out a blue ceramic bowl, and set it on the table before kicking off her thong sandals. Next, she extracted a bound bunch of sage and laid it in the middle of the bowl. She lit it with a lighter, and in a moment a thin trail of bluish smoke began to rise from the herbs, giving off a pungent odor. She picked up the bowl and began to walk around the room, doing a slow dance and chanting. I was relieved when Babs steered Esmaya away from the smoke detector.

When the last of the sage had burned, she stood at the doorway and held her arms up. "All bad vibes be gone. May this place be filled with good chi." She moved her hands as if she was gathering something up and hurled it out the door into the night. "You're good to go," she announced, slipping on her shoes. I thought she was going to leave, but she asked to stay and see how things went.

"Okay, Sheila, we're ready for you," I coaxed as I pulled the bin of yarn to the table and Dinah started to distribute small amounts of different-colored yarns. Sheila went to the head of the table and began to set up her samples and supplies.

"Here we go again," Dinah said under her breath. "Fingers crossed nothing else happens."

"What could possibly happen to wreck this?" I saw Dinah wince at me. "I know I'm tempting fate. But really, I think Sheila is going to sail through it this time."

Tony hung next to CeeCee, apparently trying to be a supportive partner.

Sheila took a deep breath and began. "Thank you for being such good friends. Really, you are my family now. And this time I'm going to get through it." She held up an airy wrap in shades of blue and started to talk about the yarn. "If you're going to use three strands, none of them can be too thick."

We all made encouraging sounds and followed her suggestion to feel the different yarns in front of us. Sheila let out her breath and seemed to be finding her way.

I nudged Dinah with a nod. "I told you nothing would happen."

But I'd spoken too soon. Suddenly and without warning the door flew open and a series of cops with their weapons drawn rushed into the room. Barry appeared through the crowd as they surrounded Tony. He took out his handcuffs.

"You're under arrest for the murder of Delaney Tanner."

CHAPTER 22

"IF YOU WOULD ALL STOP TALKING AT ONCE," THE officer behind the desk in the West Valley police station yelled. He had to yell to be heard above the racket. Tony had gone with the cops—their choice, not his. Once we kept CeeCee from fainting, she and Dinah had gotten in the greenmobile with me, and the rest of them had carpooled.

"There's been a terrible mistake," CeeCee yelled at the desk officer.

"Do you know who she is?" Babs said, stepping next to CeeCee and putting a supportive arm around her shoulder.

"Why did they arrest Tony?" Elise said.

Rhoda pushed in front and turned to me. "At least all this should erase the image of the body for Sheila." *Right, and replace it with a new upsetting one*, I thought. Sheila was next to her and appeared dazed and confused.

Adele had joined in. "I insist you contact my fiancé Eric Humphries right away. He'll get this straightened out."

Esmaya had come along, too, and was waving her arms, trying to change the vibrations. "This room is loaded with negativity," she said. She pulled out a wad of sage and a lighter.

The officer threw up his hands and came around the desk to grab the sage. "Lady, you have got to be kidding."

In the midst of all the commotion, the front door opened and Mason rolled in on his scooter followed by a frazzled-looking Brooklyn. Jaimee brought up the rear and seemed fascinated by the commotion. Mason sized up the situation immediately.

"Quiet!" Mason yelled above the din. Surprisingly, it worked. The officer returned to his place behind the counter as Mason rolled up. "I demand to see my client, Tony Bonnard."

CeeCee rushed up to Mason. "I was afraid you wouldn't come. You have to do something."

"Molly called me on her way. I'm here now. You don't have to worry. I'll take care of everything," he said.

Barry came into the lobby, took one look at the mini mob, and quickly saw Mason. The two men stared each other down for a few moments, but then Barry glanced away, and I saw his gaze rest on Mason's entourage. Barry turned to me, and for a moment, his cop face relented and he gave me a knowing nod.

Meanwhile, despite his Hawaiian shirt and jeans, Mason was all business and he repeated his request to Barry. Barry had no choice but to lead him into the back. As soon as Mason had left the lobby, the officer threw the rest of us out.

We regrouped outside in the dark parking lot. CeeCee was in no condition to be alone. Sheila still seemed rattled. Esmaya was upset that the officer had confiscated her sage, thinking it was marijuana. Adele heard from Eric on her cell, saying he'd heard there was some kind of disturbance at the station and his name was being thrown around. Rhoda and Elise said they had to get home and left.

I took charge of CeeCee, while Dinah took Sheila and got into Adele's car. Babs said she was coming with me.

"He didn't do it," CeeCee said to me as we drove to her place. "I'm sure." There was just the slightest wobble in her voice on the last word that made it seem like she wasn't really one hundred percent on that.

"Of course not," Babs said from the backseat. "How could anyone think the person who played Dr. Mackenzie Scott, saving lives for years on *The Night Before Tomorrow*, could possibly kill someone?"

I pulled the greenmobile up in front of her house. "I'll be okay," she said in a valiant voice as she got out. I didn't buy that for a minute and turned off the motor.

"I'll just walk you in," I said, and she didn't object, but it was a different story when Babs wanted to stick with us. CeeCee gave her a very clear no.

"Let me know if you need anything, chocolate or otherwise," Babs said in a disappointed voice.

CeeCee and I went inside her gate. It was strange being there without a bunch of people. Even the Yorkies' barking seemed quieter when we went inside. She walked into the living room and collapsed on the flower print sofa.

I had never really realized how much of CeeCee's appearance had to do with the way she projected herself. I had always seen her when she was "on," but she was definitely switched to "off" now, and it was as if she'd collapsed in on herself. Shadows that I'd never noticed before appeared on her face, and it was like all the light had gone out of her eyes.

"What about some tea?" I said.

"Rosa's gone," she said, misunderstanding. When I offered to make it, she brightened. "I kind of remember that you brought some biscuits, too, dear. We could add some jam. I need something sweet after getting such a big shock."

It was then that I remembered the biscuits were still in the guest apartment. I knew that Esmaya had chased away all the bad spirits, but I was still a little apprehensive about going there alone. CeeCee appeared almost comatose, so I couldn't ask her to come along.

"I'll just fetch them," I said, trying to hide my discomfort. CeeCee answered with a tired wave.

It was very quiet and dark outside. The grounds had spotlights here and there, but all those trees made for a lot of shadows. I got to the base of the stairs on the side of the garage and looked up. I was surprised to see the lights were off. I could have sworn they'd been on when we rushed out. I climbed to the top and pushed the door open, hesitating as I stared into the darkness. It smelled faintly of sage, and I reached for the light switch before I took a step inside. I was almost afraid to look when light flooded the room. It seemed okay—at least there wasn't a body on the floor. There were streaks of mud, though. I hurried across the room to grab the biscuits. Something seemed different. The box with the vent parts was gone, I realized. Had somebody come in and taken it?

I probably should have just taken the biscuits back to CeeCee and not worried about anything else, but I couldn't stop thinking about the mud on the floor. There was only one area of CeeCee's property where I'd encountered damp dirt.

I left the biscuits on the stairs and went around the back of the garage to the no-man's-land Dinah and I had ended up in when we found the gate. It was even darker and spookier than I remembered. Something ran through the ivy and over my foot, and I was glad I didn't have a flashlight to see what it was. It was easy to find the gate, since the ivy had been trimmed back after our discovery. I was sure Tony had mentioned that he was going to put a lock on it, but there was nothing there. My foot hit something on the ground. I retrieved it and held it up to catch the moonlight. It was a lock, but it had been cut open.

I didn't have to be Sherlock Holmes to deduce that somebody had come in through the back gate and taken the box of vent parts. I was guessing they were in a hurry, since they left the streaks of dirt instead of trying to cover their tracks. Cutting the lock would have been easy. They sold bolt cutters at every hardware store. The big question was, why?

It suddenly occurred to me that I had been gone too long. CeeCee would be hysterical. I left the lock and retraced my steps, stopping to pick up the biscuits.

CeeCee was standing outside when I reached the house.

"Dear, I was worried. I can't let anything happen to you." I made a silly joke to cover for myself, and we went inside. By the time I'd boiled some water and made up a tray with honey and jam for the biscuits, she seemed better. I almost thought of mentioning the lock, but I was afraid of scaring her.

CeeCee set down her cup and brushed a crumb off her outfit as I heard my cell phone's distinctive ring. CeeCee almost jumped off the sofa, and I tried to grab the phone quickly.

When she realized the voice was coming from my phone, she let out a nervous laugh.

"Hello," I said tentatively.

"Sunshine," Mason said in an upbeat voice. "I'm outside CeeCee's."

I rushed out to get him and saw that he'd lost part of his entourage. Only Brooklyn was with him now. He used the scooter to get down the path to the house, but I had to help him up the few stairs to the porch while Brooklyn carried the scooter.

I had never seen Mason doing his lawyer thing before. He gave my arm a friendly squeeze, but then it was all about CeeCee.

"Tony wanted me to come over and reassure you," he said, sitting across from CeeCee and leaning toward her. "He's going to have to spend the night." At that CeeCee let out a wail. Mason responded by taking her hands in his and assuring her that everything was going to be okay. "The important thing is they have no case against him. All they have is his business card with a note on the back that said 7 P.M. with a date."

"The date of what?" she asked.

"Well, it's the day the victim died, but it isn't Tony's handwriting. They found the victim's purse in the ivy in the area behind the garage. The card was in there."

Brooklyn stayed in the background, watching her father. Mason assured CeeCee that he could knock it out as evidence in so many ways, and CeeCee nodded with resignation.

There was some discussion as to whether CeeCee was okay to be alone after all that she had been through, and I realized that Mason acted as so much more than a legal advisor in his job.

CeeCee seemed to have recovered. "I'll be fine now," she said, standing up and making it clear it was time for us all to go. "Besides, Rosa comes early in the morning."

CeeCee saw us to the door, and I helped Mason down the stairs while Brooklyn handled the scooter. I was surprised when she walked ahead, giving Mason and me a moment alone.

"Thank you," I said. "I think you really gave CeeCee some comfort."

"No thank-you necessary," Mason said in a voice full of energy and good cheer. "This isn't how I expected to go back to work, but it certainly feels good."

"So then you don't think Tony did it," I said.

"That's not the point. They have no case."

Maybe it wasn't the point to him, but it certainly was to me.

CHAPTER 23

IT WAS MIDNIGHT WHEN I GOT HOME. THE ANIMALS were waiting by the door, full of reproach. Even Blondie had come out of her chair to join them. I gave the dogs a run in the yard, and the cats were content with some attention and having a new layer of dry cat food added to their bowls.

What a night, I thought as I flopped on my sofa. *Tired* was too mild a word for what I felt. Drained, depleted, exhausted. But at the same time, I was too wired to just go to bed. There was so much going around in my mind.

I couldn't believe that another rehearsal for Sheila had gone sour. Though, like Rhoda had said, at least we'd replaced the image of Delaney's body with the image of cops rushing in with their guns out.

The phone rang, startling me. Since it was my landline, it had a real ring instead of a disembodied voice yelling at me to answer. There were a number of missed calls on the phone, which I was pretty sure were from Dinah, so I figured she was trying again.

I grabbed the cordless, and the dogs came into the living room and began positioning themselves around me on the couch.

"Sorry I didn't call before, Dinah," I said.

"This isn't Dinah," Barry said.

"I can't believe that you're calling me. What do you want?" I didn't wait for him to say anything. "You told me the cause of death was inconclusive and you thought it was an accident or suicide, and then suddenly it's murder and you barge in with your guns out and arrest Tony in the middle of our crochet thing!"

"I'm sorry about that. The housekeeper said he was up there, and we wanted to catch him off guard. We never intended to ruin your event. It's really all because of you that everything changed."

"What?" I said, incredulous.

"After you found that gate in the fence along the street, we had a look around there. That's where we found the victim's purse and the card." He started to explain the card, and I told him I already knew. I didn't mention what Mason said about getting the case thrown out, or anything about my intention to continue trying to figure out what had really happened.

"I only called you because I knew you were still up," he said. "I'm outside. Could we talk in person?" I agreed, figuring I'd have a better chance of getting more information out of him if he was in front of me.

The dogs raced me to the front door when they heard the soft knock.

Barry looked as he had earlier, only more tired. I imagined I looked the same. By now my no-wrinkle khakis were full of creases. My shirt had come untucked, and whatever makeup I'd had on was long gone.

We didn't sit on the couch this time but stood facing each other in the entrance hall.

He apologized again, but this time for another reason. "We didn't mean to put any of you in harm's way. Like I said, we wanted to catch Tony off guard."

"You mean you were afraid he would pull a gun?"

Barry nodded and gave me a wary stare. "Then you know he has a gun?" he said. I shrugged in response, not wanting to answer, and Barry continued. "It doesn't matter—that's not the kind of information I'm really after." He seemed a little uncomfortable. "I know your group does a lot of talking when they get together. You probably complain about husbands and boyfriends." He stopped with as close to a sheepish expression as he could get, which wasn't much. "You probably bent their ear about me."

I didn't say yes or no but let him go on. I had a pretty good idea where he was headed.

"Did CeeCee ever say anything about Tony?" he asked. "He was a star on that soap opera for years, and he has some kind of web show now. All that celebrity works like a babe magnet, doesn't it?"

"I wouldn't know."

"So then CeeCee was never worried that he had something going on on the side?"

"She never said anything to me." That was the truth, but beyond that I honestly didn't know. "I'm guessing you and your other cops have a whole scenario figured out." His expression was impassive, and he had his arms crossed, but I didn't let his body language stop me. "You had your guns pointed at us. We could have been shot, and you're not going to tell me anything?"

Barry looked longingly at the couch. My legs were beginning to get tired of standing anyway. "You might as well sit down," I said. All of the dogs jumped up between us as we sat, so there was no chance for any replay of the other night, when he'd fallen asleep on my shoulder.

"All right, I'll tell you," he said finally. "We think Tony met the victim at the bank. He had recently gotten a business account, and she was the teller that covered the business line most of the time. He's a dashing TV star whose career has taken a nosedive, probably along with his ego. She's an adoring fan. One thing leads to another and he gets the idea of them having a roll in the hay together. She comes in that back gate, and he walks over from the house, leaving CeeCee with no clue as to what's going on. Maybe it becomes a regular thing. Then, maybe Delaney wants more of a relationship or maybe she threatens to tell CeeCee, who appears to be helping bankroll him while he gets his web show going. In other words, CeeCee is his meal ticket right now, and he doesn't want to lose it. So, he arranges to meet Delaney in the guest apartment. He stuffs some twigs into the vent of the heater before she gets there. He gives her a drink with some pills in it, and when she passes out, he turns on the heat and leaves. Then he waits a few days before giving CeeCee the idea of telling your group about using the space for a studio, so she'll take you up there and you'll find the body."

He seemed annoyed with himself when he finished. "I sure was loose lipped. You were supposed to tell me about Tony, and I just showed you our whole hand. Well, as long as I told you—what do you think of our scenario? Any hint things weren't going well between CeeCee and Tony?"

I thought of what Rosa had said, implying that Tony was taking advantage of CeeCee. No way was I going to repeat that. I wasn't going to say anything until I knew the whole story, so I diverted Barry with the case of the missing box of old vent parts, as well as the tracks of dirt on the floor, and the broken lock on the gate.

"Why would anybody want to steal some old vent parts?"

"I suppose your people checked out the vent when it all happened?" I answered his question with a question.

"Of course, we looked it over when it first happened. We took out some twigs and leaves but then saw there was just more of the same below it and let it go. The notes said it looked like a bird's nest, and it was left at that." His expression grew wary. He seemed to be having an internal argument. "You're back sneaking around, looking for clues, aren't you?"

I rocked my head in what I hoped was a "maybe yes, maybe no" expression. He closed his eyes halfway in frustration. "Don't go getting all excited about the missing box. Most likely someone, like maybe the housekeeper, came in to throw the box away. She was spooked by the place and hurried out without noticing she'd tracked in mud." He thought for a moment before continuing. "And the broken lock, that could have been us from last night."

I figured he'd make a move to leave after that, since he'd blown his chance of getting much information from me by telling me too much. But instead, he stayed put, looking even more uncomfortable. "I'm sorry," he said at last.

He got my attention back when he said he was sorry. Barry wasn't one to apologize at all, and this was three times in one evening. I gave him my full attention, wondering what was going to come next. "I realize I was wrong, the way I didn't put you first when we were together," he said.

"What brought that on?" I asked. As far as I'd been able to tell, when we were together, he'd felt justified keeping his job in the top position.

He looked down at the floor. "I was supposed to pick Jeffrey up after his play today and I forgot."

"You didn't," I said, shaking my head. "Poor Jeffrey. I hope he knows he could have called me."

"He got home okay, but he really let me have it. He told me I was a terrible father." Barry blew out his breath. "I'm sure I did that and worse to you. I just want you to know that I'm trying to mend my ways."

I wasn't sure how I was supposed to respond, and after a moment, he got up to go. I walked him to the door, and we stood there awkwardly.

"Thanks for stopping by, Detective Greenberg," I said, trying to lighten the moment.

He shook his head to show me he didn't think it was funny. "Stay out of trouble," he said, then he let himself out.

It was only after he left that I began to wonder about the real reason for his visit. Was it to get information on Tony, or was it really about telling me the last part?

CHAPTER 24

THE ANIMALS WERE LINED UP AT THE DOOR FOR their good-bye treats when the phone rang. I considered ignoring it, since I had overslept after the late night, but I grabbed it on the third ring and saw that it was Mason.

"Good morning, Sunshine," he said in an upbeat voice. "I can't tell you how great it is to have a purpose again." Felix realized I hadn't given him his treat and put his paws on my knees as a reminder. "I just wanted to let you know that Tony has been bailed out and is home with CeeCee." He said something to someone in the room about getting some information, then he came back to me. "Sorry. Brooklyn is helping me out, and I had to tell her something." His voice dropped as he continued. "Now that Tony is my client, you know the drill. I can ask you stuff, but I can't tell you anything. Okay?"

I had been expecting as much. "There is something you should know," I began. I told him about the old vent being there and then not being there. "There seemed to be some bits of damp dirt on the floor, too. And when I went to check that back gate, the lock was on the ground, cut open."

"Really," Mason said. I expected him to say more after that, but he seemed to be hesitating. "You have a lot on your hands right now with all the problems with Sheila and starting Yarn University. You don't have to worry about investigating anymore."

There was nothing in his tone to say he was being anything but considerate, but could he be afraid of what I was going to turn up about his client? This felt very awkward, which was something I'd never felt with him before. I wasn't sure what to say or do. Finally, I took the chicken's way out and just said nothing.

"You're still there, aren't you, Sunshine?" he said finally. I let out an *uh-huh*. "I'll see you tonight after work. We can work everything out then."

I agreed but wondered exactly what he meant by that.

"Love you, Sunshine," he said in a happy voice. He waited for my *me, too*, before he hung up.

I'd been so busy thinking about what he was saying, I'd forgotten what I was doing. In the meantime, Felix had figured out that if he jumped on the bench by the table, he could get on the table, and then onto the counter where the dog treats were. He had flipped the jar on its side, and dog biscuits were spilling out.

"I hope you were at least planning to share." I gave the gray dog a stern shake of my head as I returned him to the floor. Then there was just time for a quick cleanup, and I was out the door.

It was cold and damp, and I could smell rain in the air. Already the orange blossom petals were falling away and had become a fragrant carpet at the base of the trees. It seemed that gloom was much gloomier in Southern California because we were so used to the sun. Or maybe it just felt that way after my conversation.

The dark weather must have made everyone anxious to read, as the bookstore was busy when I arrived. I spent most of the day helping customers while trying to avoid Mrs. Shedd and Adele, particularly together. It would be too easy for something to come up about the previous night's events, which would lead directly to Sheila and her stage fright. When Mrs. Shedd finally cornered me, I was relieved that she handed me the blue pouch and asked me to make the bank deposit.

By now, I'd gotten braver and realized nobody had a clue I had a bunch of cash in my tote bag, though I did keep an eye in my rearview mirror to make sure no one was tailing me. Nobody was taking their time in the parking lot today, as it had started to drizzle. People in Southern California have themselves mixed up with the evil witch in *The Wizard of Oz* and seem to think if they get hit with a little water they will melt.

I passed several people I recognized from the bookstore as I went in. The fluorescent lights inside seemed particularly harsh contrasted with the gloom outside. By now, I knew the drill and went to the merchant line. There was one person ahead of me.

"I hope you're not in a hurry," the man said, pointing at the customer at the teller window. I had to laugh—the tall customer was certainly overdressed for the weather. His raincoat and baseball cap seemed a bit much for the amount of rain we were getting. A blue bag was on the counter, and I watched him take out stacks of bills.

"Whatever business he's in, looks good to me. I wonder if he's looking for a partner," the man said jokingly.

It seemed to be taking the teller forever to count all the bills he had.

"At last," the man in front of me said, as the customer zipped up the now empty bag and turned to walk away. The hat threw a shadow on his face, but as he walked away, there was something familiar about his profile.

When I returned to the parking lot, the drizzle had turned into a steady rain. The streets were glistening, and the sidewalks had turned a dark shade of dun.

"Mission accomplished," I said when I walked back into the bookstore and put the blue pouch on the counter. Somehow the rain made the familiar smell of paper and books mixed with the scent of coffee coming from the café more pronounced. I got rid of my rain gear and got Bob to make me a red eye to pump me up for the Hookers' gathering.

I took the steaming drink back to the yarn department. Between the rain and the events of the previous night, I wondered who would show up. Adele was the first arrival, since she just had to come from the kids' department.

She flung her tote bag on the table. "Can you believe that Eric was upset with me for throwing his name around the police station? I was just trying to help CeeCee," she said, eyeing the table while she decided where to sit. "Do you think CeeCee will be here?"

"No. Now that Tony is back home, I'm sure she's making a big fuss about him." Adele seemed surprised at the news and grumbled that nobody told her anything.

Dinah had picked up a coffee drink on her way in, too, and set it on the table as she slipped off her burnt orange raincoat and hung it on the back of the chair. Drops of rain were stuck in her short salt-and-pepper hair and had mixed with her hair gel. The light caught in the water and glistened, but her spiky style had gone flat.

Rhoda, Elise and Eduardo came in together. I could hear the two women filling him in on the previous night's excitement. He let out a sigh. "Poor CeeCee."

"Tony's out of jail," I announced as they found places around the table and took out their projects.

"It was all a mistake, then, wasn't it?" Rhoda said, looking at me.

"I don't know." It was the only answer I could give.

"But you are going to find out?" Elise said.

"I'll do what I can." I didn't want to bring up what Mason had said. "Let's just crochet for a while." I glanced around for my tote bag and realized in all the excitement I had forgotten to grab the bamboo cowl I was making for Samuel. He didn't care that men didn't seem to wear cowls. He thought he'd start a trend. Luckily, I had my purse project, as I called it. I took out the plastic bag with the worsted-weight purple wool yarn. I started to crochet as Babs came into the yarn department with a younger woman in tow.

"Is there any news on Tony?" she asked in a worried voice. Adele was only too glad to share the update that he was out of jail.

"CeeCee must be relieved, but she's probably a wreck after worrying about him all night. I better bring her some brownies. She told me chocolate is a medicinal food for her." Babs turned to the woman with her. "Is that true?" Then to the rest of us, she said, "This is my daughter-in-law, Lucille. That's Dr. Lucille Swanson." Lucille was an attractive, efficient-looking woman and gave us a friendly smile.

"Remember what I said? No medical questions," Lucille said. "When I'm off duty, I'm off duty." She looked at us. "Babs told me all about your group and promised that crochet could lower my stress level. That's just what I need."

"I wanted to show her one of your gatherings, and if she likes it, she's going to sign up for the beginning crochet class."

Adele was out of her seat before Babs reached the period on the sentence.

"You've come to the right place. I'm teaching the beginning crochet class. Ask me any questions."

"I thought I'd just watch for a while," Lucille said. She and Babs took seats at the end of the table. We went around the table and introduced ourselves and held up what we were working on.

"The crocheting is a stress reliever, but so is the company of the group. You're a doctor?" Rhoda asked. "What kind?"

"She's a dermatologist, but please forget I mentioned that," Babs said and threw her daughter-in-law an apologetic smile.

"As soon as they hear I'm a doctor, somebody always wants medical advice. I can't even go to a party," Lucille said.

Babs chimed in. "She was just a guest and they asked her to look at a rash."

Lucille threw up her hands. "If you're allergic to wool, you should know better than to wrap your arms around it."

The mention of the party caught my attention. I remembered Babs had talked about babysitting while they went somewhere on a Thursday.

"Was that at the Willises' house?" I asked, and Lucille nodded.

"It was quite the party, tented tennis court and all," she said.

"What was the occasion of the party?" I asked, and Lucille stopped to think for a moment.

"I think they had recently launched their new business. I just went along with my husband. I'm sure Babs told you, Richard has his own business management firm, and he was hoping to network."

"Did you see Tony Bonnard there?" I asked.

Babs suddenly seemed protective of Lucille and wanted to know why I was asking. Then before I could answer, she sucked in her breath as she realized why. "It was the same night that woman died at CeeCee's!" She seemed upset that she hadn't put it together before. She turned to her daughter-in-law. "Did you see him there?"

"Is he the handsome guy with the white hair who used to play a doctor in that soap opera?" We all nodded yes. "I'm pretty sure I saw him, but I can't say how long he was there. There were a lot of people."

I stopped mid-stitch, realizing it didn't really matter if Lucille had seen him or not. "Being seen at the party really doesn't give him an alibi. He could have made an appearance and then gone up to the guest apartment and killed Delaney. He could have even returned to the party after he did the deed."

"I'm here," Sheila said. We'd all been so busy talking to Lucille, none of us had noticed that Sheila had come into the bookstore. Her voice sounded upbeat, but her brows were furrowed, and she looked tense.

Mrs. Shedd was right behind her, which probably accounted for Sheila's effort to sound upbeat. I was grateful to Babs, who started raving to her daughter-in-law about Sheila's beautiful pieces and asked to show her some samples. Giving Sheila something to do took her mind off her nerves. Mrs. Shedd watched for a moment, then went back to wandering the bookstore to help customers.

With Mrs. Shedd gone, I started to suggest Sheila take a shot at just doing the introduction to her class in front of us, but I was surprised when Sheila cut me off mid-sentence.

"No. I'm not doing any more practice sessions." I started to ask why, but Sheila just shook her head in a decided manner. Even with the talk of alibis and Sheila's surprising surli-

ness, we must have done something right, because by the time
the group broke up Lucille had signed up for Adele's class.
She seemed pleased when Adele walked out with her, showing
off her beanie with the big flower on it.

At that point, Dinah and I were the only ones left at the
table. It was dinnertime now, and the bookstore had cleared
out. I let out a weary sigh and kept moving my hook through
the wool yarn. I was glad it was a simple project. I really
needed some mindless crochet.

"What are you making?" Dinah said.

"For now it's just a long, skinny strip, but eventually I'm
going to sew the ends together and make an infinity scarf." I
laid the long strip of purple stitches on the table and measured.
It was five feet long. "Just a foot or so more and I'll actually
be done." Dinah and I exchanged high fives. Dinah went back
to working on a potholder in delft blue cotton yarn. It was
one of the projects she was going to use in her class.

She didn't want to talk about her situation with Commander, and I didn't want to talk about my issues with
Mason. First it was that his daughter didn't like me, then his
ex moved in. Now, realizing he just wanted to get Tony out
of trouble, without caring if he'd done it or not, bothered
me. And then suggesting I stop trying to figure out what had
really happened to Delaney Tanner? That was what it was
really about for me. Getting justice for her.

Maybe there was just too much baggage for either Dinah
or me to have a happily ever after.

Since we didn't want to talk about the men in our lives,
we talked about Adele and her wedding woes and why Eric
didn't seem to want to pin down a date and location. We
both agreed Adele could be right. He was getting cold feet.

The topic of Sheila came up next. "There's nothing more
I can do," I said. "Maybe I pushed her too far. I've never

seen her so resolute about anything before. She actually just said no to another practice." I let out a sigh. "Maybe I'll need Adele's backup plan after all."

"Okay, enough stalling. Let's talk about what's really on our minds," Dinah said. "Tony."

I told her about Barry's theory, which opened Pandora's box. Now Dinah wanted all the details of our encounter.

"It's wasn't an encounter, except maybe for the part when he apologized for stuff he did when we were together."

Dinah insisted on a complete replay of the conversation. "Sounds to me like he wants to win you back," she said.

"I don't think so. More like stuff with his son is making him view his behavior in a new light." I shook my head to get rid of the Barry topic. "We were going to talk about Tony, remember? I hate to say it, but what Barry said made sense. Tony is at a low point in his career. It doesn't take long for people to go from saying *Weren't you in that show?* to *Who did you used to be?* I don't think it was his first choice to move in with CeeCee. Her career is on an upswing. I mean, she's an actual Academy Award nominated actress. I'm sure they're going to make a sequel to *Caught by a Kiss.* Tony's ego was probably sagging and could have needed some bolstering."

Dinah seemed disgusted. "Maybe, but how low can you go? Meeting someone in the apartment over the garage? Even as jerky as my ex was, he wouldn't have done that."

I moved my hook through the purple yarn. "And Delaney could have thought he really cared. Maybe he told her he was breaking up with CeeCee." I reached the end of the row and turned my work. "And what if Delaney threatened to tell CeeCee? Tony's trying to get that web series off the ground. CeeCee's giving him a place to live, and they're turning the guest quarters into a studio. Who knows what else she's giving him?"

Dinah finished the last row of the pot holder and reached into her bag to get her scissors to cut the cotton yarn. When she pulled them out, the strand of that variegated yarn was caught in them. It must have fallen from the table and gotten caught sometime during our session.

I thought again about how I was sure Delaney's vest had been made from that yarn, and that the whole group had denied taking it in the yarn exchange. Make that the whole group except for the one missing person—CeeCee. I didn't have to say any of that out loud. Dinah seemed to know exactly what I was thinking.

"Does that mean she was involved?" Dinah said.

"I think we should stop by CeeCee's and talk yarn."

CHAPTER 25

"We better bring something," Dinah said. "Remember Babs mentioned CeeCee needing medicinal chocolate."

There was no time to make anything, so we stopped in the café. This time of the evening was slow, and Bob was sitting at a table, hovering over his laptop. When he wasn't making coffee drinks or treats, he was working on his screenplay. Something about aliens.

Bob actually looked a little like an alien with that dab of hair below his lip. I know it was called a soul patch, but I called it a mistake in shaving. By this time of the day, there wasn't much food left, but he managed to make up a package with some double chocolate bars.

I wasn't sure what kind of a reception we'd get at CeeCee's, since we were basically dropping in unannounced and uninvited, but the chocolate offerings had gotten Babs access, so I figured it might work.

Actually, CeeCee sounded almost tearful when she heard it was us. As soon as we came inside, she took us right into the living room. Tony was sitting in an overstuffed wing chair, writing something down. CeeCee took the package of sweets and looked inside. "It has been such a trying time—these cookie bars are just what I need. But if you want something to go with it, you'll have to make it yourself. We're having to rough it since I gave Rosa a couple of days off."

We passed on the drinks but accepted her offer to sit down. CeeCee helped herself to a bar and then set the bag on the coffee table.

"Tony is such a trooper," CeeCee said. "He's writing down notes from his experiences last night and is going to use them in his web series." Tony looked up from his work.

"Of course, I have to drama it up a bit. The truth is pretty dull."

"I suppose they questioned you," I said.

He shook his head. "Hey, I've been in enough television shows to know you get lawyered up right away. The thing that was so amazing was the way Mason Fields magically appeared when I said that." He patted CeeCee's hand. "It was brilliant thinking of hers to call him on the way to the police station." I laughed inside at the comment. I'd been the one to call Mason, but I was fine with her getting the credit. He set the papers aside and gave his full attention to the group of us. "I was kind of surprised that when Mason and I had some time alone, he didn't actually ask me if I did it." Tony seemed to find that amusing, but CeeCee seemed upset.

"You shouldn't joke about that," she said. "This is serious."

"I'm not worried. Mason Fields is the best. He doesn't think they have much of a case. And do you have any idea how much publicity I'm going to get for my series?"

"You and that series," CeeCee grumbled.

I could almost hear Mason telling me to let things be, but I ignored the imagined comment and plowed ahead. "Why did you say you didn't know Delaney Tanner?" I asked Tony.

"Because it was the truth," he said casually. "The cops gave me her name first, and I didn't recognize it. To be honest, I barely glanced at the photograph they had. It was only when the cops brought up the business card and said she'd worked at the bank that I realized who she was."

"Tell them how she got your business card," CeeCee prompted.

"I have a business account at the bank. With all that bullet-proof glass they have now, I barely noticed the teller I was dealing with. But she recognized me. She was a big fan of the soap I was on and kept telling me how great I was in it." He put up his hands in a helpless pose. "It was music to my ears, particularly since things weren't going so well. She wanted to hear about the web series, and I was glad to have a willing ear. I had forgotten, but last week when I went in there, she said something about how it would be a dream come true if she could be an extra on the show. I gave her my business card and told her to call and leave a message. Whatever was on the back of that card came from someone else."

"You're being awfully cavalier about this," CeeCee said. She seemed upset and medicated herself with another cookie bar.

"I will tell you this," Tony continued. "Delaney bordered on being too friendly. I was happy to talk about the web series, but I was a little uncomfortable when she made comments about the checks I was depositing and then talked about other customers. If she talked about them, she'd talk about me. I wasn't sure I wanted it on the street how much I was strug-gling. I said something about my small deposits, and she brought up Evan Willis and his partner, saying they came in a lot to deposit cash."

Tony suddenly looked embarrassed. "It was a lot easier when somebody was paying me. I asked her about what he was doing, thinking maybe he'd want to have a piece of my web series. She told me the name of his business. I was expecting something in the entertainment industry, but it was a day spa or something like that. She could have said there was a chain of them; I'm not sure."

For a minute I just sat there thinking about Kelsey Willis and how she had acted so high-handed. There was a world of difference in status between being an executive in a studio and owning a massage parlor. What Tony said sounded like it could be true, but there could also be more to the story. Like maybe he was meeting her to give her "acting lessons."

Dinah nudged me to remind me of the reason we'd come, and I took out the length of yarn I'd found earlier and put it on the coffee table. "I was just wondering if you had any more luck in working with this yarn than I had," I asked CeeCee.

CeeCee had a blank look on her face. "Remember, you took it at the yarn exchange?" I said.

CeeCee picked up the length of variegated yarn and examined it more closely.

"Oh, that wool yarn you didn't want," she said finally. "Now I remember. I believed Adele when she said she was sure that the yarn would work for crochet." CeeCee turned to me. "Dear, I know you said it wouldn't work for you, but I have been crocheting a lot longer than you, and I have wrangled with some tough yarn."

"And," I coaxed, "what did you make with it?" CeeCee responded with another blank look.

"I'm not sure. Let me look at my yarn stash." Dinah and I followed her to the den, which looked out on the yard. She had a closet with shelves for her yarn supply. It was far neater than mine. She looked through all of it. "That's right," she said. "I realized I was never going to use it, so I gave it to Rosa." She looked at me squarely. "Why is it so important?"

"Do you think she really knew why we were asking about the yarn?" Dinah asked. We were back in the greenmobile on the way home.

"She seemed genuinely surprised when I mentioned the vest Delaney Tanner was wearing was made out of it."

"But remember, pretending is her business," Dinah said, and I nodded in agreement. "I hate to say it, but CeeCee's not remembering and then looking around for it could have just been a stall while she figured out something to say. It seems very convenient that she claimed she gave it to Rosa, who wasn't there. And then when you suggested calling her, CeeCee refused to let us bother her during her time off."

"All we can do is wait to talk to Rosa," I said.

The streets of Tarzana were quiet, and I was in front of Dinah's in no time. "I guess that's a wrap for tonight," I said. Dinah opened the door but hesitated before getting out.

"I can't keep telling Commander I'm thinking about it. I don't want to keep him dangling. I care about him too much. I'm going to call him right now." She shut the door to the car before I could ask her what she was going to say. I planned to keep plenty of tea and sympathy ready in case things didn't go well.

CHAPTER 26

As expected, Dinah called me in the morning and wanted to meet up. She wouldn't give me a clue about how things had gone with Commander but just told me to meet her at Le Grande Fromage. It was amazing how as soon as the sun came out, the rain was almost forgotten, even though the cold air still smelled of wet earth as I crossed the yard. I had finally learned not to look back once I left the house. That way I wouldn't see Felix with his paws up on the glass door with a look beseeching me to take him along.

The windows on my car were fogged up from the chilly dampness, and I had to wipe them all down before I could drive anywhere.

I left the car in the bookstore parking lot then headed down the street to the neighborhood bistro. I passed Luxe, which wasn't open yet, and noted a display in the window. The hazy blue color of the blanket was an instant giveaway that it was one of Sheila's pieces. One of the flyers was lying next to it. I hoped that meant she wasn't expecting to bail out on the class.

I had snagged a table and ordered breakfast for us before Dinah arrived in a flash of brightness with her long, rainbow-colored scarf.

"Well?" I said as soon as my friend had sat down. She certainly knew how to build up tension. Other than greeting me, she didn't say anything else as she surveyed the café au lait I'd gotten for her along with a croissant sandwich.

"I can't take the suspense. Did you tell Commander you would marry him?" I said.

Dinah took a sip of her coffee and smiled. "I didn't tell him anything yet, but I have decided that I'm thinking of telling him that I will marry him."

I was about to say something, but Adele swooped in, apparently hearing the end of Dinah's sentence. "You're going to get married?" Adele plopped down in the chair and immediately went into full pout. "It's not fair if you get married first." She set the crochet magazine that seemed to be her ever-present companion on the table.

Dinah and I rolled our eyes at each other, then Dinah took a deep breath and tried to console our fellow Hooker. "Adele, I just said I was thinking of telling Commander I would marry him."

"How come nobody told me that he asked you in the first place?" Adele turned to me, and I waited for her to bring up our French toast sister thing and reproach me for not sharing. Thank heavens Dinah stepped in and said she had only told me and insisted I not tell anyone.

As soon as it seemed clear that Dinah's possible nuptials weren't going to steal Adele's thunder, she brightened up and opened the magazine to show us a picture of a bride's hands encased in lacy crocheted gauntlets. "What do you think?" she asked. I started to say the hand covering was pretty, but Adele tapped the bride's nails, which had been painted white with a flower stenciled on them. "I was thinking I'd do this, but in mauve. I'm going to show the picture to the place down the street to see if they can do it.

"You should come with me, Molly," she said in a possessive manner. "You could get your nails done, too." She flipped the page and showed me a photo of the bridesmaid's hand. Her nails were done in stripes of magenta with glitter in between. I looked at my plain nails and swallowed a laugh.

Since they hadn't even set a date, it did seem a little premature to worry about getting my nails done, but sometimes the best way to deal with Adele was just to go along with whatever she said. "Sure," I said.

Dinah said she'd go with us. "Who knows, maybe I'll want one of those fancy manicures, too." She saw Adele's expression fade and quickly added, "If and when I actually get married."

I didn't want to say anything, but I fully expected the new salon on the corner to be closed. So far, I'd only seen it open once. But I was glad I'd kept my thoughts to myself when I saw the open sign on the door.

Adele went in ahead of us, directly to the front desk, and asked to speak to a manicurist. She had no idea the receptionist was one of Dinah's students and got upset when the young woman seemed more intent on greeting Dinah than fulfilling Adele's request.

"My friend wants to talk to someone about a fancy manicure," Dinah said. I saw Adele's face light up at being referred to as a friend. It meant so much to Adele, but she made it so hard.

"You can go on back. She just finished doing the nails of one of the owners." Emily directed us to go around the partition that blocked part of the view.

A woman with long black hair was cleaning up after her work and looked up at the three of us. "Be with you in a minute," she said as she went to straighten a lambskin pad on the seat.

"Mind if I try it?" Adele asked, settling into the chair.

"It's a pretty good fake, don't you think?" the woman said as she put away the footbath and straightened the polishes. "The owner is allergic to wool," she added as an explanation. "Now what can I do for you?" She looked at the three of us.

Adele showed her the magazine pictures, and the woman glanced them over and set the magazine down. She seemed confident she could replicate the designs and had a bunch of questions about how many people would be getting manicures, would they be coming to the store or did Adele want her to do them on location, and when was the date. As soon as the woman heard the date hadn't been set, she seemed a lot less interested and just gave Adele her card. "You can always reach me at this number." She glanced around her surroundings. "Who knows about this place?"

As we walked outside, Adele linked arms with us. "Getting your nails done is such a girlfriend thing to do." It didn't seem to matter to her that we hadn't actually gotten anything done to our nails. "I suppose Dinah wants you to be her maid of honor, too," Adele said, suddenly looking glum. "And if she gets married first it won't be so special to be in my wedding."

"Believe me, Adele, being in your wedding will definitely be a unique experience," I said when we reached the bookstore. Dinah pulled free and hugged each of us good-bye then went on her way as Adele and I walked inside.

I went toward the information booth, and Adele headed to the kids' section to get ready for story time.

Mrs. Shedd caught me as I was going across the store. "Before you get situated, could you take the deposit? I forgot to put in a bunch of checks yesterday."

By now I'd run through the whole gamut of emotions about handling the deposits. First I'd been honored that she trusted me with them, then scared that I was carrying the cash all alone, and now it was just something to get done with.

I grabbed the blue plastic pouch and headed outside before Adele had a chance to see what I was doing. I didn't want her to insist on playing bodyguard again. The drive down Ventura Boulevard to the bank was uneventful. With the sun out again, people were taking their time walking in from the parking lot, and there were a lot of people coming and going.

I had the routine down now and without thinking about it went right to the merchant teller. It was the same teller I had dealt with before, but then she'd said there were just two of them who worked the business accounts.

When it was my turn, I handed her the deposit. As long as I was here, I thought I might as well see if I could get any more information about Delaney.

I mentioned the business card with the note on the back of it. "Do you know what it was about?" At first the woman shrugged, but then her eyes lit up and she nodded.

"Now that you mention it, Delaney did say something about going to a party. I forgot all about that after what happened. Delaney showed me the back of the card and said she'd been invited to a party by a customer—I mean client."

"Did she mention who it was?" I asked.

"No. A lot of people treat us tellers as if we're invisible. Delaney never could handle that and made sure she was noticed by remembering details about clients and commenting on their transactions. I think the idea that one of them invited her to a party meant a lot to her."

She handed me the deposit receipt, and I saw her eyes go to the line that had formed. I thanked her and moved away. I stopped for a moment to put away the receipt, and when I looked up, Evan Willis had just joined the end of the business line. As before, he was dressed in track pants and a matching jacket, and he carried a sports bag. Like the rest of the people in the line, he was gazing at his smartphone. I hung off to the side and watched as he moved up the line. When it was his turn, he unzipped the bag and began to unload packets of cash. He didn't make any conversation with the teller but just slipped the cash through the window as she put it in the machine to be counted.

I thought back to what Tony had said about the Willises buying a business. It must have been doing well, because his deposit was a lot bigger than the one I'd made for the bookstore. I know I should have just left, but I was curious now about what was doing so well. I stayed just out of sight until he headed back to the door, then I walked behind two women who were also going outside. Evan had parked his white Maserati close to the door, and I had parked toward the back of the parking lot. As he got in his car, I sprinted toward mine.

He had pulled out on Ventura Boulevard, and I hit the gas hard to catch up. I got a few dirty looks as I raced through the parking lot. As I turned onto the main street, Evan's car was only a few ahead of mine. After a few blocks, I saw him put on his left turn signal. It was only when I got behind him that I realized he was turning onto the street that bordered the bookstore. He made it through before the light turned red, but I was caught waiting. I saw the Maserati pull into what I considered the bookstore parking lot. Really, though, it served the whole block of stores with entrances to the lot on both streets.

I made it through the next stoplight and pulled into the lot. I drove around until I saw the Maserati, then I parked a distance away. The greenmobile wasn't great for tailing somebody—the color and the vintage style made it stand out.

I got out and crouched low as I saw him get out of his car. He had the blue bag with him but seemed a lot more relaxed than he had at the bank. He seemed to be crossing the whole parking lot. I zigzagged through the parked cars in case he turned around. Just as I was about to walk behind a silver Honda, it began to back up. I stopped so suddenly that I almost tripped over my own feet, and when I looked up, Evan was just going into the back door of the store on the corner. It was closed by the time I reached it. The small sign on the door said Nail Spa. I thought back to the time I'd seen him at the bank before. I'd been nervous about making the deposit, and the teller had tried to reassure me that she'd just had a cus- tomer bring in a lot more cash than I had. Adele had asked what kind of a business it was. I thought the teller hadn't answered, but now I got it. When she called after us and I thought she said Manny or Molly, she was saying mani, as in manicure. And the customer must have been Evan. How odd. When I went around to the front, the "Closed" sign was up and it was empty and dark.

I had to get back to the bookstore. Considering when I'd left to deposit the money, if I didn't show up soon, Mrs. Shedd would probably call the cops. For a minute I laughed to myself, thinking of Barry hearing there was an APB out for me because I'd disappeared with a bag of cash.

CHAPTER 27

I DIDN'T HAVE ANY MORE TIME TO THINK ABOUT Evan or Delaney. The bookstore was busy, and we had two groups meeting there that day. At noon, it was open mic for the poetry group. They were an emotional bunch who didn't take criticism well, so I had to be there to referee. The romance readers were meeting as well, but they were easy, since they were just about love.

I spent the rest of the afternoon making sure everything was up to date for Yarn University. Mason and I had been in touch during the day. He wanted to make sure I was coming by that evening. I was still dealing with his suggestion that I stop investigating Delaney Tanner's death. He hadn't said it, but I knew it was because he was worried about what I might turn up about Tony. I understood that Mason's job was solely to defend Tony, but I needed to know what had really happened. And I thought dealing with Brooklyn scowling at me and Jaimee staying there was a problem!

Eventually, I tried to put all my conflicted feelings in the back of my mind, convinced everything would work out. Once he didn't have the scooter and the two women were gone, things would be different. And I *had* been the one to call him to help Tony. Life was just a bumpy ride.

It was just getting dark when I drove over there. As I walked to the front door and took out my key, I mentally prepared myself to face his sullen daughter and over-the-top ex-wife. I opened the door, and Spike came running into the foyer, barking to announce my arrival. Something smelled delicious. Mason came scooting down the hall to greet me and was upbeat and energetic as he gave me a welcome kiss. "I just want to thank you again for giving me the push I needed to get my life back by throwing a client at me." He let out a satisfied sigh. "Brooklyn has been helping me all day."

I sagged at the mention of her name, but Mason continued. "I told her to take the evening off. She went off with her sister somewhere. And Jaimee is gone, too. I didn't ask for details—all I know is she isn't here."

We'd reached the den, where his favorite detective was on the screen in freeze-frame mode. "Enough of his shenanigans," Mason said. "It's back to real life." He used the remote to turn it off.

"Dinner's waiting." He took my hand and scooted alongside me as we went to the dining room. No food containers and paper plates this time. Instead the table was set and the food was actually in serving dishes. My mouth watered from the smell of garlic from the Caesar salad.

"It's from Fabrocini's, isn't it?" I looked over the array of items from our favorite spot for Italian food. The stuffed mushrooms looked delicious. There was ravioli with marinara sauce, a platter of grilled vegetables and flatbread with tomatoes and cheese.

"We've got cheesecake with strawberries as well," Mason said. "Brooklyn went and got it, and I did the rest." He did a mock bow as he gestured for me to sit. "It's just the two of us for the rest of the evening. I won't need this much longer." He gave the scooter bell a slow pull, and the bell barely rang before he pushed it off to the side and hopped into a chair adjacent to me. We started to pass the plates of food around. "Soon life will go back to normal, and in the meantime we can make some plans." He turned to me with a happy smile. "How does that sound?"

I put a mound of Caesar salad on my plate and added a sprinkle of freshly ground pepper. "That sounds wonderful. So, tell me again about money laundering."

"What?" he said with a chuckle. "I thought we'd talk about us. The first day I'm done with this scooter, we're going to the beach. We'll pick up cappuccinos and watch the sunset." He looked at me for a reaction and saw that I was serious about my request.

"I can't believe we're going to waste our evening alone talking about money laundering." He sighed in resignation. "What do you want to know?"

"How to do it."

Mason's face broke into a big grin. "Are you planning on starting on a new venture?"

"Very funny," I said. "Just tell me how it works."

It was such a relief to see the Mason I'd come to love make an appearance as he began to talk. "It's all about taking money, usually cash from some nefarious activity, and passing it along as money from a legitimate business." He stopped to collect his thoughts. "It's better if I give you an example, like from that show I was watching. The PI was depositing cash in an account for a chain of Laundromats." Mason rolled his eyes at the cliché before he continued. "As long as the deposits were small enough, the bank accepted them without any question. It makes perfect sense—if you have a business that deals with a lot of cash, you will be making lots of deposits. Once the money is in the bank account, it can be used to pay for anything—a boat, a house, big credit card bills. You could even send it to someone else. The big thing is just getting rid of all those dollar bills." Mason stopped to take a sip of water. "I hope this is just curiosity on your part and not something you're investigating because of Delaney Tanner's death?"

I had been hoping he wouldn't say something like that, so I was contemplating how to answer when the doorbell rang.

"We could ignore it," Mason said in a playful voice, clearly having no idea I was unhappy with what he'd said. But the words were barely out of his mouth when the chimes sounded again, so Mason got off the chair and onto the scooter, and I trailed behind as we went to the front door. "I hope it's a Girl Scout selling cookies. We can buy some and get rid of them in a hurry." He opened the door, but there were no cookies or girls in green uniforms, just Jaimee's ex.

"Todd, if you're looking for Jaimee, she's not here," Mason said.

"I know. I thought you might be able to help," Todd said. Mason hesitated, then sighed and told Todd to come in.

Mason leaned toward me and spoke under his breath. "Anything to get them back together and get her out of here."

Todd seemed really upset as Mason took him in the den. The two men sat down, and I wasn't sure what I should do, so I basically hovered at the back of the room and tried to pretend I was looking at the pool.

"I took your advice and tried to woo her, and it's not working. She won't even pick up my calls. Has she met someone else?"

Mason shook his head and chuckled to himself. "It's really weird for me to be trying to help you mend fences with my ex. I have to ask—why? You're a young guy, an athlete. There must be other women you give tennis lessons to who would love to be your—" Mason hesitated, and I knew he was trying to find the right term. "Uh, your girlfriend," he said finally. "Why Jaimee?"

Todd took a moment. "Everybody has different turn-ons. For me it's a woman a few years older than me. Jaimee and I had something special. You should see the rackets she had made for me." He glanced around the room. "She didn't bring my stuff here, did she?"

"I think she said she put everything in storage while her house is being redone," Mason said. Todd hung his head, and when I saw his profile, I had a feeling of déjà vu. He must have held his head that way last time he was there.

I thought Mason was going to choke when Todd started going on about how sharp and clever Jaimee was and how much he missed her.

"She felt neglected by you," Mason said. "She told me you had something else going on." The way Mason said it, it was clear that he thought the *something else* was another girlfriend, one probably richer and younger than Jaimee.

"Is that what Jaimee thinks?" Todd asked, clearly getting Mason's implication. "I don't know what to do to convince her that she's wrong."

I had been staying in the background, but I wanted them to get back together, and the sooner, the better, so I jumped in. "Maybe I can help you. Give you a woman's perspective. I heard what Jaimee said, and I think she was the most hurt that you didn't invite her to stay with you while her house was fixed up."

"I just have a small place," he explained.

"Just call it cozy," I suggested. "If you want her back, that's what you need to do." He seemed to be mulling it over.

"If that's what it takes," Todd said. "I'll do it, but don't say anything to her. I want it to be a surprise."

"Don't worry. I wouldn't do anything to mess it up. So, then, the problem is solved," Mason said, easing himself back onto the scooter to show Todd to the door. Jaimee's boy toy seemed more optimistic as he followed Mason.

When Mason returned, we tried to enjoy the rest of the evening, but the mood never really bounced back after Todd left. The worst part was that after Mason's comments about me investigating, I couldn't even discuss what I'd found out.

The greeting committee was waiting when I got home, so I took care of all their needs then made myself a cup of rose tea and sat down at my kitchen table. I had a lot on my mind as I stared out at the dark yard. It was one of those times when I really wanted to talk to someone. Dinah must have been having the same sort of feeling, because a moment later she called and invited herself over.

She was knocking at my back door just as I finished putting together a mug for her. She dropped her coat in the kitchen, and the scent of roses surrounded us as we took our drinks into the living room. Dinah was already unloading before we even sat down on the couches.

"After listening to Adele talking about wedding dresses, bouquets, fancy manicures . . ." Dinah looked at me. "I'm leaning toward saying 'no' again. I don't know if I'm up for all that fuss."

"No one is saying you have to make the same big deal out of it that Adele is. I'm sure Commander would be fine if you didn't have flowers on your nails." I chuckled at the idea of my friend having an elaborate manicure, since I'd never seen her wear any polish. But the mention of manicures made me think of what had happened after we'd left the nail salon earlier that day.

I told her about my trip to the bank and following Evan Willis afterward. "He got away before I could see exactly where he went, but I'm sure he went in the back door of the nail salon."

Dinah set her mug on the coffee table. "Well, I can see why they might be keeping it quiet. From everything you've told me about his wife and how she thinks she's one step above everybody . . . well, owning a nail salon doesn't quite go with that image, even if Emily did tell me the other day after class that there are three of them."

"But that's not really the issue," I said. "Twice I've seen him at the bank depositing a lot of cash. A whole bag of cash."

"I hear you," Dinah said. "And we know the nail salon doesn't seem to be open much. Even when they are, they don't have much business." She stopped to think for a moment. "So when Emily said the owner had been in there getting his nails done, it must have been Evan." Dinah started to say something, but she stopped herself. "Oops—can't say anything bad about men getting their nails done. Commander gets manicures. Though no polish," she added quickly.

"So what do bags of cash for a business that doesn't seem to be doing well say to you?"

"He's got money coming from somewhere else and he wants it to look like it's coming from the nail salon." Dinah picked up the cup and put it down again. "And it's a pretty sure bet that it isn't something legal."

"Exactly," I said. "And Delaney handled most of the transactions. Everybody I talked to said she took the friendliness a little too far. Suppose she started to ask questions and figured out the same thing that we just did." I backtracked to the note on Tony's business card. "I didn't realize it at first, but that note wasn't about a rendezvous with Tony; it was for the

Willises' party. The teller I talked to confirmed that Delaney had said she was invited to a party."

Dinah had forgotten all about her wedding worries and was caught up in our Sherlock Holmes game. I was pretty caught up in it myself. "Here's what I think happened," I said. "Delaney went to the party and was given a drink with something in it. When she got all woozy, somebody took her to CeeCee's guest apartment. I remember now that there was some dirt on the front of her shoes, as if she'd been 'helped' through the back part of the yard and her feet had dragged. The somebody could have turned on the heat and then stuffed something in the vent after they left."

There was something rattling in my brain that wouldn't quite come together. "The vest," I said loudly. "It was wool. Babs's daughter-in-law said somebody at the party had a reaction to wool. She said something about how if people were allergic to wool they ought to know better than to put their arms around it. If somebody was helping a half-passed-out Delaney, they would have had their arms all over that vest." I was on a roll now.

"And remember at the nail salon, when Adele asked about the lambskin pad? The manicurist said it was fake because the customer she'd just had, which Emily told us was the owner, was allergic to wool.

"It's Evan, I'm sure." I had remembered something else. "Kelsey returned that cream because she said it had lanolin in it. Lanolin comes from sheep, and if you're allergic to wool, you're allergic to lanolin as well."

Dinah was nodding along excitedly, and I felt sure we'd really made a breakthrough. Now, what to do with that information?

CHAPTER 28

It was chilly the next morning, so I put on a multicolored wool infinity scarf and wound it around a few times as I got ready for work. I was still thinking about what to do with what I had figured out. Dinah had suggested I call Barry and tell him about Evan Willis and the bags of cash and how I thought it was connected to Delaney Tanner's death. But I had two concerns. When I went over it all in my head again, I thought it might sound a little crazy, and also like I was just trying to get the heat off Tony. And I thought Barry might take it all as just an excuse to call him. No—before I told him anything, I had to be sure.

I thought I had put it all on the back burner of my mind, but as I started to drive to the bookstore, I felt a sudden desire to take a detour. I turned in the opposite direction and drove to the street behind CeeCee's property. I pulled to the curb and looked at the wall of greenery along the back of her place. I could tell by the dip in the curb where the gate was, which was almost directly across from the Willises' house, though that didn't really prove anything, especially since Babs had found out that the gate was common knowledge.

As I was staring at the fence, I saw the gate across the driveway opening as a car waited to pull out. Inside the yard, Evan, dressed in shorts and a T-shirt, was crossing toward the house, bouncing a small ball.

I didn't stop to think but rather just seized the moment and rushed across the street. The car pulled out and cleared the driveway, and I slipped in just before the gate shut.

A voice in my head screamed, *What are you doing? Get out of there while you can!* But I couldn't stop now, though I did pause to compose a text message to Barry, just in case I got in over my head. It had happened before. But my tote bag swung forward, and I must have hit the phone, because the partial message seemed to have disappeared. There was no time to fuss with my phone to find it. Besides, I had just come up with a plan.

I got to the front door and was going to knock, but it pushed open easily when I touched it. "Yoo-hoo," I called as I went in. I added a few more *hellos* but got no response. Nobody was in the living room, and the soft soles of my shoes didn't make a sound on the terra-cotta pavers in the hallway. As I got closer to the kitchen, I heard water splashing.

I called out another *yoo-hoo* as I went into the room and put on a friendly smile. Evan was standing at the sink—the noise of the running water must have covered up my greeting. He jumped when he saw me.

"What are you doing here?" he demanded.

"Oh, I'm sorry if I scared you," I said in a breezy voice.

"The gate was open and I wanted to show something to Kelsey. It's about the baby shower." I held up the tote bag.

"She's not here," he said, coming across the kitchen in an obvious attempt to guide me out of there.

"Well, then, you can help me," I said. I barely stopped to breathe, continuing to talk, doing my best impression of Babs. "You must be in shock about Tony being arrested for Delaney Tanner's murder. I know you said you didn't know who she was, but I'm sure by now you realize she was the teller at the bank. And of course you know about the back gate at CeeCee's."

He had been nodding noncommittally as I went on, but he finally interrupted. "Until the other night, I didn't know anything about that gate. How about you just get to the reason why you're here?" He sounded annoyed.

"I know you own the nail salon," I said. His face registered surprise and displeasure.

"It's nail salons, plural," he said with an edge. "What's your point? That it doesn't have the same prestige of my former job?" he asked. He was clearly getting impatient and irritated—not a good combination in a possible murderer. "I'm busy now. Why don't you come back when Kelsey is here?"

"I know more than that," I said. "I know what really happened to Delaney Tanner."

Evan didn't lose an ounce of his calm. "And so do the cops. They arrested Tony Bonnard."

He had taken my arm and was walking me to the door. I only had moments left to get any evidence against him. "Okay, then," I said, stopping. "The real reason I came here was to show Kelsey a sample of this." I reached in my bag, feeling around for a project. "I wanted to make sure she thought it was soft enough." All I came up with was the cowl

I was making for Samuel. Bamboo yarn wouldn't do any good. I needed wool. We were almost to the door when I remembered my scarf. I grabbed the longer loop of it and rubbed it against his cheek. "It's one hundred percent wool," I said. I took a step back and waited for the fireworks to start.

CHAPTER 29

"NOTHING HAPPENED?" DINAH SAID INCREDU-lously. "Maybe it takes a few minutes for the allergy to kick in?"

"I don't think so. I made it clear it was wool, and he didn't say anything like, 'Get that off me.' Well, he did say something to that effect, but it wasn't because of the wool. He seemed to think I was coming on to him." I rocked my head, reliving the embarrassment as Dinah tried not to laugh. We were seated in the café at the bookstore. I'd called Dinah as soon as I'd gotten to work. Her house was barely a block away, so she'd come right over and bought me a red eye so I could drown my sorrows in caffeine. I took a long drag on the drink. "How could I have been so wrong? He wasn't allergic to wool. And he just seemed impatient when I brought up the idea that I knew stuff about Delaney's death."

We sat, brooding over our coffee for a few minutes. "All I can say is, I'm sure glad I didn't go running to Barry pointing an accusing finger at Evan. Or send that text message."

Dinah leaned across the table and gave me a consoling pat. "And I'm glad you didn't listen to me when I suggested it." She hesitated. "I really hate to say this, but what if the cops have it right this time? Maybe Tony invited Delaney to meet him at the party. It sounded like there were a lot of people, so she might not have been noticed by the hosts. Didn't they tent part of the yard?" Dinah picked up the end of her scarf and waved it around. "Maybe we should do the wool test on Tony."

I shook my head at the suggestion. "It's complicated. Mason told me not to investigate, and I'm certainly not supposed to do anything that involves his client."

"And you're going to listen?" Dinah asked.

"I don't know." I was about to explain my dilemma with Mason when Mrs. Shedd came into the café and interrupted.

"There you are," my boss said. "We need to talk." She had that sound in her voice that made it clear we weren't going to be talking about anything good.

Dinah gave my arm a reassuring pat. "I'm sure you can handle it whatever it is. And now I have a class to teach." Her chair scraped the floor as she got up. I followed Mrs. Shedd into the bookstore. When she led me to her office, I knew it was really trouble.

"Sit," she said, indicating a chair. "Molly, we are days away from starting Yarn University, and I just found out that Sheila is having a problem. I heard she couldn't even make it through a practice class!"

I saw her point. The office was filled with boxes of Yarn U T-shirts, tote bags and knitting and crochet tools. "I'm afraid you've gotten distracted with this latest murder business."

"I was the one to find the body," I said.

"Okay, but that doesn't mean you have to find the killer. Besides, the police already arrested Tony Bonnard. Just let it go and do something to solve the Sheila problem."

It was clear she was finished, so I got up and went back to the yarn department.

It was one of those moments when everything seemed to be caving in. I'd been wrong about Evan, I wasn't happy with what Mason had said about me investigating, and what Mrs. Shedd said about Sheila was true. Maybe I could at least do something about the last one.

I marched over to Luxe and walked in as Sheila was handing a customer her package. I waited until the customer had left the store before reading Sheila the riot act. "I know you said you didn't want to do a practice class, but you absolutely have to," I insisted. Sheila didn't seem happy with the idea but agreed to come to the bookstore during her lunch break.

Then I marched back to the bookstore and called Adele out. "I know you told Mrs. Shedd about Sheila," I said.

"I didn't mean to. I was trying to help by telling Mrs. Shedd that if anything went wrong I could step in," Adele said. I shook my head. Adele couldn't help being Adele. I told her about the practice class.

"Just be there," I said.

I agreed with Mrs. Shedd that Yarn University should be my first concern, but I couldn't help thinking about who killed Delaney Tanner. I still couldn't believe I could have been so wrong about Evan. All the pieces seemed to fit. I pulled out my cell phone. I knew Dinah was teaching a class, so I sent her a text asking her to get more details from her student about the owner of the nail salon and his manicure.

I didn't care what Mason said to do or not do. I had to be true to myself. I called CeeCee, prepared to ask her straight out if Tony was allergic to wool and if he'd had a rash recently. But I got her voice mail. I left a message asking her to call me back.

I felt better now that I had taken steps to deal with

everything. But the good feeling was short-lived, as I saw Jaimee and Todd come into the bookstore a few minutes later. I had the feeling they were going to be trouble. Jaimee was dressed in her usual expensive-casual look, and Todd was in tennis clothes. Seeing him from a distance reminded me of something, but I couldn't sort out what. Mrs. Shedd went over to them, and the next thing I knew, Jaimee was pointing in my direction. Todd held on to her hand and then reluctantly let it go, before he turned to leave. Did that mean they were back together?

Jaimee had a big smile when she reached me in the yarn department. I almost fell over when she hugged me.

"I understand you're the one who explained to Todd why I was upset. I am a little surprised, though. I thought I'd made it really clear to him what the problem was, but I guess he didn't get it." She stopped for a breath. "He's invited me to stay with him until the house is done. Then, who knows?" She seemed as giddy as a teenager. I waited for what was to come next—I didn't really believe she had just come here to share her news.

"Now I realize how petty it was to keep Todd's things, but I was so angry. Anyway, I want to get everything back to him." She looked around, as if she was worried he was still there. "I don't want him to know that I lied to him when I told him everything was in a storage unit, when it was really at my place. Brooklyn is against us getting back together, so she won't help, but I want to get his things and surprise him. Todd dropped me off here. He thinks you and I are having lunch together. Could you give me a lift to my place and help me get the stuff? You can drop me off at Mason's." When I didn't say yes immediately, she went on. "I'm sure you want me out of the house so you and Mason can get cozy."

She definitely hit a nerve with that comment, so I agreed

to take her during my lunch break. Sheila was coming into
the bookstore as we were walking out, and she seemed
relieved when I said I'd have to postpone her practice class.

JAIMEE COULDN'T MAKE ENOUGH COMMENTS ABOUT
the greenmobile and all the modern amenities it was missing. "I'm surprised it has seat belts," she said, putting hers
on. I started to react to her comment, but she claimed she
was just joking, which I doubted since she seemed to have
no sense of humor.

She directed me through Encino and then up into the
hills to Mulholland Drive. My phone made a few noises to
announce something, but I ignored it. We had a mesmerizing
view of the Valley below us as the road curved around, until
she had me turn off into a small development of luxury
homes—really just a long street that ended in a cul-de-sac.
They were all similar but had slightly different designs done
in off-white stucco with terra-cotta tile roofs. It seemed very
quiet, like nobody was home in any of the houses. There
were a few cars parked on the street and in some of the
driveways. Jaimee pointed out hers, and I pulled in.

There was a Dumpster out front, but it appeared the
workers were gone for the day. I expected the inside of her
place to be stripped down, but as we passed the living room,
it looked intact. "I thought you were redoing your house," I
said. What I didn't say was that it looked like she didn't
really have to move out.

"I'm redoing the den," Jaimee said, pointing out the next
room we passed. It had been emptied, and the flooring had
been stripped down to the concrete. A workbench with a
saw and other tools was in the middle of the room. I noticed
a stack of lumber and some cinder blocks. The room seemed

dimly lit, even with the French doors leading outside. Then I saw that the patio outside was covered, which cut down on the light that made it inside.

I followed her to one of the bedrooms. She folded back the closet door, and I saw an array of men's clothes hanging from the rack and a stack of blue gym bags on the ground. She seemed surprised by the amount of stuff. "Maybe we'll just take some of it now."

I was really trying to be better about my cell phone. Remembering that it had chirped with the sound for messages, I pulled it out and looked at the screen, but it said "No service." Jaimee noticed what I was doing. "Cell service is spotty up here. You might have to drive around the cul-de-sac. Just keep an eye on the screen until you see that you've got service and stop there," she said. I guess I gave her a look, because she told me they were putting in a tower nearby that was going to assure consistent service. Of course, that was no help to me now.

I got in the car and backed out of the driveway and then started toward the dead end of the street, going about five miles an hour. I reached the end and came back around and still, no service. I turned around where the street fed into Mulholland and tried again. I finally had to drive out onto Mulholland before the phone would work. I checked through the phone and saw that I'd received a text.

"What?" I gasped as I read it over. Dinah had gotten some information from her student Emily that absolutely changed everything.

I quickly drove back and went into the house to get Jaimee. When I passed the den, I saw that she had moved some of the gym bags in there. I went to have a look at them. The first couple held tennis balls and rackets, but the next one was full of cash. There were bundles of singles and five-dollar bills. And then I heard voices. *This is not good*, I thought. I couldn't tell where the voices were coming from, so I grabbed the first hiding spot I could find. It wasn't very original, but the closet seemed like it would work. The door had louvered slats, and I could see into the room, but I was pretty sure I couldn't be seen. I tried my phone again, but it still had no service.

"Yes, I followed you, sweetie," Todd said. "I knew it would be too much for you to manage. I'll just take all the gym bags. You can bring my clothes if you want."

"Bring them where?" Jaimee said.

"Just take them back to your ex's. I'll come by later or call you." He grabbed three gym bags and started to walk toward the front door. *Let him go, let him go*, I thought, hoping Jaimee would pick up on my mental telepathy.

"Wait a second," Jaimee said. "Was this all just a plan for you to get your stuff back?"

"No, honey. Like I said, you take the clothes, and we'll meet up tonight."

Jaimee went for one of the gym bags. "No way. *You* take the clothes, and I'll take the gym bags." She unzipped the one she'd grabbed and then squealed. I couldn't see what she was seeing, but it seemed like a safe bet it was filled with cash, like the bag I'd seen.

"I don't understand," Jaimee said. "What are you doing with bags full of money?"

Todd grabbed the bag from Jaimee's hand and swore under his breath. "I was a dead man if I didn't find these," he said. "You don't cross Mr. X."

"Who? Where did the money come from?" Jaimee asked. Apparently she hadn't paid any attention to the TV show that Mason had on incessantly.

Todd looked like he was going to ignore what she said, but

then he seemed to have a need to explain. "One of my clients asked me to do him a favor. He had a lot of cash from something. He asked me to deposit the money in my account, then transfer it to an offshore account he had. He offered to pay me a percentage for doing it. It was easy money, so how could I turn it down? Then he asked me to do it again, and again after that. All I had to do was go to the bank a lot. As long as the deposits were small, nobody asked any questions. At least that's how it was supposed to be. I was ready with an answer just in case—I gave clients a discount if they paid me in cash for lessons. I was a victim of my own success, and pretty soon I was accumulating bags of cash faster than I could deposit them. I started bringing some of them here."

"Okay," Jaimee said. "Just do what you have to with these bags of money and then tell him you quit." She went to hug him. "We'll work this out together." I watched in horror as he turned her sign of affection into an opportunity to grab her.

"There is no quitting. I made a deal with the devil. When I tried to tell him it was more than I could handle, he just told me to get help." Todd zipped up the bag and added it back to the stack. "Why couldn't you have just made this easy and let me leave with the bags without interfering?"

"You should have told me there was a problem," Jaimee said. "I can help you."

She couldn't see it, but Todd rolled his eyes and gave her an angry look. "You really don't understand, do you?"

"I can help you make the deposits," she said. "We can work this all out together." Her tone was cajoling. I had no idea what she was thinking. Did she really mean she wanted to help him, or did she realize she was in danger and was trying to act like she was on his side so he would let her go?

"I have help. When that woman at the bank started asking all those questions and commenting on how odd it was that all my tennis students paid in cash and in small bills, I got a partner. I thought it would shut her up when I told her I was a partner in some nail salons, too, and was making deposits for them. But she only talked more. Evan said to ignore her like he did, but when she joked more than once that it was almost like I was laundering money, I knew I had to get rid of her."

"What do you mean get rid of her?" Jaimee squealed.

His demeanor and voice changed, and it almost seemed that he was talking to himself. "It turned out to be very easy. Delaney was flattered when I invited her to the party. She didn't have a clue that I'd doctored her drink. And then I took her into the Collins place through the back gate. I arranged her on the floor and turned the heat on full blast. On the way out I stuffed up the vent."

"Todd, honey, it doesn't matter what you did. None of it matters. We could take the money and go buy some plane tickets. I hear Switzerland is nice this time of year." There was no doubt that Jaimee understood she was in real danger now. No matter how cajoling she tried to sound, the high-pitched squeaky sound of her voice gave away her panic.

"That won't work," he said in a cold voice. He was looking around the den now. "This room looks like an accident waiting to happen. That's what Mason's girlfriend will think if she comes back to pick you up." Jaimee tried to pull away, but Todd was much stronger, and he punched her in the gut. She bent over in pain, and he took the opportunity to grab her hands and tie them together with an electric cord. He looked around the room, clearly considering his options. Then he saw the cinder blocks.

"Wouldn't it be terrible if you tripped and hit your head?" he said. The calm tone of his voice made his words even scarier. He grabbed the back of her shirt and pulled her around like she was a rag doll as he tried to decide the best way to smash her head. Jaimee kept struggling, trying to pull free, but Todd held her tighter and smacked her face.

Jaimee looked around with a dazed, helpless expression. I had to do something fast. All I had to work with was a phone with no service and a purse with no weapons. What was I going to do? And then, suddenly, I had a plan.

Todd had his back to the door, and I could see that all his attention was on what he was doing, and not what else was going on in the room. I also had the advantage that the room was pretty dimly lit and he thought they were alone. I got on the ground and opened the door without making a noise. I crawled toward Todd as I unfolded my secret weapon—I'd remembered that the killer had an Achilles' heel. I held my breath as I got close to him. For a moment, I was afraid he was going to step on me, but luckily, Jaimee was squirming, which kept his attention while I carefully slid the purple wool scarf across his tennis shoes.

"Let's get this over with," he said, positioning her so that several cinder blocks were right in front of her. He was about to give her shoulder a shove when I pulled hard on the purple scarf. It jumped off the top of his tennis shoes and wound around his bare legs. I pulled the scarf from behind so it moved back and forth against his skin and he yelped in surprise and discomfort. It must have burned and itched at the same time. He let go of Jaimee and bent forward to pull at the scarf and scratch the rash that was already starting to form, but leverage was on my side, and I gave him a shove from the back. He went forward and hit his head on the cinder blocks. He collapsed to the floor. I rushed to untie Jaimee, who had started crying.

"I thought you left me here!"

"We need to get out of here," I said. I grabbed her hand. But as we turned I saw a blond woman holding a small blue handgun pointed at us. I recognized the tattoo on her finger.

"I told you, you should have taken the gun," she said to Todd, who was trying to sit up.

My mouth fell open in surprise as it sunk in who she was. "Pia Sawyer!" I exclaimed.

"Who?" Jaimee said. "This is who you were cheating on me with?" she yelled at Todd.

"Shut up," Pia said to her. "Should I just shoot them?" she asked Todd. He was using his polo shirt to sop up the blood from his head while still frantically trying to pull the scarf loose and scratch his legs at the same time. He seemed a little out of it, but he glared at me. "Yes."

Pia seemed to realize she couldn't shoot us both at the same time and moved the gun back and forth. "Who should I do first?" she asked Todd.

He glared at me again, reaching down to give the rash another scratch. "Do her first. And do it so she dies slow."

My mouth had gone dry, and my knees felt suddenly wobbly. Was this going to be it for me? Shot by some former PTA mom? "You know, there could be another way," I said, trying to stall.

"Don't listen to her," Todd yelled. "Go on, shoot her."

Suddenly, loud noise sounded at the glass doors that led outside. We all turned at once, and it seemed like nothing was there. Then there was another loud noise, and I thought I saw something hitting the French door.

"Ignore it," Todd yelled. "Pull the damn trigger."

I closed my eyes and cringed, waiting for the end. I felt something push me, and the gun went off and then— darkness.

CHAPTER 30

I COULDN'T SEE ANYTHING, BUT SOMETHING WAS on top of me. Or was it someone? Suddenly, I was being helped into a sitting position and there was light. "Barry?" I said, looking at the figure next to me on the ground. "Is this a dream?"

His cop face cracked, and he smiled. "More like a nightmare. I'm sorry if I hurt you."

I was completely confused. "I saw the gun aimed at you, and I pushed you out of the way," he said. "And landed on top of you." He stood and held out his hand to help me up. "We're both lucky she isn't much of a shot." He pointed toward the ceiling, where a bullet was lodged. He kept his voice light, but I got the point—he'd thrown himself on top of me to protect me.

"I'm okay," I said, though really I was a little shaky on my feet. "This is nothing compared to the pain and suffering Todd was hoping for." I managed a weak smile. Looking around for the first time since the gun went off, I noticed that there were a couple of other cops in the room. Pia was in handcuffs. Todd was still on the floor, handcuffed as well and loudly demanding that someone cut the scarf off his legs. For her part, Jaimee was having a total meltdown. I was in better shape than she was, so I went to try and comfort her.

"It's all over. You're safe now," I said, putting my hands on her shoulders. "You're okay." She had bruises on her face from Todd's smack, so when the paramedics arrived, I waved one of them over and got an ice pack for her face.

I was functioning on the outside, but inside I was in a total daze and operated solely on nerve as I answered a bunch of questions about Todd, Pia and the bags of money. Eventually, Thursday came and got her mother, saying she'd take her to a doctor to be checked out, and Barry drove me and my car home.

Everything was getting a little clearer now, so I asked the obvious question.

"How did you happen to show up?" I said as he pulled into my driveway. A police officer driving Barry's Crown Vic pulled in behind us. He got out and brought Barry the keys, then walked to the cruiser that had pulled up to the curb.

"We got a call about an old, oddly colored Mercedes that seemed suspicious. It was driving slowly, like it was casing houses."

"Or looking for cell service," I said.

"Yeah, well . . ." He blew out his breath like whatever was coming was uncomfortable. "The caller gave the dispatcher the license plate number, and they ran it." He shut off the engine and pulled out the key. "There was a note saying I was to be notified anytime there was a call about your car. I guess I forgot to remove it when we broke up." He handed me the keys and opened the door to get out. "I might have ignored it, but I got a weird text message from you. All it said was, *Need you*."

"Oh," I said. It was my turn to be uncomfortable. Somehow the text I had started to write at the Willises' had gotten sent in my fussing with the phone. It was supposed to have said, *Need your help with suspect*. I quickly changed the subject. "And then what happened?"

"Some uniforms and I responded to the call, and we had a look in the windows and saw what was going on. I didn't want to wait for a SWAT unit to show up, so I did it the old-fashioned way—I distracted them by throwing pebbles against the window."

"Thank you," I said. The reality of everything had finally sunk in, and my eyes filled with water.

"Just doing my job," he said, trying to keep his tone professional. "You look a little shaky. Let me walk you inside." He put his arm around me for support, and I leaned into it gratefully.

ONCE THEY PATCHED UP TODD, HE WAS TAKEN TO jail and charged with first-degree murder, money laundering, fraud, tax evasion and trespassing. It turned out that he was the only one who knew about the gate at CeeCee's—Babs admitted to me that it was Todd who had told her it was common knowledge when he'd come to give her grandkids their tennis lesson, and she'd accepted it as true. He'd found it by accident when he was giving lessons to Evan and Kelsey—so many tennis balls were ending up in CeeCee's yard that he looked to see if there was a way in and had found the gate. He found the guest apartment when a tennis ball landed on the top of the stairway and the door was open.

Dinah was the only one to acknowledge it, but if it hadn't

been for me, the coroner might have left Delaney's death as inconclusive. It was because I found the gate that the cops looked around the area behind the garage and found Delaney's purse with the business card.

The mystery of what had happened to the box of old vent pieces was solved when they found it at Todd's place—the cops had seen the twigs and leaves in the vent and left it at that. It turned out that Todd had stuffed some tennis balls in first, and they happened to have his name on them. They were still in the box with the old vent parts.

But there was one thing Todd would not give up—the identity of Mr. X. He claimed it would mean instant death for him. All I could figure was that he lived in the area and liked tennis.

They wanted to charge Pia with attempted murder and a bunch of other stuff, but she thought if she talked she could make a deal. Barry actually let me watch them question her. Well, on a TV screen with not the best reception. She admitted that she and Todd had been in a relationship for over six months and she'd known from the start about the money laundering. Apparently, she'd watched one too many cable shows and had gone a little crazy with the idea of being outside the law. Pia had introduced the idea of Todd and the Willises working together. After Evan lost his job, the couple had invested in some nail salons, but by the time they opened the one near the bookstore, they'd realized they didn't know what they were doing and needed money. They already knew Todd, because he had helped both Kelsey and Evan improve their backhands. They were fine with using the nail salons as a front. Evan made the deposits and wired the money but convinced himself that it was just a temporary measure. Kelsey was simply happy to have her old lifestyle back.

Pia insisted that she knew nothing about Delaney's death.

She and Todd had gone to the Willises' party together but then gone their separate ways at the event. She confirmed that the Willises knew nothing about Delaney Tanner's death and really had believed that Tony Bonnard had done it. Because she gave up so much information, the D.A. knocked out Pia's conspiracy charge, but still charged her with attempted murder and accessory to money laundering. They should have added one for bad judgment, in my opinion.

Kelsey and Evan Willis were charged with fraud, money laundering and tax evasion. Both of them were facing prison time. But before they even went to trial, they had both started writing books, and I heard Evan was shopping the idea of their story for a TV show.

I had gotten justice for Delaney, but I still lamented the fact that if she hadn't talked so much, she might be alive today.

CeeCee couldn't stop thanking me for the fact that Tony was out from under the cloud of suspicion. She invited Elise, Rhoda, Adele, Eduardo, Sheila, Dinah and me over to celebrate the next day. I convinced her to include Babs, too. The afternoon had the softness of spring, and we sat on the tree-surrounded patio between the house and garage. As it got a little later, CeeCee turned on the heat lamps and the string of lights, illuminating the whole area in a festive way.

Dinah and I had pulled our chairs close together. "I'm sorry I wasn't there with you yesterday when everything hit the fan. It's just lucky that Barry showed up when he did." She squeezed my hand. "I don't know what I would do without you." I was glad when she didn't go into the details of what he'd done. I was still having trouble processing the idea that Barry had been willing to take a bullet for me.

"It was your text that tipped me off," I said. "When you told me how your student described the nail salon owner who'd gotten the manicure as some kind of tennis pro, I thought about Todd. Then all the pieces fell into place. The figure I'd seen at the bank in the rain gear who made the cash deposit looked familiar because it was Todd. And remember the guy we saw at the café with the rash? I realized that was Todd, too."

Dinah considered what I'd said for a moment. "Right, that was the day you found Delaney. The rash was from her vest when he 'helped' her get to CeeCee's."

Tony made a beeline for us. He looked at me with his most charming smile. "Good work, Molly. And thank you."

"I hope you got an apology from the cops," Dinah said.

"I did, but I don't care. It was worth the hassle. I got so much publicity for the web show from getting arrested that I have people lining up to invest in it. A major distributor wants to release it. Life is good." He moved off to take a call on his cell phone.

"I still don't know how my yarn ended up in Delaney's vest," I said. Rosa came outside with a tray of drinks.

"Last I heard you'd tracked it to CeeCee, who claimed she'd given it to Rosa. Ask her," Dinah suggested. A few moments later, the housekeeper reached us. We passed on the drinks, but I brought up the yarn. Rosa seemed to be drawing a blank, then she remembered. "Miss CeeCee was right. I tried to use it, but the yarn won in the fight between us."

"What happened to it?"

"She saw me trying to knit with it and suggested I try some other needles." Rosa threw up her free hand. "Life is too short, so I gave it to her."

"Who is 'she'?" I asked.

Rosa pointed, and Dinah and I said in unison, "Rhoda?"

I was determined to get to the bottom of this once and for all, so we walked right over to where Rhoda was sitting. I brought up the yarn, and Rhoda seemed upset.

"Why didn't you tell me you had the yarn?" I asked.

"I didn't want to be connected with the dead woman. Next thing you know I'd be a suspect. Besides, you asked who took it in the yarn exchange." Rhoda seemed obstinate.

I had a sudden memory of her quickly putting away some felted items right after I'd brought up the yarn. "That's why you put away that pouch purse so quickly. Not that I could recognize the yarn once it had been felted. So did you make the vest Delaney was wearing?"

Rhoda nodded. "I know what's coming next. How is it Delaney Tanner had it?" Rhoda seemed to come undone. "I didn't want to tell anyone, but my daughter is getting a divorce. She moved back home with no job and two kids. Plus, Hal got laid off. So, I started selling things I made to bring in some extra money. I was too embarrassed to say anything after making such a point that I gave away the things I made. When I set up a business account at the Bank of Tarzana, I dealt with Delaney. I showed her the vest I'd made as an example of my work, and she bought it."

"Rhoda, you don't have to keep anything from us. We're family, remember?" Rhoda answered with a slow nod.

"It's a relief to have everything out in the open," she said.

We were distracted from Rhoda when we saw Adele coming toward us, clutching onto Eric, who was in his motor officer uniform. They whispered to each other for a moment, then Eric broke away.

"I have an announcement," he said. Everyone stopped talking and listened. "I want you all to know that I was not trying to back out of our wedding by not agreeing to a date and place. There's something I have to run past Adele first."

He turned to his intended. "Cutchykins, my mother gave up her place in San Diego, and she's moved in with me. That means she will be living with us."

Poor Adele. She looked like she didn't know whether to laugh or cry. But in the end, she just said, "Okay."

We all offered our congratulations, and I turned back to Dinah. "What about you?" I asked. "Any more thoughts on your wedding plans?"

"Actually, yes," my friend said. She took a deep breath and began to talk. "I figured out the problem. This is so lame, but I think I'm addicted to difficult men. You know, the ups, the downs, the breakups, the makeups. But with Commander, it's more like a straight line."

"You mean, as in dull?" I asked.

"Yes, but in a nice way," she said.

"So, what are you going to do?"

"What I should have done in the first place," she said. "Tell him the truth about why I'm still thinking about it."

"Poor guy gets in trouble for being too nice," I said.

Sheila had just arrived and was saying hello to everyone. She stopped next to us, but before I could suggest that it was a perfect time for her to do a practice class, she shook her head.

"No, Molly, no more practice classes," Sheila said firmly. "I am not doing another practice class, ever."

I started to argue my case, but she interrupted.

"Don't you get it?" Sheila said, seeming more in command of herself than I was used to. "I dealt with a dead woman at CeeCee's and cops rushing in to arrest Tony. If I could get through that, I can do anything. A class of people who are just there to crochet will be a snap."

I think I believed her.

The get-together ended with us all talking about Yarn University and planning to meet at our regular spot the next day at Happy Hour. After, Dinah went home and I headed to Mason's. I used my key to let myself in and was surprised to see that he was waiting for me with a huge smile. His knee was resting on the scooter, but he quickly lifted it and set his foot on the ground. I was staring, with my mouth wide open. "When did this happen?"

"This afternoon. The doctor gave me the all clear on everything. Walking, driving, dancing." He did a little cha-cha. "I can go back to work!" Brooklyn walked into the hall from the wing of bedrooms. I expected her usual scowl, but she gave me a one-armed hug.

"Thanks for saving my mother," she said before heading to the kitchen.

This was the first time I'd seen Mason since the episode with Todd. We'd talked on the phone briefly, but I could tell that he was overwhelmed dealing with his daughters and Jaimee. The truth was, I was more used to dealing with that kind of chaos and I recovered faster.

When Barry had brought me home after the incident at Jaimee's house, we'd sat drinking peppery chai tea until he was satisfied that I was okay. When he got up to go, I'd walked him to the door.

"Thank you for everything," I'd said as we stood in the entrance hall. At that moment, Samuel came in the front door with his suitcase and locked gazes with Barry.

"What's going on?" my son asked.

"Your mother will tell you all about it. She had quite a day." Just before he went out the door, Barry had turned back. "I'm glad I could be there for you."

I didn't bring up anything about Barry to Mason now, but I did mention that my mother's tour had ended and my son Samuel was home, so at last I'd have some help with the animals.

Mason walked over and put his arms around me. "I am

so glad you're all right. Even when you try to stay out of things, you end up in the middle of them."

"About that," I said. "You need to know that I didn't take your suggestion to stay out of the investigation. I understand where your head is. You're just about getting your client off." I paused for a moment, knowing he probably wasn't going to like what I was about to say. "And I am all about getting the bad guy caught, no matter who he is."

Mason grinned. "I think we're going to have some interesting conversations in our future. Speaking of which, I have something to tell you." He leaned close and then looked to make sure no one was in earshot. "I found out why Brooklyn left San Diego in such a hurry to take care of me. Her life fell apart when she lost both her job and her boyfriend within a week. The good news is, she has a new plan. She liked working with me for those couple of days that Tony was a client, and she's decided to go to law school here," he said. I nodded in acknowledgment.

"I don't think you understand," Mason said. "She wants to go to school here in the Valley and stay here with me."

"Oh," I said.

"There's more," Mason said. He paused just like I had, and I had a feeling it was for the same reason. He knew I wasn't going to be happy with what he had to say. "Jaimee says she's a changed person after yesterday. She doesn't want to go back to that house, ever. The *Housewives* people were on the phone with her this morning, rolling out the red carpet for her to come back—they didn't even care when she said she wasn't going to be living on Mulholland Drive anymore. Jaimee had out-drama-ed them all."

"So, you're trying to tell me she's going to be staying here for the moment—or a lot of moments." Mason nodded and watched as my expression wilted.

"Ah, but I saved the best for last. They're here, but we can go somewhere else, for the weekend, anyway." He kicked his leg out and shook it to show he had full use. "I was thinking a villa at the Del Coronado hotel. It's the off-season, so we'll have the island to ourselves. We can walk on the beach and finally watch a sunset."

"That sounds great. It'll be the calm before the storm of Yarn University next week," I said. "When do we leave?"

Mason called Spike and grabbed his car keys. "How about right now? Before anything can happen to stop us."

Sheila's Hug

Easy to make

Supplies: 2 skeins Louisa Harding La Salute, dark blue,
79% kid mohair, 21% nylon (115 yds, 105
mtrs, 25 g)

1 skein Knit One Crochet Too Douceur et
Soie, dark blue, 70% baby mohair, 30%
silk (225 yd, 205 mtrs, 25 g)

1 skein Trendsetter Super Kid Seta, shade,
70% super kid mohair, 30% seta silk
(230 yds, 212 m, 25 g)

Crochet hook P-15/10.00 mm

Tapestry needle

Stitch markers (optional)

Gauge is not important to this project.

    Dimensions before sewn together are approximately 10
inches by 44 inches.

Note: Three strands of yarn are crocheted together throughout. It is easier to see the stitches on either end if they are marked with stitch markers.

Chain 21 using all three yarns.

Row 1: Single crochet in the 2nd chain from hook. Single crochet across. 20 stitches.

Row 2: Chain 1, turn. Single crochet across. 20 stitches.

Repeat Row 2 until piece is approximately 44 inches long, fasten off and weave in ends.

Finishing:

Lay flat and fold so that the A and B on the side match the A and B on the bottom. Use tapestry needle with all three strands of yarn to sew the matched A to B together. Weave in ends.

To wear, slip over head and arrange so point is in the middle.

Adele's Hug

Easy to make

Supplies   1 skein Lion Brand Homespun, Windsor,
bulky weight, 98% acrylic, 2% polyester
(185 yd, 169 m, 6 oz, 170 g)
Hook P-15/10.00 mm
Tapestry needle
Stitch markers (optional)

Gauge is not important to this project.
Dimensions before sewn together are
   approximately 10 inches by 44 inches.

Note: It is easier to see the stitches on either end if they are
marked with stitch markers.

Chain 23
   Row 1: Double crochet in 4th chain from hook (counts as
2 double crochets). Double crochet across. 21 stitches made.

Row 2: Chain 3 (counts as first double crochet). Double crochet across. 21 stitches.

Repeat Row 2 until the piece is approximately 44 inches long, fasten off and weave in the ends.

Finishing:

Lay flat and fold so that the A and B on the side match the A and B on the bottom. Use tapestry needle with yarn to sew the matched A to B together. Weave in ends.

To wear, slip over head and arrange so point is in the middle.

Vegetable Stew

Package of Lawry's Beef Stew Spices & Seasonings mix
2 tablespoons olive oil
12-ounce bag frozen pearl onions
½ cup sliced leeks
1 cup celery hearts, cut into 1-inch pieces
2 cups mushrooms, sliced
1 cup baby carrots
2 cups gold potatoes, cut in quarters
8 half cobs of corn
6 cups water
10-ounce bag frozen baby peas
Sour cream for garnish

In a large pot or Dutch oven, mix the seasoning mix, oil, onions, leeks, celery and mushrooms. Cook, stirring often, for approximately 10 minutes. Add the carrots, potatoes, corn and water. Bring to a boil then simmer for about 30 minutes or until the vegetables are tender. Turn off the heat and add the baby peas. Cover the pan and let sit for 10 minutes. Add a generous tablespoon of sour cream as garnish. Serves 8.

Molly's Delicious
Drop Biscuits

2 cups unbleached all-purpose flour
4 teaspoons non-aluminum baking powder
1 teaspoon salt
4 tablespoons butter
1 cup buttermilk

Sift the dry ingredients together. Work the butter into the flour mixture until crumbly using a pastry cutter, fingers or food processor. Make a well in center. Pour in buttermilk all at once. Stir until the flour is just moistened. Drop by spoonfuls into muffin tin. Preheat oven to 450 degrees and bake for approximately 10 minutes. Makes 12 biscuits.

Turn the page for a preview of
Betty Hechtman's next Yarn Retreat Mystery . . .

GONE WITH THE WOOL

Coming in July 2016
from Berkley Prime Crime

WHY HADN'T I REALIZED THIS PROBLEM BEFORE? The bright red tote bag with Yarn To Go emblazoned on the front fell over as I tried to cram in the long knitting loom for my upcoming yarn retreat. My selection of round looms rolled across the floor before falling flat on the floor. The other long looms scattered at my feet. Julius, my black cat, watched from his spot on the leather love seat in the room I called my office as I gathered up the odd-looking pieces of equipment.

I might be able to get them into the bag for my meeting, but it would simply not work to hand out such ungainly and heavy bags to my retreaters as they registered.

Julius blinked his yellow eyes at me. "I know what you're thinking," I said. "This is the fourth retreat I'm putting on and I should have figured this out already." The plan had been that after my meeting, I was going to pick up the boxes of looms and stuff the bags for the retreaters.

I looked around the small room, as if there might be an answer for me. There were reminders of my aunt's handiwork with yarn everywhere. My favorite was the crocheted lion who patrolled from the desk, though his face was too amusing to appear threatening. And then there was the sample of my handiwork that I was the most proud of. It had taken me a while, but I'd finished making the Worry Doll from the last retreat. I loved the doll and the concept. You were supposed to give her your worries and she would take care of them. I'd given mine a face with an attitude, which made her appear up for the job.

"Worry Doll, how about some help with this?" I pointed at the bag, which I had smartly propped up at my feet when I'd refilled it. It fell over on its side anyway.

"I'm talking to cats and dolls," I said, shaking my head in disbelief as I grabbed the handles and lugged the bag out of the room.

Julius followed me to the kitchen, making a last play for a serving of stink fish. I started to ignore it, but such a little effort made him so happy, and eventually I gave in. The can of smelly cat food was wrapped in plastic and then in three layers of plastic bags, yet somehow the strong smell still got through. I held my nose before giving him a dainty portion and then starting the involved job of rewrapping and resealing it. He was busily chewing as I went out the back door.

Julius and I had only been companions for a short time and he was the first pet I had ever had—though I was beginning to think he viewed me as the pet. He had definitely chosen me, and he seemed to be doing a good job of training me to give him the care he desired. I'd wanted him to stay inside initially, but he'd had no intention of being strictly an indoor cat and had pushed open a window to show me how to leave it open just enough so that he could come and go as he pleased.

Outside, the sky was a flat white. That was the average weather here on the tip of the Monterey Peninsula. White sky, cool weather, no matter the month. It just happened to be October, though you couldn't tell by looking around. There were no trees with golden leaves—mostly, there were Monterey pines and Monterey cypress, which never lost their foliage and stayed a dark green year round. The cypress tree on the small strip of land in front of my house had a typical horizontal shape from the constant wind. Somehow it made me think of someone running away with their hair flowing behind them. It seemed funny, since I had run here to Cadbury by the Sea, California.

My name is Casey Feldstein and to make a long story short, I'd relocated to my aunt's guest house in Cadbury when I was faced with moving back in with my high achieving parents (both doctors) because I was once again out of a job. Sadly, my aunt had been killed in a hit and run several months after I moved in. She'd left me everything—a house, a yarn retreat business and, as it was turning out, a life.

I might have moved almost two thousand miles away from Chicago, but that didn't mean I had severed my ties with my parents or, I was sorry to admit, my need for their approval. It still stung when my mother ended our conversations with her usual, "When I was your age I was a wife, a doctor, and a mother, and you're what?"

So, maybe I was thirty-five and it's true that I've had a rather spotty career history that, until recently, seemed to be headed nowhere. Of all the things I had done, my two favorites were the temp work at the detective agency, where I was either an assistant detective or a detective's assistant, depending on who you talked to, and my position as a dessert chef at a small bistro. I would have never left either of those jobs—they left me.

Though my mother had a hard time acknowledging it, these days I did have an answer for her usual comment. I had taken over my aunt's yarn retreat business, even though I hadn't known a knitting needle from a crochet hook when I'd started. And I'd turned my baking skills into a regular job as the dessert chef at the Blue Door restaurant, plus I baked muffins for the assorted coffee spots in Cadbury.

I started to walk past the converted garage that had been my home when I'd first moved here and then made a last-minute decision to go inside and check the supply of tote bags, as if the new ones I'd had made up might somehow be bigger than the one I was carrying.

The flat light that made it through the cloud cover was coming in the windows and illuminating the interior. The stack of bags sat on the counter that served as a divider between the tiny kitchen area and living space. I folded one out and measured it against my stuffed one. No surprise, they were the same size. As I flattened the bag and put it back, I noticed the worn manila envelope that had been sitting there for months. I still hadn't figured out what to do about its contents.

I hadn't told anyone about the information the envelope contained, not even my best friend Lucinda Thornkill, who owned the Blue Door with her husband Tag, so there was no one to go to for advice.

There was no reason to deal with it now, except to procrastinate from dealing with the bag issue. I guess there was *one* person I could go to for advice. It was two hours later in Chicago and, even though it was Saturday, my ex-boss at the detective agency was probably leaning back in his office chair considering his lunch options, which meant it was a good time to call.

I punched in the number and he answered on the third ring.

"Hi Frank," I said. Before I could say more he interrupted.

"Oh no, Feldstein. Don't tell me there's another body in that town of yours, with the name that sounds like a candy bar." It was true that when I had called him in the past, it was to get advice about a death—well, a murder in town, to be exact.

"No, no, Frank. No dead bodies this time. All the citizens of Cadbury by the Sea are alive—as far as I know. I wanted to ask your advice on something else."

"Okay, Feldstein. I get it. You've got boy trouble again. Shoot."

I laughed. I'd never called him about boy trouble, as he called it, or ever would. "It's something else," I began. "Do you remember I told you I had some information that would shake up the town? Well, now I have even more. I know who it is—"

"Who what is, Feldstein? You're going to have to bring me up to speed if you want my advice. You do know I have a life here that has nothing to do with that town you're living in, right?"

I was hoping that I wouldn't have to start from scratch, but I could see his point. What was going on in Cadbury was hardly of earth-shaking importance to him. I began by telling him about the Delacorte family, who were the local royalty. The family owned lots of property around town. Vista Del Mar, the hotel and conference center across the street from my house, where I held the yarn retreats, had belonged solely to Edmund Delacorte.

When Edmund had died, it had been very specific in his will that Vista Del Mar was to go to his children. His only son had died in an accident a year or so after Edmund's death, and since it seemed there were no other children, the hotel and conference center had gone back into the family estate. All that was left of the Delacortes now were two sisters, Cora and Madeleine. I explained all of this to Frank.

"It only *seemed* there were no other children," I said. I debated with myself if I should go into the whole story of how I'd come to the conclusion that Edmund had a love child. Frank only had limited patience and I was afraid it would run out if I went through telling him I'd found an envelope of photos that was marked "Our Baby" in a dresser that had belonged to Edmund. The baby was clearly a girl and, as far as everyone knew, he had only had a son. Even though Frank had helped me figure out that Edmund had made money drops to the mother through them both accessing a safety deposit box, I didn't bring it up and got right to the point. "I found out that Edmund had a love child, but I didn't know their identity, not until I found some evidence that made it clear who the baby is. Well, she's not a baby anymore. All I have to do is tell her who she is, and then she can get a DNA test. I have samples of both Edmund's and the baby's mother's DNA."

"Details, Feldstein. What kind of samples?"

I didn't have to look in the large envelope to know there was a sample of Edmund's hair with the roots I'd gotten from an old hair brush. It was amazing—you could be dead for years, but hair stuck in an old hair brush survived. The mother had licked an envelope and I had that. I listed them off to Frank with a certain amount of pride in my detective skills.

"Okay," he said. "Now what evidence led you to the baby's identity?"

"A teddy bear in the photos," I said, imagining his expression as I said it. He didn't disappoint. I heard him choking on whatever he was drinking as we talked.

"A teddy bear," he repeated in an incredulous tone. "I got to hear this one. How did a teddy bear give the kid's identity away?"

Frank didn't know anything about needle craft. Actually, I hadn't known much either until recently. I struggled, trying to find a way to explain it so he would understand. "There was a one-of-a-kind handmade teddy bear in the pictures next to the baby girl. The style is distinctive, like a fingerprint. I know who made it and I'm sure the woman will recognize it."

"Now it's coming back to me," Frank said. "I think I asked you before what was in it for you?"

"Nothing," I said.

"Then I recommend you sit on it. Those Delacorte sisters aren't going to be happy with someone trying to claim part of their estate. From the way you describe that town, I don't know that anybody would be happy with you for sharing your information."

"I bet Edmund's daughter would like to know who she is, and I happen to know that an inheritance would certainly help her out."

"Don't be so sure, Feldstein. My advice is to keep quiet a while longer. Once the cat is out of the bag you can't put it back." There was silence on my end and after a moment Frank said, "Is there something else?" His mention of a bag had brought me right back to my problem, but I was pretty sure he wouldn't be any help there.

"That's it," I said finally.

"Then I've got to go, the delivery guy is here with my sub sandwich." I heard a click and he was gone.

There was one thing he was definitely right about: the

whole cat in the bag thing. I left the envelope where it was.
There was always tomorrow.

The red tote bag banged against my leg as I walked and
I had to stop more than once to pick up a loom that tumbled
out and force it back in as I walked to my yellow Mini
Cooper, which was parked in the driveway.

My house was on the edge of Cadbury. The look was
wilder here, with more trees, no sidewalks, and of course
Vista Del Mar across the street. I glanced toward the hotel
and conference center as I pulled onto the street. Something
large and cumbersome was being pulled down the driveway.
It was impossible to see what it was, as it was covered in blue
tarps. This was the beginning of the biggest week of the year
here in Cadbury and I had a feeling it was connected.

Cadbury by the Sea's real claim to fame was not the
moody scenery, but the tens of thousands of striking orange
and black butterflies that arrived in October to overwinter
in a stand of trees behind a pink motel. There was even a
statue of a Monarch butterfly near the lighthouse. Tomorrow
was the kick-off of Butterfly Week in Cadbury. There were
going to be events each day, ending with a parade and the
coronation of the Butterfly Queen.

I might live on the edge of Cadbury, but it was still a
small town and it only took five minutes or so to get down-
town. There was an authentic feeling to the place. No ye
olde anythings—if anything was old here, it was because it
had been around for a long time. The buildings were a mixture of Victorians that were built when that was the current
style and some more streamlined mid-century style struc-
tures that looked plain in comparison.

Grand Street was the main drag in town. The two directions of traffic were divided by a park-like strip of grass and

trees, with some benches thrown in. I found an angled parking spot near my destination.

There was more than the usual Saturday morning activity on the street. Several people on ladders were putting up banners on the light posts, and the shops along the street were decorating their windows. The theme to all of it was the Monarch butterfly.

I lugged the bag out of the car, somehow managing to keep everything inside it as I threaded past all the activity and turned onto a side street that sloped down toward the water. I was so used to being able to see the Pacific from just about everywhere that it almost didn't register. I'd also gotten used to the constant hint of moisture in the air and the background sound of the rhythm of the waves. "Of course," I chuckled to myself—today there was a parking spot right in front of my destination, Cadbury Yarn.

The store was actually located in a small, bungalow-style house. As I crossed the front porch I noticed they had added a banner covered with butterflies that flapped in the ever-present breeze. Inside, the store seemed busier than usual. The table in what had once been a dining room was filled with a group of women chatting while they worked on their yarn projects.

Gwen Selwyn, the shop's owner, was ringing up a sale at the glass counter in the center of what had been the living room. She looked up as I came in and offered me a welcoming wave. It was strange to realize she had no idea that she was the love child of Edmund Delacorte. I went over what I knew about her. It was obvious from her appearance that she was more interested in serviceable than stylish. She was somewhere in her fifties, and I would have laid down money that the nubby brown sweater she was wearing was her own creation. Making something like that was still only a dream to me, but Gwen was one of those people who could knit without even looking at her work. I was sure that any color in her cheeks came from the cool damp air. She was not likely to wear makeup any more so than she was to do anything about the streaks of gray that had begun to show up in her short chestnut hair. Even though she was widowed, I'd also bet that she would never be caught hanging out in the local wine bar looking for a hookup. As far as I could tell, all her energy went into trying to keep the yarn store and her family afloat.

Today I noticed there seemed to be an extra furrow to her brow and for a moment I considered ignoring Frank's advice and pulling her into the storage room and blurting out that she was the secret Delacorte heir. But the place was busy and that's not the kind of news to just dump on some-one between ringing up skeins of hand-dyed yarn.

"We're over here," Crystal Smith called to me, waving from a room off to the side. A table sat in front of a window that looked out into the strip of space between the house and its neighbor. Three captain-style chairs were around it. Crystal was Gwen's daughter, though any resemblance was well hidden. Gwen leaned toward neutrals, while her daugh-ter was all about splashes of color. Her dark hair fell into tight ringlets and she had a thing for wearing pieces that didn't match. I couldn't remember ever seeing her in a matched set of earrings or a pair of socks that were the same. She managed to wear all kinds of eye makeup and have it work. The one time I'd tried to emulate it, I came out looking like a sad raccoon.

It was just the two of us for now, and Crystal offered me a chair. "I hope Wanda shows up soon. I have to leave for the football game so I can cheer on my son. Go Monarchs!" Crys-tal said, shaking her fist in a supportive gesture. "It was very nice of you to bring the corn muffins last night," she said.

"It was my attempt at showing town spirit," I said. As soon as I'd heard about the tradition of a chili dinner the night before the team's homecoming game, I'd decided to make a contribution. The event was held in the multipurpose room of the natural history museum. Long tables had been set up and the walls decorated with pennants for the Monarchs. I had just gone into the kitchen and dropped off the muffins.

"Too bad you didn't stay for the dinner," Crystal said. "The boys were all excited being served by their parents and the coach. There was lots of cheering and 'we're going to win this year' kind of stuff."

"The woman making the chili didn't seem that happy with my donation or my presence," I said. "Besides, I had things to do."

"That would be Rosalie Hardcastle and I'm not surprised she wasn't gracious," Crystal said. "She's very possessive of the dinner. She started the tradition and she cooks the chili from her recipe. If it's any consolation, the boys really scarfed down those muffins."

"Well, that's history now anyway, so on to the present. We've got a problem," I said, hoisting the bag onto the table. Wanda Krug came in just as the bag flopped over on its side and all the long looms fell out and hit the floor.

Though Wanda was a golf pro at a local resort, which made her an athlete, somehow whenever I saw her all I could think of was The Teapot Song. She was short and stout as the lyrics proclaimed and she had a habit of putting one hand on her hip and gesturing with the other. The funny thing was that with her bland style of dress—polo shirts and comfortable loose slacks—it seemed like she should be Gwen's daughter.

Crystal and Wanda had become my regular workshop

leaders for the yarn retreats. They were both much better with yarn craft than I was and never agreed on anything. Somehow I'd thought that would balance things out.

I retrieved the long looms, thinking how much they resembled something you'd put on the wall to hang coats on. I left the bag on its side and shoved them back in. "And that's without any yarn. There's no way I can give bags out with all this." I mentioned that I'd planned to pick up the boxes of looms and stuff the bags later today.

The loom idea had been Crystal's, and she had given me a quick demonstration on how to use them, making a point of telling me that knowing how to knit wasn't necessary. I had trusted her to come up with a plan for the workshops. Apparently, she hadn't thought about the logistics of how to handle the looms.

I regretted that I had waited so long for the three of us to meet about the upcoming retreat. Wanda tried to lift the bag. She had good upper body strength and had no problem holding it.

"You're right. You'll get somebody complaining they got muscle strain from carrying this around." She set it back down. "I guess Crystal didn't think about that." There was a tiny bit of triumph in Wanda's voice.

Crystal ignored the comment as well as the bag problem. "We should really talk about the plan for the workshops." She had a plastic bin and began to take out knitted items and lay them on the table. I looked at the array of hats, scarves, and shawls.

"These were all made with the looms?" I asked. In my basic lesson I had just made a swatch using part of a circular loom. I was going to be almost on the same level of my retreaters when it came to skill with the device.

Crystal nodded and encouraged me to handle the pieces. I was surprised how thick and soft some of the scarves were.

"But what's the plan?" Wanda said. "I know how to use the looms, but if I'm going to be instructing and helping, I have to know with what."

Crystal shrugged. "I thought we'd just offer them patterns that went with the different kinds of looms and let them pick what they want."

Wanda assumed her teapot pose. "Obviously you aren't a teacher. You have to have structure, a plan for how you're going to direct the workshop. We should tell them what to make." Crystal blanched at the criticism.

I wasn't an expert with the looms or really any yarn craft, but I had spent time as a substitute teacher and I knew what Wanda was saying was true, but I didn't want to alienate Crystal.

"Isn't the point of the workshops to teach the group how to use the looms and then guide them through their projects?" I said. The two of them agreed. "I know one of the reasons the looms seemed like a good idea is that it's quick to make projects, which means the group ought to be able to make a number of them during the retreat. What about this for a plan: after you teach them the basics of how to use the looms, have everybody make one of these using the circular looms." I picked up a plain navy blue beanie. "Then have them make something like this." I draped a thick scarf over my arm. "And after that they can make whatever they choose."

I think because I suggested it rather than Wanda, Crystal saw the point of telling the group what to make and having them all doing the same thing at the same time. "Okay," she said, "but we have to give them some freedom of choice. Who wants to see them all making their hats in the same color? It'll look like a factory instead of an expression of their creativity. I'll go along with having the whole group make the same first two projects, but we have to let them be able to pick their own yarn."

I looked to Wanda to see if she would agree. "It's your retreat, so if that's what you want," Wanda said with a shrug.

"It seems like a compromise," I said. "I'm not very good at imposing my will, and I'd rather we all agree. I do better when I get everyone on my side. That's what I did when I was a teacher."

"All right," Wanda said finally. "And as for the tote bags— I would suggest stuffing them with the folders like you have in the past. They can get a schedule, basic instructions for the looms, and probably something about Butterfly Week this time. Maybe put in some yarn. Then we'll hand out the looms at the first workshop. They can just carry around the one they're working on and leave the rest in the meeting room. At the end of the retreat, they can take their whole set with them. By then it will be their problem, not yours."

I looked to Crystal, who rocked her head back and forth in a semblance of agreement.

"We'll deal with the people who fuss about using the looms when we get to it," Wanda added.

"What?" I said. I had expected the group to love the whole idea of using the looms.

"Knitting purists might not be so happy," Wanda said. "It doesn't have the same grace as knitting with needles. And the novices still have to learn how to do something."

Crystal didn't seem happy with the comment. "Wanda, you'll see. It will be fine."

With that settled, we started to talk about Butterfly Week. This time I had planned a longer retreat and had arranged for my retreaters to take part in all the town's activities.

"Did I tell you that Marcy is in the running for Butterfly Queen?" Crystal asked. Marcy was her daughter and I still had a hard time realizing that the free spirit had teenage kids. She went on for a few minutes about how she'd been in the princess court one year. "It was pointless," Crystal said. "I know there was a committee, but that woman ran the show and I'm sure really picked who she wanted to be queen. What is she doing here now?"

Both Wanda and I followed Crystal's gaze into the main room to see who she was talking about. I recognized the woman from the chili dinner as she went by.

"Rosalie Hardcastle," Wanda said. "She likes to think she's a big mover and shaker in town. My sister is in the princess court, too. I better go and say hello to Rosalie. Then it's off to the football game with the rest of the town. Go Monarchs." Crystal and I watched as Wanda went up to the woman and really laid it on thick.

"If she thinks that's going to help her sister, she's crazy," Crystal said, clearly perturbed—maybe because she hadn't come up with the idea first. Rosalie gave Wanda a haughty smile in response to her greeting, then Wanda sailed out the door.

I noticed that Gwen's brow seemed even more furrowed as Rosalie pulled her aside, taking her away from the customer she was helping.

"What does she want with my mother?" Crystal said. I was surprised at her tone. Crystal always seemed like a free spirit type who kind of rolled with the punches. But then, I supposed she was protective of her mother. I knew that Crystal had come back to town with her two kids when her rock musician husband had taken off with a younger woman and left her stranded. Gwen had taken them in with no question, even though her house was small and money was tight.

"It doesn't seem like good news," I said as I got a better look at Rosalie's expression. She was a pretty woman, probably somewhere in her late forties. But by now her personality was catching up with her looks, and I noticed a harshness about her expression. "But maybe that's just the way she always looks," I said. "That's pretty much the expression she had when she said 'thank you' for the muffins."

"She appeared a little softer when she came out of the kitchen last night so the team could thank her," Crystal said. "Kory is such a good kid. He's the one who said they should give her a 'hip, hip, hooray' for the chili."

I thought of the dark-haired, gangly boy. "I just can't get used to the idea that you have a sixteen-year-old son who is taller than you."

Crystal smiled. "I got an early start. I would say it was a big mistake running off with a musician, but I wouldn't trade my kids for anything. Rixx doesn't know what he's missing." I remained silent, but all I could think was, *What a pretentious name.*

"You probably don't know this, but Rosalie thinks of herself as being one of the movers and shakers in Cadbury," Crystal continued. "She's a piece of work. She was Butterfly Queen three times and even tried to get the town council to make it a permanent position for her." Crystal rolled her eyes. "She made the chili dinner a tradition when her kids were in high school and her son was on the team. Someone suggested changing it to maybe a spaghetti dinner or having someone else make the chili, but no, it had to be her secret recipe and she always has to make it the morning of, in the community room, with no one around." Crystal laughed. "It's no wonder she didn't appreciate your corn muffins. She acted like they were some kind of invaders. I'm sure she would have conveniently managed to drop them into the trash and not served them, except I showed them off to the other parents before she had a chance. We put them out on the tables."

Rosalie finally left, and Crystal looked at the wall clock. "The game is about to start. I have to go."

"Go Monarchs," I called after her.

By the time I went outside, the street was much quieter. It seemed the whole town was going to the game, except me. I could only make my town spirit go so far, and I had bags to make up.

A police cruiser pulled up behind my car and an officer got out as things began to topple out of the tote bag again. "Need some help?"

Before I could say yes, Dane Mangano stuck his foot in a round loom that had started to roll down the street. He hopped on one foot as he reached forward to pick it up. Dane was my neighbor and a Cadbury PD officer. Really he was more, though I kept trying to fight the feeling. There was definitely a spark between us, which he seemed anxious to pursue, but I had put the brakes on. I didn't have a good track record of sticking with places or people, and even though I seemed to be settling into Cadbury and my aunt's business, I couldn't predict the future. So why start something? And if I were to stay, it could turn out even worse. What if we dated and broke up? I was still an outsider and he was a town hero.

"Why aren't you going to the game?" I said as he took the bag from me and managed to fit the loom pieces all back in. He set it down on the floor of the front seat and waited until it settled.

"Somebody has to protect the streets of Cadbury," he said with less than his usual enthusiasm. I knew the truth was that Dane had gotten in trouble with his superiors because he'd helped me in the past, and as a result was now working every holiday and the worst shifts the rest of the time.

"I'm sorry," I said.

Dane shrugged and gave my shoulder a quick squeeze. "It was worth it. But you've got to give me another chance."

He was referring to our attempts at a date. There had been two, and neither had turned out well. The first time, we'd gotten the business from the locals sitting around us. I blushed thinking of all their comments about what a cute couple we were and when we got married would I make my own wedding cake. The next time we tried going to a tourist trap out of town, where we were sure not to meet anyone who knew us. That part of it had worked out, but someone had choked on a hunk of chicken. Dane had jumped into action and gotten the chicken piece out. I won't go into gory details, but it was a lot more messy than the typical Heimlich maneuver. The guy's wife fainted, a bunch of EMTs showed up, and the restaurant was closing, so we ended up getting our dinner to go and eating in his truck. So much for a romantic evening.

Dane was so much more than a pretty face. He practically oozed character. When his father had disappeared, leaving him and his sister with an alcoholic mother, Dane had taken care of the family. I'd heard he did a good job pretending to be a bad boy, but he was also the one who took his sister shopping for her first bra.

Growing up that way could have left him angry and bitter, but instead he really did want to keep the streets of Cadbury safe. He knew bored teenagers were likely to get into trouble, so he converted his garage into a karate studio and gave the kids lessons and let them hang out. On top of that, he fed them copious amounts of spaghetti with sauce so delicious my mouth watered at the thought of it. He fed me, too.

While I might excel at dessert, I sucked when it came to regular food and mostly ate frozen entrees. But the relationship wasn't all take on my part. I left him muffins and cookies a lot of the time.

It was probably because he was such a great guy that made me hold back even more. I had tried to explain my hesitation to him and his answer floored me. He actually said he'd gladly have his heart broken if it meant he'd gotten to spend time with me. Was he sure he was talking about me?

I apologized again. I knew some of the kids who hung out at his place were on the football team and I was sure he wanted to cheer them on.

"It's okay," he said, not sounding too convincing. "I have more things on my mind." He looked up and down the street. There didn't seem to be any need of his services, and he continued. "Chloe lost that job at the diner in Gilroy and everything that went with it—including her own place."

"So she's back staying with you?" I asked. He nodded.

Chloe was Dane's sister and was kind of a wild child, the kind of woman my mother would have described as hard. She dressed to show off as much skin as possible, had hair that looked like she used crayons to color it, and though Dane had never said anything about it, I had the feeling she wasn't too picky about who she went home with. I didn't mean to be judgmental, but she was somebody I couldn't understand at all.

"If only that was all there was," he said. "She's decided that she wants to be Butterfly Queen. She's in the princess court."

"Then she made it into the finals?" I said, surprised.

"It doesn't work that way. Anyone can get into the princess court. All they need is a sponsor. I wish she had talked to me first." He sounded dejected. "She went straight to the owner of the beauty supply store. Apparently, she's a big customer." Dane rolled his eyes as he gestured toward his hair. "I guess it's nice that she got something out of buying all that hair dye." Dane rested his hands on his equipment belt as he checked the street again for criminal activity, but there was just an old man walking a beagle. I guess the only chance he'd do something requiring Dane's attention was if he didn't pick up after his dog.

"She's really into this princess thing. She told me she thinks it's going to open some doors for her. She won't listen to me. Maybe you could help her pick out something to wear that looks like a princess for the event tomorrow night?"

"You're kidding, right?" I said, and he let out a weary sigh. I'm sure he knew that Chloe wouldn't listen to me either.

"I just hope there isn't any trouble," he said.